# Death Rules the Night

## Rosemary and Larry

# MILD

Magic Island Literary Works • Honolulu, Hawaii • 2021

Interior book design by Larry Mild.
Cover design by Larry Mild

Original photo of The Olde Victorian Bookstore: by Tyler McLaughlin. Photo reprinted by permission.

The image of the house on p. 71 is a composite of four different house photos, shrubbery, fence, etc.

Library of Congress Cataloging-in-Publication Data

Mild, Rosemary P.; Mild, Larry M.
***Death Rules the Night,*** A Dan and Rivka Sherman Mystery
Mild, Rosemary P.; Mild, Larry M.

ISBN 978-0-9905472-6-6
First Edition 2021


10 9 8 7 6 5 4 3 2 1

# Dedication

For our beloved grandchildren—
## Alena, Craig, Ben, Leah, and Emily
For our precious new great-grandson—
## Kai Benjamin
For our wonderful daughters—
## Jackie and Myrna
For our marriage—soul mates, partners, lovers

# Acknowledgments

We could fill an entire volume with the names of all the family members, dear friends, and acquaintances who are loyal fans of our books, essays, and short stories. And you, our readers, are all precious to us and give us the ultimate push to continue our writing.

Our special thanks and hugs to:

Sisters in Crime/Hawai'i Chapter and Hawai'i Fiction Writers, for their friendship, encouragement, and advice.

Diane Farkas, our close friend, for her outstanding proofreading skills.

# Disclaimer

**Death Rules the Night** is a work of fiction. The plots and events therein are of the authors' imagination and invention. All characters therein are fictitious and any resemblance to persons living or dead is purely coincidental. A few real locations have been altered to accommodate the narrative. The supposed *historical* work of Arthur C. Atkins is totally fictitious and any connection therein to actual historical events, people, and places does not, in fact, exist.

# Table of Contents

# Table of Contents (Continued)

## Special Credits

Gothic Leaf font was chosen by the authors of **Death Goes Postal** to represent what Gerheardt Koenig's floral font might have looked like, as in the illuminated first character in each chapter. The authors have chosen to continue the practice in **Death Takes A Mistress, Death Steals A Holy Book**, and **Death Rules the Night.** Many thanks to Rob Anderson and the Flight of the Dragon organization.

This font was created by Rob Anderson of Flight of the Dragon, using CorelDRAW version 5 and 6. This font is freely available, and may be distributed in any way as long as this message is included:

"The author of the font makes no guarantee about the viability and usability of this font and is not responsible for any damages related to the use. © All rights reserved. Copyright 1997, Flight of the Dragon."

# Books Coauthored by the Milds

The Dan and Rivka Sherman Mysteries
- Death Goes Postal
- Death Takes A Mistress
- Death Steals A Holy Book
- Death Rules the Night

The Paco and Molly Mysteries
- Locks and Cream Cheese
- Hot Grudge Sunday
- Boston Scream Pie

Adventure/Thrillers
- Cry Ohana
- Honolulu Heat

Short Story Collections
- Murder, Fantasy, and Weird Tales
- The Misadventures of Slim O. Wittz
- Copper and Goldie, 13 Tails of Mystery and Suspense in Hawaii
- Charlie and the Magic Jug and Other Stories

Science-Fiction Novella
- Unto the Third Generation

\* \* \* \*

Also by Rosemary
- Miriam's World—and Mine
- Love! Laugh! Panic! Life with My Mother
- In My Next Life I'll Get It Right

Also by Larry
- No Place To Be But Here, My Life and Times

# Cast of Characters

**Rivka Sherman:** Former editor turned bookseller.
**Daniel Sherman:** Former engineer turned bookseller and husband of Rivka.
**Ivy Reubens Cohen:** Bookstore clerk engaged to Mark Schwartz.
**Mark Schwartz:** Son of Leo and Heddy.
**Leo Schwartz:** Father of Mark Schwartz.
**Tom Dwyer:** Truck driver.
**Laura Bancroft Dwyer:** Wife of Tom.
**Frank Mulhaney:** Truck driver trainer.
**Arthur Atkins:** Author and patriarch of the Atkins family.
**Gillian Lear Atkins:** Deceased wife of Arthur.
**Cordelia (Cora) Bacon:** Daughter of Arthur and Gillian.
**Daisy Bacon:** Daughter of Cora Bacon.
**Samuel Atkins Bacon:** Daisy's baby.
**Regan (Rae) Atkins:** Daughter of Arthur and Gillian.
**Goneril (Gloria) Atkins:** Daughter of Arthur and Gillian.
**Budreau (Muddy) Atkins:** Son of Arthur and Gillian.
**Anne Atkins:** Missing wife of Muddy Atkins.
**Helen Margoles:** Purchaser of the Atkins house.
**Leland Margoles:** Husband of Helen.
**Michelle T. Monahan:** Police detective sergeant.
**Emma Rathbone:** Librarian.
**Lord Byron:** Bookstore cat.
**Lady Annabella:** Stray cat that wanders into bookstore and has kittens by Lord Byron, named: **One**, **Two**, **Three**, and **Four**.

~

# Members of the Mystery Writers' Critique Group

**Dan Sherman:** *Shadow of Fear*, A Kasper Brasse Mystery.

**Rivka Sherman:** *Driven into the Woods*, A Deputy Glenda Glide Mystery.

**Ivy Reubens Cohen:** *Diary of My Murdered Mother*, A True-to-Life Mystery.

**Frieda Fraume:** *Ginger's Secret*, A Clara Taylor Horse Mystery.

**Joel Wise:** *The Law and Mickey Mann, Esq.*, Short Stories.

**Katie Silver:** *Boxcar Bertie,* An On the Rails Mystery.

**Esther Reubens:** *The Trial of Lizzy Harrington*, A Joan Ruben Mystery.

**Emma Rathbone**: *Petticoat Mysteries*, Lady P.I. Short Stories.

**Helen Margoles:** Wannabe writer.

**Cordelia (Cora) Bacon:** Wannabe writer.

**Tom Dwyer:** *Confessions of a Truck Driver.*

~

## Chapter 1
## Split Seconds
Monday, May 8th, 1989

The worst thing about accidents and missteps is that we don't know when or how to anticipate them. If we were able to see the when and how, we might learn to avoid them altogether. But alas, we are only human and can neither choose nor recognize those ill-fated moments when it isn't safe to let our guards down. A near-miss might cause us to reflect on our whole lives. A direct hit might do the same. Two truck drivers, Tom Dwyer and Frank Mulhaney, will learn this the hard way and react differently to its twenty-year consequences.

At 5:45 a.m. Tom Dwyer and his wife, Laura, were eating breakfast at their tiny Formica kitchen table. Laura had an unremarkable round face, a thick mass of light brown hair, and rimless bifocals. Today, the thirty-nine-year-old woman wore a tan cardigan sweater over a brown print dress. She worked for the telephone company in bill adjustments.

Tom drove a truck for a fast-growing package delivery service based in Baltimore, Maryland. A towering muscular man with clean-shaven gray cheeks, he wore his company's dark blue slacks and chambray shirt with "Tom" emblazoned across one pocket. He ate his usual Raisin Bran cereal with milk and a packet of artificial sweetener. He held a spoon in one hand and a folded newspaper in the other, while Laura nibbled away at a buttered English muffin. Wielding a pencil in her free hand, she worked at completing a shopping list.

1

"Where are you off to this morning, dear?" she asked.

"Let's see, today's Tuesday. I'll be learning the Annapolis route with some guy named Frank." He finished his cereal and pushed his bowl toward the center of the table.

"Will you be late tonight?" Laura took the last bite of her muffin, picked up his bowl and her plate, and placed them in the dishwasher.

"Don't think so, hon," he said as he put the paper down and got up from the table. He collected his uniform coat and cap from the hall and left for work. "Bye, see you tonight."

"Bye," she called from behind the bathroom door.

\* \* \* \*

By 9:45 the two drivers were completing their fifth delivery of the morning. Their Express Package Delivery truck sat idling next to the curb at 2320 Slate Street, a deserted one-way thoroughfare close to downtown Annapolis, Maryland. Tom Dwyer, an experienced driver just riding along to learn the more efficient delivery routes, carried a cardboard carton upstairs to an apartment in the adjacent building. Obtaining a signature of receipt, he returned to the truck and climbed in the cab beside the driver.

Frank Mulhaney, a hefty driver with twelve years on this job, had waited behind the wheel. As soon as Tom slammed his door shut, Frank released the emergency brake and lightly tapped the gas pedal. The truck pulled away from the curb and rolled slowly toward the red traffic light at the corner.

In the parking spaces across the street and to the left of the moving truck were six vehicles—a pickup truck, a line of four sedans, and an unmarked white panel truck.

"Where to next?" asked Tom.

Frank gazed up at the traffic light, just turning green, and then down at his delivery list to see his next address. It only took that split second for him to look at the rectangular metallic box holding the packing lists with the addresses, but it would turn out to be the most terrible split second of his life. As his vehicle rolled abreast of the panel truck, Frank returned his attention to the windshield once more and gasped.

"Look out," shouted Tom.

Bigger than life, Frank saw a woman with outstretched arms and legs plow into their truck's windshield. He instantly panicked. His foot briefly mis-hit the accelerator before jamming down on the intended brakes. Too late. The woman's body slid underneath the truck frame. The heavy box truck did come to a stop, but not before the drivers felt the tires *thump-a-thump* in the road below. Frank applied the emergency hand brake as a matter of habit. He sat shaking for a few seconds, then flung the door open, slid off the seat, and slammed his extra-wide shoes down onto the macadam street.

Tom heaved his six-foot-three body down from the passenger side of the cab and hurried around to join Frank on the other side of the truck. He could feel his heart thumping at a painful rate. His mind was still fixated on the woman's distorted face as she appeared through the windshield.

Kneeling down, the two men discovered the woman's battered body lying beneath the cab of the truck. There was no way Frank could move their truck without further mutilating the body, so the two men reached underneath the truck, grabbed the woman under her arms, and dragged her to the opposite sidewalk.

The green lightweight coat on the blonde twenty-something victim had fallen open, revealing a pink housedress with a gray diagonal tire track drawn across its middle. One pink slipper dangled from her left foot. The other was surely still under the truck.

Once they had hauled the woman from the street to the sidewalk, Frank's thick fingers felt her carotid artery. Feeling no signs of life there, he stood up straight, shook his head, then began scanning his environs for anyone else who might have observed the accident scene. No one. Not a soul in sight. Like a child who'd sent an errant baseball through a neighbor's window, Frank felt a new wave of panic wash over him, as he bolted for the cab and climbed in, slamming the door behind him.

"You can't leave her lying there like this," shouted Tom.

"I can't? You just watch me," answered Frank. "Get in quick

before someone sees us."

"Shouldn't we call it in?"

"Not unless you want to lose your license," said Frank. "I need mine to make a living."

Tom reluctantly climbed up into the cab and pulled his door shut. Frank released the emergency hand brake and drove off.

* * * *

At 9:15 that same morning—a very different breakfast scene. Budreau Atkins sat down at the kitchen table in his Annapolis apartment. The lanky thirty-two-year old sometimes went by the nickname Buddy, but mostly everyone who knew him called him Muddy. That name stuck because of the many shady deals and troubles he got himself into. Muddy's large nose tapered to high cheekbones and hollow hawkish eyes. Powerful allergies laid claim to his sinuses that morning and, by painful association, his poor temperament as well.

Anne, Muddy's wife of eight years, stood in front of the gas range in her faded, thin housedress—one hand holding an iron skillet handle. The three eggs in the skillet sizzled and popped from the excess butter under heat.

"Aren't them damn eggs done yet?" he demanded. "What's taking so long?"

"Coming right up, dear." Anne half-flipped the pan over a large dinner plate and slid the contents onto it. She carried the plate to the table and set it down in front of him. "There!"

Muddy picked up a fork, dug in, and conveyed several bitefuls to his mouth before carping, "These blasted eggs are runny again. You know how I hate runny eggs."

"I know," she said. "But you're always so impatient. You hurried me up."

"Don't you go blaming your incompetence on me, woman."

Anne thought seriously about beaning him with the skillet she was rinsing in the sink, but pure reason stopped her. "Why are you starting up with me this morning? I didn't do anything to you."

Muddy ignored her question. "Did you pick up my dress shirts from the cleaners like I told you?"

"No, I'll get them first thing."

"You dunce, can't you do anything the first time like I tell you?"

Anne approached him, arms folded across her chest. "I'm your wife, not your damn slave. Treat me with some respect. Just because your sisters were so cruel to you growing up, doesn't mean you have to take it out on me."

His chair made a scraping sound on the floor as he pushed it back and stood to face her. A half-dozen seconds passed before he slapped her hard on the right cheek, stunning her, knocking her a step aside. "You dumb bitch! I ought to throw you out on your ear."

Anne, a 110-pound lefty, responded defiantly with a loud stinging slap to his right cheek. Muddy made a fist and jabbed it deep into her stomach. The blow sent her across the room onto her backside. Facing him, her eyes glazed with surprise followed by pure anger. Then fear set in. She wriggled her way across the floor to the nearest corner and cowered there.

Muddy looked down on her with a sneer and said, "You dumb bitch! I'm not through with you yet."

"You sonofabitch," she cried. "One of these days I'm leaving you for good and I ain't coming back."

"Go ahead, leave. Ain't no one here gonna miss you anyway."

She stumbled out the door and slammed it behind her.

\* \* \* \*

At 7:45 that same evening Tom Dwyer walked in the door and went directly to his favorite recliner, without even announcing his arrival. He and Frank had driven through all the rest of their deliveries like automatons, neither one speaking his troubled mind. Now he sat there sulking in silence, rehashing his dark day in the dimness of his own living room.

"I thought you weren't going to be late, dear," Laura called from the kitchen. When she heard no response, Laura went to see for herself why. She perceived something was awry with her husband, who usually came home in a reasonably pleasant mood.

"Why are you sitting there in the dark?" she asked. She entered the living room and flipped the light switch to ON. As soon as she saw him sitting there, she knew for sure something was eating at him. "What's wrong, dear. Your face is as white as my dish towel."

"Today we accidentally murdered someone, a woman," he muttered with his eyes turned down.

"Murdered?" she repeated. "A woman?"

"Yes! Somebody's wife, maybe, or somebody's mother," he whined.

"Where? How?"

"Annapolis...we ran her over with the company truck."

"We? Who was driving?"

"Frank."

"Are you sure she's dead?" Laura asked. "Maybe she's still alive. Did you stop and check?"

"Of course we did. We both checked for her life signs. There just weren't any."

"So how is that murder?" she asked. "It sounds more like an accident to me."

"But we drove off without getting any help."

"You left the scene?" Laura asked slowly, as though she didn't want to hear the answer.

"Yeah. There weren't any witnesses, so Frank panicked and took off."

"Tom, why are you so sure of that? No witnesses, I mean."

"Damn it, Laura, it was a deserted side street. I looked it up and down. I even looked at the windows in all the next-door houses. There was no one about. I didn't want to leave without calling the police and an ambulance, but Frank insisted. He was worried about losing his license."

"Have you any idea who she was? Did you look in her purse?"

"No, I didn't! Come to think of it, I don't remember seeing any purse."

"None? What kind of a woman leaves the house without her purse?"

"It could have been under the truck. I didn't look there."

"Come, let's have a bite to eat. Your supper's getting cold. We'll talk more later."

"I don't feel like eating anything," he said.

"Come to the table anyway," she coaxed. "Maybe you'll change your mind." Laura sat across from him at the supper table with hardly a word said by either one. She ate slowly and sparingly, looking up at him periodically, her mouth parting as though she intended to say something, but she never did.

Tom tried to eat several times, but whatever reached his mouth seemed both tasteless and intolerable. The distorted woman's face stuck relentlessly in his mind. Whenever he saw Laura raise her head to speak, he didn't know whether it would be to admonish him or comfort him. Ultimately, she did neither. He was left to deal with his own conscience.

What scarce sleep Tom had that night came with repeated nightmares of the same accident scene—the frightening flash image of the outstretched woman in the windshield in that horrifying instant before she fell beneath the wheels of Frank's rolling truck. The *thump-a-thump* sound and smell of the braking tires, the hammer pounding against his chest, and the dominating fear hovering over him. It took possession of him and his life. He was no better than Frank—they had both left the scene of the crime. The future held little or no relief, for he was to be plagued with endless nights full of that awful lifeless image. And, of course he could seek no help, nor could he tell a soul beyond Laura.

The next few mornings they rushed to search the local newspapers for coverage of the accident. The *Baltimore Sun* carried no mention of an Annapolis hit-and-run, and the *Annapolis Journal-Gazette* over several days mentioned two similar incidents with few details: different locations and both at night. These items only added to the couple's consternation.

# Chapter 2
## The Fling
### Saturday, October 16th, 2004

It's extremely difficult to avoid the consequences of one night's indiscretion when you are normally a person of decency and principles. Lying, evasion, and denial are not easily found in your arsenal. But excessive celebration sometimes clouds behavior. You submit and you are left with guilt, and the consequences linger long after. Fifteen years have passed since the hit-and-run accident and there is yet another misstep in the making.

Consider the plight of Mark Schwartz, an undergraduate junior majoring in physics at Johns Hopkins University in Baltimore. He and fellow students Bradley Billingsly and Paul Scarbrough were simply out celebrating the end of midterm exams. The venue for this celebration was the Blue Jay Tavern deep in the heart of the Homewood section of the city. The three were seated in a brown vinyl booth toward the rear of the noisy establishment.

"Say, Brad, are you going out for lacrosse again next year?" asked Mark.

Brad took a long drag on his mug of craft beer before answering. "It all depends on whether my torn hamstring heals in time for spring practice."

"That was a bummer, Brad—ending the season after only one game," said Paul. "How'd it happen anyway?"

"I was chasing the ball at midfield, when I got cross-checked, and the Maryland midfielder stole the ball. I planted my right foot to go after him, and as I quickly changed directions, I could almost feel the muscle tear. I went to the ground and couldn't get up. I had to be helped off the field."

"Hey, sorry, man," said Mark. "Hamstrings hurt like hell. My Dad pulled his and he bitched for a week." Mark picked up his mug and drained it to the bottom.

"I thought I had only pulled mine, but then they told me it was a tear. I got this huge lump in the back of my upper leg and I couldn't walk without a cane for a couple weeks," said Brad. Then he too drained his mug to the last drop.

"It looks like no one's servicing the tables tonight," said Paul. "I counted more than a dozen bottles on the table. Who's ready for another round?"

Mark nodded yes.

"Count me in," said Brad. "I'll get them."

"No, it's my turn to buy," insisted Mark.

The young man slid out of the booth and wavered a little before completely standing. He headed for the restroom first, and on his way back to the bar he passed a table with four attractive young ladies. Mark recognized none of them, so he kept going until he heard his name called. He turned and saw one of the young ladies standing.

"Mark," she repeated, "Mark Schwartz. Don't you remember me?"

"I, I'm sorry. I don't," he replied, sheepishly.

"So soon they forget. It's Daisy," she replied. "Student nurse, Daisy Lynn Bacon. I attended to you at the university hospital. You had pneumonia, I believe."

"Ah, yes," he admitted. "Now I do. You sat on the edge of my bed, and we talked for nearly an hour before that mean old head nurse caught you goofing off."

"Yeah, I really got chewed out for that," she said. "I never got a chance to see you again."

"I had been bored out of my gourd until you showed up. I wanted to see more of you, but they discharged me the next day."

9

Mark put a hand on her back and steered Daisy to a nearby empty booth. She went willingly.

"Why didn't you call?" she asked, as soon as they were seated.

"I tried, but by the time I did, you had been shifted to another service. I had no way of tracking you down. All I remembered was your first name. I apologize, my bad."

Paul poked his head around the edge of the booth. "So that's where you wound up. We were wondering what happened to the beers you were getting us."

"Sorry, something more pressing turned up. I met Daisy here," said Mark with a guilty grin.

"Hi, Daisy," said Paul. "Can I get you two something from the bar?"

"A Natty Boh draft for me and…" Mark looked to Daisy.

"I've been drinking white Zinfandel," she replied.

"Got it," said Paul as he headed for the bar with their order. He returned shortly, deposited their drinks on the table, and disappeared.

Mark and Daisy chatted freely and consumed two more rounds of drinks before he caught her staring bleary-eyed at him. She seemed to be concentrating, soaking up every last word he uttered. Her hand let go of her half-empty glass, and he reached across the table to touch and soon hold it. She smiled and then pursed her lips into a short oval pucker resembling a kiss. He did the same. This state of pleasurable existence lasted for the better part of an hour with only a smattering of wordy exchange.

"We could catch a cab and go back to my place, but I'm not sure who would be home at this hour," suggested Daisy.

"I've got a better idea," said Mark. "We could walk three blocks to my apartment, which is guaranteed free of roommates for the entire weekend."

"Umm."

"Is that all you can say?" he challenged.

"It's as good as a yes, isn't it?" she replied. "Maybe I should have said "Yum!"

Mark paid the bar bill with a healthy tip, and the two half-staggered and half-strolled out onto the sidewalk. The crisp October air and bright streetlight perked up both of them for the walk to his place. They climbed the stairs to his second-floor apartment in a four-story, red-brick row house. The two leaned on each other in front of the door to the right-rear apartment while Mark fumbled for his keys. As soon as the door closed behind them, they shed their coats and dropped them on the floor where they stood.

Daisy jumped into his arms and straddled his hips with her legs. As her legs slipped downward, she began to kiss any part of Mark she could reach and he responded in kind.

As her feet touched the floor, she said, "I want you, but the damn room won't stand still."

"I want you, too, but first, let me put up some coffee." He led her over to the big blue sofa, where she collapsed in a sitting position.

"I'm not sure I want any, but you go fix yourself some," mumbled Daisy in slurred words. "I'm feeling a buzz right now—too good to spoil with coffee." She wore a great big grin of contentment.

*I'm not sure what's happening here. I've got a dilemma. If we try to hook up now she'll fall asleep on me in the middle,* thought Mark. *If I make the coffee, I'm not sure she'll be awake enough to drink it. In any case, we're not doing it while she's passed out cold.*

Mark decided to head to the kitchen and make the coffee anyway. Upon his return to the living room he found she had not only stretched out on the sofa, but fallen fast asleep and was even snoring. He returned to the kitchen and had his coffee by himself. Before retiring, he fetched an extra blanket from the closet and draped it over her sleeping form.

Toward morning, but not yet light, Mark sensed someone else in bed with him. He felt Daisy's nakedness all the way from the cleft between his shoulder blades down to her knees, fitted into the back of his own. She truly had come to fulfill the promise she'd made the night before. *Veni, vidi, vici;* she came, she saw, and she conquered while they found the pleasure in each other.

But when he awoke, Daisy was gone. He had no way to thank her for the pleasures in the night. He still had no way to get in touch with her, as he couldn't remember her last name.

\* \* \* \*

**D**aisy never showed up at the Blue Jay Tavern again, nor did she bother to contact him in any way. That is, until four months had passed. It was one snowy Friday, February 11th, 2005, when Mark's landline phone rang at 8:20 that evening.

"Hello...Who?...Daisy who?...Ah-ha, er, that...Daisy...No, I haven't forgotten you...How are you?"

"I'm four months pregnant with *your* baby," replied Daisy.

"Whoa, *my* baby? How do you know it's *my* baby?"

"It's been a year since I had sex with anyone else. That's how. What do *you* intend to do about it?"

"Do?" he exclaimed. "Oh! So you need help with an abortion. I could probably get some cash from my dad if you need it. But I'm not looking to be a father any time soon, nor do I want to be a husband, if that's what you have in mind."

"You sonofabitch," she blurted out. "Don't you have any sense of decency? Abortion is out of the question. Four months is too late. Besides, I'm Catholic and I'm pro-life. I've even protested in two marches."

"So why did you wait four months to tell me?" he retorted. "And let's get this straight. It was *you* who first suggested we go back to your place. What were we going to do there? Play Tiddlywinks?"

"I would have made coffee and we could have talked."

"Yeah, sure," said Mark. "Second of all, we went back to my place, and you were all over me before the damn door was even closed. And when I went to make coffee, you fell asleep on me."

"I did?" she questioned.

"Yeah, so I covered you up on the living room sofa and I went to bed all by myself. Sometime later, you climbed into bed with me of your own free will and without your clothes. Since you didn't ask about protection, I just assumed you were on The Pill."

"I don't use birth control. It was supposed to be the wrong time of the month for me to conceive. I must have figured it out wrong. So maybe I'm bad, but you had a part in this, too. And you got some enjoyment as well. Are you going to step up or not?"

"Not!" he returned. "However, I will still help to support an abortion. I don't feel so totally responsible in this case. You were the aggressor here. It was nothing more than a one-night stand, a fling, for the lack of a better word. You have to admit that you had no lasting feelings for me that night. Hardly any more than lust, I suspect."

"How do you know what I was feeling back then?"

"It sure didn't feel anything like wedding bells."

"I told you I'm not aborting and I don't care about your money. That's not a problem on this end. What about marriage?" she asked in a tearful voice. "Don't you care that you're gonna have a child out of wedlock?"

"Out of the question is more like it," he replied. "We are of different faiths and ideas. We're incompatible on so many things. A marriage wouldn't work. The child is your choice, your mistake."

The line went dead.

\* \* \* \*

Five months later Mark received a second phone call from Daisy. It was Monday, July 23rd at 3:30 p.m.

"I just called to inform you that you are the father of a beautiful eight-pound, five-ounce baby boy. He is nineteen inches long, and I've decided to call him Samuel Atkins Bacon, that is, unless you plan to step up at this late time."

"That is still a definite No, my dear Daisy. I have no interest in becoming a father at this time."

"Don't you have the least interest in a child that you helped to create, that you helped to bring into this world—not even a teensy bit of curiosity as to what your son looks like?

"Please stop this harassment, Daisy. You already know my attitude on this subject. I'd like to remain your friend and I can be of some help financially if you ever need it. But that's all."

"That's not the kind of help I need. I need someone to help

me raise Sam. Sammy needs a father."

Mark could almost hear the tears in her plea, and then she hung up. The young man wasn't heartless. He felt a measure of guilt, but he was pretty damned sure his life was meant to take him elsewhere.

# The Olde Victorian Bookstore

## Chapter 3
## The Olde Victorian Bookstore
Five years later. Monday, April 6th, 2009

The Olde Victorian Bookstore faced East Franklyn Lane in Historic Annapolis. A bold black-and-white sign stood over the entrance at the head of seven gray steps up from the sidewalk. White trim—with balusters, spindles, and even a sunburst—offset forest-green, cedar-shake siding. Originally build in the 1850s and renovated roughly every twenty years, this Victorian-style house had a small second-floor porch overlooking the main wraparound veranda. On the far-right side of the house, a thirty-foot octagonal turret rose from the basement to a dramatic pointy roof. Sandwiched between the front entrance and the turret stood a quaint iron-strapped wooden door marked The Dungeon. It led to the spooky store basement with additional book stacks. Four more years have passed, a total of twenty since the  hit-and-run incident.

An Express Package Delivery Service vehicle, an over-the-cab box truck, pulled up and parked curbside in front of the bookstore. Tom Dwyer, the driver, tooted his horn, for he routinely had cartons of books to deliver. Climbing down from the cab, he opened the double doors at the rear, and slid out the hand truck. Inside, there were three good-sized cartons clearly marked for The Olde Victorian Bookstore at 123 East Franklyn Lane, Annapolis, MD 21043. He loaded all three of them onto the hand truck and started toward the ground-floor Dungeon door. Just as Tom arrived, a pleasant-looking woman wearing a man's dress shirt over tight jeans, emerged from the front steps and held the door back for him to bring in the hand truck load.

"More books, I guess, Mrs. Sherman," Tom said in a friendly voice.

"Sure, what else do we get here?" returned Rivka Sherman with a laugh. "Just set them down inside the reading room, and my husband will check them in later."

The Dungeon reading room comprised two wooden tables attended by eight metal folding chairs and was surrounded by full bookshelves on three walls. Foot-high windows above two of the bookshelves shed natural light into the room, while fluorescent lighting supplemented the natural light. The fourth side opened to the actual Dungeon, a very large room full of loaded book stacks. Massive three-dimensional images depicted a medieval castle's dungeon. Chains, irons, axes, or fake webbing were fastened to the many stanchions supporting the house above it.

"I love what you've done with the room's atmosphere down here," said Tom. "It's like no other bookstore I've ever seen. Those scary three-dimensional effects, they're called trump something. Aren't they?"

"Why thank you, Tom. It's from the French. They're called *trompe l'oeil*, and we had a lot of fun creating an intriguing place to buy and read books," offered Rivka.

"Well, I better get on my horse now. I have a gazillion other deliveries to make." He headed out the iron-strapped door, closing it behind him.

* * * *

"Here kitty kitty. Here kitty kitty," called Daniel Sherman as he hopped off the last step down from the family apartment on the third level. "Hey, Rivka, have you seen Lord Byron lately? He hasn't eaten any of his food, and I can't find him anywhere. We fixed up that plush litter box over the poetry stack, and now he spends less and less time there."

"Nope, I haven't seen him," she replied. "Maybe he's found himself a juicy fat mouse to play with."

"Or a snazzy lady cat he's romancing," said Dan. "Don't forget, he's quite a sophisticated charmer, our Lord Byron. By the way, didn't I hear someone tooting out front?"

"Yeah. Tom brought another load of books for you to check in and label. They're stacked just inside the reading room over there."

"Oh, I see 'em. Did he mention that he wanted to do some original writing?"

"No, nothing about that at all," answered Rivka. "Why, what did he say to you?"

"Tom said he wanted to write a book, some kind of confessional. I asked him if it was an autobiography or family history, and he answered, 'sort of.' But he didn't know where to start, so I suggested that he join our writers' critique group at our next weekly meeting on Thursday. He said he'd try to make it."

"Why not? The more the merrier," said Rivka.

Dan and Rivka had bought the store from Bernie and Edythe Bender a few years earlier. Originally, they had no intention of becoming entrepreneurs. What did they know about bookselling, or running any business for that matter? In their mid-fifties, who would think of making such a life change? But they mustered the necessary nerve—*chutzpah* in Yiddish—and why not? Dan, an electronics engineer, and Rivka, a newspaper feature editor, had what it took to abandon their careers to embrace four floors of erudition and precarious adventures.

Daniel Saul Sherman and Rivka Manx Sherman were empty nesters, with each of their two children having married well and now living out of state. Their family now included two grandchildren. Our senior Shermans lived on the third level of The Olde Victorian Bookstore. The Dungeon in the basement; a main level where the cash register sat; the apartment; and the tower on the top floor comprised the rest of the converted Victorian home. There were stacks of books on every floor, including the original great room on the third floor.

Rivka, a substantial five-foot-six woman of fifty-five, usually wore her curly dark brown hair turned out at the collar and pulled slightly back to reveal her favorite hoop earrings. Deliberately untamed bangs nearly touched her eyebrows. Full lips, with a slight clockwise twist, sat in the center of a creamy, unlined face. When Rivka chuckled, her cinnamon-brown eyes sparkled with warmth. Every soprano word she spoke seemed to draw almost everyone's attention.

Stepping into the Dungeon reading room, Dan regarded the newly arrived cartons of books. He started by lifting the first one onto the table. A box knife with a slide-out blade, taken from a table drawer, cut through the carton's sealing tape. He slid out a chair from under the table and fitted his large frame into it. Slouching, he stretched his long, lean legs under the table.

The tallish, clean-shaven, square-chinned bookseller hardly looked his fifty-seven years. Pushing his horn-rimmed spectacles to the rise of his prominent, slightly crooked nose, Dan tackled the carton's contents. Buried in the packing material lay twelve mass-market paperback romances that had come indirectly from the printer via the distributors. His hands flipped though the pages while his eyes scanned for margin uniformity, print density, and page-to-spine integrity. Having passed those tests, he checked each book against the order manifest. One book had a few loose pages, but the rest he entered into the store inventory and placed them on a rolling cart for Ivy, their clerk, to sort and meld into the stacks in the proper rooms. The maverick with the loose pages would be returned to the printer.

Rivka, who had been going through the morning mail in the adjacent room, stuck her head in the reading room. She glared across the room at Dan's bushy black hair, with a touch of gray threading through it. The lineup of wisps decorating his neck meant he needed a haircut badly. She knew Dan got the message, but he'd always wait another two weeks just to bug her. *It was a guy thing*, she thought. Dan crossed his arms over his turtleneck sweater and scowled at her—*just a guy asserting his independence.*

"Say, who's on the register with the two of us down here?" she asked.

"Ivy. She took over from me when I went to look for Lord Byron," replied Dan, attacking the second carton.

"I didn't see her come in. Besides, I thought she had the day off. I'll go up and see how she's doing."

Rivka climbed one flight of stairs to the main store level, and, sure enough, Ivy was processing a purchase—a family history of Harry S. Truman. She decided not to disturb her.

Ivy Cohen Reubens was more to the Shermans than a trusted bookstore clerk. In a sense she had become their adopted daughter—born in London, England, as Ivy Cohen to a single mother who was murdered when Ivy was only three months old. Sympathetic neighbors, Wayne and Janice Sachs, took her in, raised her, and paid for her college education. In 2005 Ivy vowed to avenge the murder of her mother and bring the killer, who was never identified, to justice. At the age of twenty-three she followed a number of leading clues and migrated to the U.S. and particularly Annapolis to find her birth father and possibly the murderer of her birth mother. She eventually found both with the help of Dan and Rivka. From the beginning, when they hired her they treated her like family.

Through her many kindnesses to Irma Riley, her beloved friend and elderly landlady, Ivy eventually inherited Irma's fine old four-story, house and all its contents. Irma had no close family and few acquaintances. Ivy had been a tenant in a single fourth-floor room when Irma became incapacitated. Their relationship grew from there until Irma's passing.

Instead of interrupting Ivy, Rivka decided to empty the overflowing wastebasket behind the register counter. At the back door she encountered a mostly black cat curled up and asleep in the open-door supply closet. At first she assumed it was Lord Byron. "So that's where you've been hiding, M'lord." But as Rivka got closer, she discovered that this cat was definitely not Lord Byron. No, it was an unknown female and a very pregnant female at that. *It must have come in through Lord Byron's pet entrance in the back door*, Rivka reasoned. Continuing out the back entrance she emptied the wastebasket in the trashcan. Rather than confront the strange visitor, she sought to find the missing Laird in his home on top of the poetry stack on the main floor.

Arriving at the poetry stack, she noted that several books appeared to be out of place on the bottom shelf, so without giving the cats another thought, Rivka sat down cross-legged on the tiled floor and attempted to bring order to the misplaced mess.

Atop this stack was his kitty basket, lined with a Strathclyde tartan plaid in blue and purple. From his high perch, a reincarnated Lord Byron looked quizzically over the edge at her, but not for long. Three graceful bounds brought the full-grown feline to the floor, landing smack in the middle of Rivka's lap. She tickled the black fur behind his kitty ears and whispered to him, "I'll bet you know all about the strange cat at our back door, M'lord. Maybe you'll tell me who she is and where you found her. Maybe not?"

His amber eyes looked up at her as if to say "I'm busy now." Then he closed them and curled up in her lap for his second snooze of the day.

Rivka put the last book in place, shoved the Laird off her lap, got to her feet, and climbed the next flight of stairs to the kitchen, where she filled one bowl with water from the tap and a second bowl with dry cat food. She carried them downstairs to the back door and left them for the expectant cat. Without waiting for any acknowledgment, she returned to the Dungeon reading room and informed Dan of Lord Byron's return and her discovery of the newest visitor in the bookstore.

"We can't exactly turn the poor thing out on the street." said Dan. "After all, she's going to be the mother of our Lord Byron's children."

"Literally his litter," his wife added with a chuckle.

"Oooh," he said. "So what are we going to do about this new arrival?"

"I already gave her some water and cat food. That ought to show we care. I don't know if she'll even want to stay with us for the entire gestation period or if she'll seek someplace more permanent."

"Well, if she stays at all, we'll need to give her a name," said Dan.

"What do you suggest?"

"The poet's wife was the Baroness Annabella Byron. His two daughters were Ada Lovelace and Allegra."

"I like Lady Annabella," said Rivka. "It has a ring to it, pizzazz, too."

"But what are we going to do with a whole litter of kittens, pray tell?" asked Dan.

"We'll worry about that when the time comes. Meanwhile, I should go back up and talk to Ivy."

"I thought you already did that."

"Nope, not yet," she replied from the stairs.

Ivy, in her white blouse, pink sweater, and denim skirt, looked up from jotting a few notes on a lined pad as Rivka approached.

"Ivy, I didn't think you were coming in today. You said you had a few errands you needed to attend to."

Ivy tossed her shimmering, coal-black hair to one side and answered in her familiar soft voice. "I'm waiting for a wedding planner to call me back. I foolishly gave her only the store number and not my home number when we exchanged information. So I decided I had to come to work anyway." As usual, Ivy's long, loose hair flopped over her left eye.

"I think it's all so very exciting," replied Rivka. "How are your wedding plans coming along?"

"Well, not far enough along, according to Mark. He graduates from Johns Hopkins next month with his doctorate in physics and wants us to be married as soon afterward as possible. I'm afraid I've fallen down on the job. I'm being harassed by his father, Leo, and Alice Zimmer, his father's live-in lover. They're pushing us to set a date for the wedding, and I haven't even found a venue yet." Her voice tapered off to nothing.

"Why hasn't Mark taken a more proactive part in the planning then?" asked Rivka.

"He's way too busy preparing for his oral exams. He meets with the committee one last time in two weeks. He says whatever I decide is fine with him. But I'm afraid I suck at this sort of thing."

Ivy, with her petite build, oval face, and normally perky, jubilant personality, had proven herself to be a driven woman in the past, but somehow she'd let this wedding planning and preparations business slip away from her.

*Why?* she wondered. *Is this a sign I'm really afraid or unsure of marriage, or somehow I don't want to be married? I do love Mark and I want to be with him. We've been going together for three years now. That should be enough time to make up my mind. Shouldn't it?*

"Ivy! What's wrong?" asked Rivka.

"Oh, nothing. It's just that my mind is jumping from one thing to another. I think I'd better get this whole wedding under control before I lose it altogether. And this pressure from Leo and Alice isn't really helping any."

"Do you mean to say they haven't tied the knot yet, and they're hurrying you guys to marry?"

"Well, Leo's been through two hard marriages already, so I think he's gotten a little gun-shy. The first love he lost through illness and I believe he's still in love with Katie, his second. She remarried after their divorce."

"So how does this Alice fit into the picture?" asked Rivka.

"He rescued her from an abusive boyfriend and felt responsible for her afterward. It's more than that, though—they both show signs of being in love—only he doesn't want to make any commitment, nothing official anyway. He does take good care of her, from what I've seen."

"I still think they've got a lot of nerve imposing their will on you," said Rivka. But she needed to change the subject. "I bet Dan's ready for you to put away the new books by now. Why don't I take over the register for a bit. I'll give you a yell if your planner calls."

"Okay," agreed Ivy as she slid off the behind-the-counter stool and headed downstairs.

A half-hour later, Dan appeared at the register. "Hey, Rivvie. Do you remember selling the book *The Atkins Family History, 1768 to 1934*? It was a used book in the Local History section."

"I don't recall selling a book about the Atkins family," she answered. "There hasn't been much action in that section for a long time. Why?"

"It's missing," he replied. "It was there yesterday morning when I looked something up in an adjacent book, and today it's gone, a hole between two other books. I asked Ivy, but she's never heard of it."

"You think someone took it?" Rivka asked. "Or is it just misplaced?"

"It might be misplaced, but I seriously doubt it," reasoned Dan. "A theft, but why? It's just a history of the Atkins family from colonial times in Annapolis to the 1930s when old man Arthur Akins wrote it."

"What makes you so sure it isn't misplaced, dear?"

"It's not likely that a book is misplaced out of its home stack, and, just now, I went over that whole stack with a fine-tooth comb."

"Well, then, I believe we have another mystery," said Rivka. "Oh-oh, I can't believe I said that."

"Don't worry, this one seems tame enough," said Dan. "After all, it's only a missing book."

## Chapter 4
## The Hunt Begins
Tuesday, April 7th, 2009

The phone near the register began to ring in the bookstore, and no one seemed to be answering it, so Rivka picked it up from the kitchen, where she had just started preparing sandwiches for the three of them. She laid the handset down on the counter, went to the stairwell, and yelled down, "Ivy, telephone!" She listened until Ivy picked up the phone downstairs, then hung up. The Shermans had their lunch in the kitchen and, twenty-five minutes later, Rivka brought a baloney sandwich, a glass of iced tea, two pickle slices, and a handful of corn chips down to Ivy.

When Rivka arrived with her lunch, Ivy's green eyes were alive with excitement, and she appeared to be bursting with news that couldn't wait.

"That was Francine, my wedding planner, and she has all kinds of good ideas. I told her we were thinking of inviting about one hundred guests, and she suggested the William Paca House in colonial downtown Annapolis. I said I'd meet her there after work today for a tour. Would you like to come along?"

"Thank you, no, Ivy. I wish I could, but I have a 1:15 dentist appointment this afternoon."

"Just a checkup, I hope," said Dan, walking into the room in his usual uniform—tan Docker slacks and a polo shirt. Today's shirt color was a solid blue and he wore New Balance sneakers.

25

"No, dear, I've got this persistent dull pain right up here." she replied in a mushy nasal voice, pointing to the enamel offender in the top rear inside her mouth. "It's probably another damn cavity. And I just had one filled six months ago."

"I'm available to take you there," said Dan, while looking at Ivy.

"Why would I want you to drive me to the dentist?" asked Rivka. "I'm perfectly capable of walking. It's only a few blocks from here."

"No, not you. I was volunteering to take Ivy to the Paca House, if she doesn't mind if I tag along. I haven't been to the place in years."

"Great!" said Ivy. "My appointment's for five o'clock. Maybe you could help me with some of the decision-making and food selection."

"It's a date, then. I'll see you at 4:30 and I'll be sure to bring my taste buds along." Dan turned, reached over the sleeping Lady Annabella to retrieve his blue and white warm-up jacket from the wall hook in the back hall, and started for the front exit. *I wonder if Lady Annabella belongs to one of the neighbors,* he pondered. *Or have we adopted another dependent, and maybe a whole litter of them pretty soon now?*

"And where are you off to already?" inquired Rivka, frowning, before he reached for the door handle. *Why did Dan volunteer? Why couldn't Ivy wait 'til tomorrow when I'm free?*

"I'm off to the West Street library to see if I can find another copy of our mysteriously missing book. Maybe I can find out *why* anyone would want to purloin our lone copy of the Atkins family history. I'll be back way before three, especially if they'll let me check it out. Ivy can handle the store for a couple hours."

"You're making far too much of that missing book, dear," said Rivka. "It's only worth a paltry few dollars. Let it go. We can write it off."

"I'm just curious, that's all," he replied.

"What if there's an even simpler explanation for where that

book went? What if all the library copies are out on loan? And what if the library never had a copy?"

"I might look into other books of the same period. I'll think of something, maybe not." Dan blew her a kiss and swiftly disappeared outside the store.

Rivka turned to Ivy. "Have you and Mark set a date yet?"

"Francine said that Paca House had a cancellation for Sunday afternoon, May 24th. I really wanted more time to get ready, but between Memorial Day and the following week, Graduation and June Week at the Naval Academy, all the hotel and motel rooms and their facilities will be booked solid. She thinks that I ought to grab the date, because no matter where I look, I'll find that most bookings for weddings take place six months to a year ahead of time."

"So you two *have* agreed on the wedding date?"

"Only if I like the facility," she answered. "They're only holding the date for the next twenty-four hours, so I'll have to make a quick decision this afternoon."

"Speaking of decisions, just how do you think my husband can help you make any decisions this afternoon?"

"Well, there may be a selection of facilities and subvenues and, of course, there's always a sample menu to be tasted and picked from. I don't know the first thing about wedding foods. I just wish you were coming with us."

Rivka bit her tongue before answering. "Oh, don't worry, Dan is an excellent taster. It's what he does best."

A customer approached the register with two books.

"Hi, Cora, It's good to see you," greeted Rivka. "Ivy, this is Cora Bacon, one of our most loyal customers."

Ivy beamed her best smile and proceeded to scan, ring up, and check out the two books laid on the counter. After Cora left the store Ivy said, "She signed the credit slip 'Cordelia Bacon.' With a name like Bacon, It makes you wonder if her husband's name is Francis?"

Rivka smiled. "I don't think so. I believe her husband's name is Raphael, but nice try anyway. Whoops, I'm going to be late for my dental appointment." She grabbed a heavy green wool sweater from the back of the register stool, tucked her purse under her arm, and left.

\* \* \* \*

Twenty minutes later, the bell over the bookstore's main entrance jingled again, and a fiftyish woman with coarse shoulder-length brown hair hobbled into the store on a crooked cane. She suddenly stopped, looked over the store's layout, and turned back to face Ivy behind the counter. A bewildered look appeared on her face.

Ivy broke the silence. "How can I help you?"

"I'm here about the ad," the woman replied. "The one in the *Journal-Gazette.*"

"You mean the one about our Mystery Writers' Critique Group?"

"Why yes, that's it. Are you Mrs. Sherman?"

"No, I'm Ivy Cohen Reubens, a bookstore associate. Rivka Sherman is out just now. How can I help you?" she repeated.

"Mrs. Reubens, I would..."

"Call me Ivy, please, and I'm engaged but not married yet."

"Congratulations, Ivy. I'm Helen Margoles, and I would like very much to join your critique group."

"I'm not familiar with any Margoles living here in Annapolis," said Ivy, taking note of the Jewish star around her neck. "Are you new in town?"

"Why, yes, my husband, Leland, and I will be moving down from Baltimore in a few weeks. We bought the old Atkins house in West Annapolis. Meanwhile, we have a room at the Maryland Inn. We'll be moving into the house pretty soon."

"How very interesting, Helen. I've heard of the Atkins family. Our critique group meets upstairs at 7:00 p.m. every Thursday. We're always looking for new blood—if you'll excuse the pun."

"Who are the store owners?" she asked. "If I'm not being too nosy, that is."

"Not at all. Rivka, along with her husband, Daniel," Ivy replied. "What mystery subgenre do you prefer to write in?"

"I love the historical mystery because I like doing the associated research. I majored in English and minored in history at American University in D.C., but that was ages ago. I'm afraid I haven't done much actual writing since. I've been a full-time mother and homemaker, but I'm an empty nester with the last kiddie long out of house and college. I'm hoping I can learn enough from the group to get started."

"You should fit in with the group very nicely," said Ivy. "I'm glad to meet you."

"See you then," said Helen, as she left the store.

\* \* \* \*

Rivka rushed into the dentist's waiting room, up to the receptionist's counter, and signed in. She looked at her watch. It was 1:19, four minutes late. "Am I too late for my appointment?" she asked.

"No," said the woman behind the glass in a curt voice. "I'm sorry to tell you Dr. Fillmore is running about forty-five minutes late."

Rivka had mixed feelings about the woman's response—she wasn't considered late, yet she wouldn't see the dentist for some time. She settled into a wooden armchair next to the magazine rack. Shuffling through mostly year-old issues, she decided on a vintage *Reader's Digest*. Staring at the clock didn't help much either. Finally, at 2:15 she was shown into a mobilized torture chair and cranked up to height by a dental technician, who began taking repeated x-rays for the next fifteen minutes. Rivka wryly wondered if the woman was trying to achieve something aesthetic with them.

When the technician began probing her mouth with a mirror and an assortment of picks, Rivka wanted to let the busy young lady in white know she was there for a specific problem, but with a mouthful of stainless hardware it was difficult to convey her meaning. So the technician kept working and repeating that the dentist would see her shortly. Then the technician made her way around to the ornery tooth and Rivka let out an unearthly scream.

The young lady withdrew. "What's wrong?" she asked with an innocent face.

"I came here to fix whatever is causing my tooth to hurt like hell. I'm damn well not here for a simple cleaning. You did that four months ago."

The technician looked down at the chart and shook her head. "Let me speak with Dr. Fillmore for a moment."

She left the room and Rivka heard her enter an adjacent room. There was an unintelligible exchange of voices and, at last, Dr. Fillmore entered her space, all mask, blue scrubs, and tennis shoes of him.

"And what is our problem today?" he asked.

*Our problem,* Rivka thought. *You mean he wants to share half my pain?* She pointed to the tooth. "It hurts like hell," she told him.

He explored her mouth and clunked in on the baddie, letting her know he'd found it in the worst way. Then he examined the x-rays for a minute or two. Rivka heard every tsk-tsk that came out of his mouth until he made his diagnosis known to her.

"There's nothing left of the tooth below the gum line," he proclaimed. "It needs to be extracted as soon as possible. Do I have your permission?"

"Yes, it hurts too much to go on like this."

"You shouldn't have waited so long to come in," said Dr. Fillmore.

"I was here four months ago," Rivka said in her defense.

He shrugged his shoulders and made a face of disapproval.

It went rather routinely after that. A swab of numbing lidocaine, a partial syringe of Novocain, a pair of bent-nose pliers, a few crunching twists, and, *voila,* the tooth surrendered peaceably.

Rivka was discharged with a prescription for an antibiotic, instructions to rinse with salt water, and orders to take an aspirin substitute if necessary. She was informed that she had three choices: live with a permanent hole in her mouth, have a bridge made, or have a manufactured tooth implanted. She was given a shocking price tag and a lengthy schedule for choosing the latter.

* * * *

Earlier, at noon, Daniel Sherman had climbed into their

'98 Toyota Corolla and driven to the public library on West Street. He parked beside the one-story building. Inside, he approached the desk and recognized librarian Emma Rathbone, a member of their Mystery Writers' Critique Group for the last year-and-a-half. Tall, blonde, and sturdy, at age twenty-eight she portrayed the flawless image of the stereotype Nordic beauty. But that was only the half of it. The woman could recall more local history than anyone he knew. She came out from behind the checkout desk with open arms and gave him a token hug.

"Hi, Emma, maybe you can help me find a copy of *The Atkins Family History, 1768 to 1934*. I'm trying to find out why a used copy of it would be special enough for someone to steal it off our shelves rather than purchase it outright for a mere $12.95. It doesn't make sense. I wondered if you, by any chance, had a copy here."

"I believe there's at least one copy," Emma said, as she returned to her side of the desk. "But let me check the computer." She studied several screens and told him, "We have two different books on the Atkins family history, one copy of each. The older book, written by Arthur Clement Atkins, matches the title you asked me for. It traces the family history from 1768 to 1934. The newer book, by Regan Lear Atkins, *A Continued History of the Atkins Family*, traces the family history from 1900 to 1968. Unfortunately, the older book has been checked out. And wow! Here the screen says there's a series of overdue notices that have been sent out and then returned to sender."

"Does the computer tell you who checked the book out?" asked Dan.

"I'm not supposed to tell you, so you didn't hear it from me. Okay?"

"Of course. Well?"

"Don't be impatient—I've got to bring it up again. Ah, here it is: Robin Tobbler."

"Do you have an address or telephone number?" he pleaded.

"That I can't give you," she said, "but I'm sure you can look it up easily enough—that is, if it's an authentic name and address. I do have a photocopy here of the library card taken at checkout time, but that could be phony, too."

"Very strange," said Dan. "But do you think the Pratt Library up in Baltimore might have a copy of the Atkins book?"

"It's possible. Here, let me check." Emma's fingers flew over the keyboard once more and a dozen seconds later she had her answer. "They own one copy, but it is also checked out and two months overdue."

"Ah, even stranger yet," said Dan. "I think we've got a real mystery going here. What is written in that first edition that someone wanted kept from everyone else? Is it embarrassing family dirt or directions to some family treasure?"

"That's a lot of speculation, but it's your mystery to solve or not."

"If the older book should show its face, would you give me a call?"

"Of course," she replied. "Do you want to check out the book by Regan Atkins?"

"Sure, why not."

"Give me a minute and I'll get it for you."

Dan turned around and leaned against the desk while he waited for Emma to return.

She scanned the book and his library card and handed them to him.

"Thanks for the help," he said. "I'll see you on Thursday."

* * * *

Outside in the car, pulling out onto West Street, Dan turned right, making a deliberate decision to go for coffee rather than immediately returning to the store. Crossing Solomon's Island Road, he turned right and parked in the front lot of the Double T Diner. Inside, and before choosing a table, he searched for Frieda Fraume, so she could wait on him. Within a minute she came out of the kitchen balancing a large tray of sandwiches and drinks. He followed her to a nearby empty booth in her section.

"How's my favorite waitress?" asked Dan, as she passed by

with an empty tray at her side.

"Great," she returned in her usual raspy voice. "Give me fifteen more minutes, I'll be on break and then I can sit with you. Meanwhile, can I get you anything?"

"Coffee, black..." he hesitated.

"And..." she prompted.

"Oh, you're evil, Frieda," he said. "Well, maybe a slab of that strawberry-topped cheesecake."

The short, chunky waitress delivered the cake and coffee and disappeared from view once more. Dan dug into the cheesecake with a relish, simply because Rivka wasn't there to admonish him.

Ten minutes later Frieda reappeared sans apron. She slid into his booth opposite him. "So what brings you to the diner during the workday?"

"I needed to do a little research at the West Street library, so I was only a few blocks away. How does it feel being married again after all those years?"

"I'm still getting used to it. Yesterday I signed a check 'Frieda Forester.'"

"That's still the name on all your horse stories, isn't it?"

"Sure, but Garry wants me to use Fraume in the future. He says it makes us sound more like a family. I like the sound of it, too, but it's like I'm two people. I don't know how good that is for an author. Maybe it's too confusing for readers and fans."

"Maybe. How's Garry doing?"

"His plumbing business is overflowing—excuse the pun. More business than he can handle. He's even thinking of taking on a partner. As much as he enjoys the critique group, he doesn't have the time for writing anymore."

"That's a damn shame—I kind of like what he did with *The Unspun Web*. I think he got disillusioned when he hooked up with that phony literary agent."

"I think you're right, Dan," said Frieda as she slipped out of the booth and headed for the kitchen.

Dan scraped the last crumbs of cheesecake off the plate,

licked them from the fork tines, and sipped the last of his coffee. He got up and left for the bookstore. There was still a whole afternoon before he had to take Ivy to Paca House.

## Chapter 5
## Wedding Plans
Same Day

As the minute hand passed 4:00, then 4:15, then 4:25, Rivka had not yet returned to the bookstore from her appointment. Dan became concerned. *Maybe the dental work was more complicated than she had first anticipated,* he reassured himself. *Someone would have notified me if it had turned out to be a major problem.* Dan wrestled with his dilemma. He'd promised to take Ivy to her appointment with the wedding planner. *But I can't leave the bookstore open with nobody here, so I'll wait another fifteen minutes. Rivka should be home soon.* At 4:40 he turned to Ivy and said, "Let's go." He locked up. They climbed into the Toyota and Dan drove off.

\* \* \* \*

Ten minutes after they left, Rivka returned to the bookstore with a hard lump in her jaw and a painful decision to make. When she got back, she discovered the bookstore abandoned and the front door locked. She looked at her watch—*4:50 and no one here? Oh-oh, Ivy's appointment.* Reaching in her purse, she found that her keys weren't there. Neither was her cell phone. They weren't really missing; she knew where they were. She'd left them in her other purse on the dresser in the bedroom. She sat down on the second step in front of the main entrance and cried.

\* \* \* \*

A few minutes after five, Dan and Ivy managed to find a

35

parking space on Prince George Street beyond the East Street crossing, and they walked the rest of the way. The William Paca House faced Prince George Street, and the garden and grounds extended through to King George Street. The colonial brick home was built on a small rise. They had to climb eight brick steps to reach that level and ten more wood steps to the front veranda of the five-section Georgian mansion built around 1763. William Paca, the third governor of Maryland and a signer of the Declaration of Independence, had raised his family here. A gray-green patina plaque to the right of the entrance attested to the home's listing as a National Historic Landmark.

Wedding planner Francine Miller met them just inside the main hall. In her mid-thirties, she had a brunette ponytail pulled back with every hair strictly in place. She wore a royal blue business suit with a knee-length skirt, a white frilly blouse, and stiletto heels. Francine wasted no time with small talk. She led them on a quick tour of the four main rooms on the first floor of the central section, hoping to give them a sampling of the colonial ambiance. Each room had its own fireplace, heavy red or blue drapes, and etched glass windows. She explained that much of the delicate furniture and superb cabinetry work was attributed to master craftsman John Shaw, who had a workshop and home on State Circle across from the State Capitol. He was known for his Federal Period designs and craftsmanship. Several other pieces with tiny fist-and-paw-shaped feet reflected a French influence in the décor.

"Where is the actual wedding venue?" asked Ivy, worried where she'd put all the guests.

"None of these rooms are nearly large enough to accommodate a hundred guests," said Dan. "By the way, where's Carvel Hall, the old hotel where they used to hold all those big fancy parties?"

"I'm afraid it was torn down around 1965 to restore the original garden area beneath it." said Francine. "The hotel abutted the rear of the home and faced King George Street. Today there is no indoor venue except for the Summerhouse, which accommodates a mere dozen guests. When we step outside, you'll see the huge tents erected mainly for receptions, but they also serve as backups for ceremonies held during inclement weather. They accommodate roughly 125 people, including a small dance floor and a food service area. Now our weddings are usually performed outdoors, either near the Summerhouse or on the bridge overlooking the fishpond. Come, follow me outside, and I'll show you."

She led them through a rear door to a stunning panorama of landscaping—a broad lawn, lined with thick five-foot-high hedgerows. A stone path down the center wound its way over a small bridge, descending in levels gradually, until it reached the tiny domed white Summerhouse situated in front of a high brick wall. Up close to the main building, to their immediate right, were three massive white canvas tents.

"What's that big dome on the other side of the wall," asked Ivy.

"That's the chapel on the campus of the United States Naval Academy," replied Francine, "where John Paul Jones, naval hero of the Revolutionary War, is buried."

"So where are the actual gardens I've heard so much about?" asked Dan. "There isn't a blooming flower in sight."

"The gardens are on the far side," their guide answered. "Here, let me show you."

They followed Francine through a breach in the hedgerows. Red colonial brick walkways outlined dozens of individual garden plots laid out almost like city streets on a map. But to their great disappointment, only a few scattered blooms could be seen.

Noting their dismayed expressions, Francine hastened to explain. "Don't be alarmed. By mid-May, the gardens will come alive with all kinds of blooming floral arrays. I promise you won't be disappointed."

Feeling a bit restless and skeptical, Ivy broke in. "I'm really anxious to know about the reception."

"Of course," Francine replied, quick to shift focus. "Your timing is perfect. Now we'll move on to some of the reception details. I think you'll enjoy the food, and of course you'll get an idea of overall cost. If you'll follow me into the kitchen, our chefs have prepared a sampling of their wares for you to taste and select."

Ivy and Dan trailed along behind her as she led them up a short flight of wooden steps to a colonial kitchen in one of the brick side buildings. Several chefs were busy preparing for an event that evening; still, a few looked up, smiled, and waved. A long, narrow sampling pantry just off the kitchen was next on the agenda. Inside, on a wide wood-block table, lay a broad array of foods, specially cut in size and amount, for the purpose of taste sampling. A per-guest price tag accompanied each bite-sized morsel. Hors d'oeuvres, meat, fowl, and vegetarian offerings were followed by five side dishes and four desserts, including small squares from two different-style wedding cakes. Given Melamine plates and kitchen-type silverware, they started at one end of the great block table and ate their way to the other, partaking of the fare and making choices while Francine recorded their preferences.

"What if we need a half-dozen kosher meals as well?" asked Dan.

"Good thinking, Dan," Ivy remarked, relieved that he had thought of it.

"A Baltimore caterer delivers as many main courses as you need," replied Francine, as she ushered them into an adjacent office. She handed them a separate schedule of prices for the kosher meals. After several minutes at a computer keyboard, keying in their selections, Francine hesitated and asked, "You did say 100 guests and six kosher meals?"

"That's correct," said Ivy.

Francine entered those facts, clicked PRINT, and they heard a noisy printer produce a complete, precisely detailed contract for Ivy's wedding. Francine handed them the document and indicated the required places to sign. "Of course, we will need a deposit of one-third today in order to reserve everything you've chosen. The total will be $27,198."

"Wow! All that much!" said Ivy.

Dan raised his eyebrows, but said nothing.

Ivy and Dan each took the time to read through the contract before Ivy actually signed it. She took out her checkbook and wrote in the requested $9,066 deposit amount. They shook hands with Francine before they took their leave.

"I'll be in touch," were the planner's parting words.

As they walked away, Dan said, "This is heavy-duty stuff, Ivy. It might be a good idea to let Mark know of these arrangements as soon as possible."

"Yes, of course. It's a good thing I have the money I inherited from Irma Riley or none of this would be possible," said Ivy, as they walked back to the car. "I think of Irma almost every day and marvel at what she has done for me. She was a no-nonsense woman with a heart of gold."

"But think of what you did for her, the companionship you freely gave, and how you managed to care for her in her last days."

"I didn't do it for the inheritance, Dan. I did it because I was so fond of her."

"I know that, and I have to believe she did what she did because she cared for you as well. What would you and Mark have done otherwise?" asked Dan.

"Unless Mark's family came up with a donation, I'm afraid we'd have to have said our vows in front of a county clerk," she answered.

"Speaking of vows, have you given any thought to *who* you want to perform the ceremony?" asked Dan.

"It has to be a rabbi, but I haven't spoken to Rabbi Goldfish yet. I do know the social hall at Beth Israel was booked for every weekend we wanted, but do you think he would perform an off-site ceremony for us?"

"I can't see any reason why he wouldn't," he replied. "It would mean careful scheduling. Would you like me to give him a call when we get back?"

"Would you?" she asked.

"I would."

* * * *

39

When Dan and Ivy returned to the store, they found Rivka sitting on the front steps sulking. Her right cheek was as much swollen as her temper.

"It's about time you two goof-offs got back" Rivka hesitated. "Dan, I know what you're thinking and you're right. I forgot my keys. Still, the store has been closed all this time? What if we had a real live customer, one who actually reads, or knows someone who does?" Her speech was still impaired from the Novocain. "So unlock the Dungeon door already, before a customer threatens to enter and, God forbid, gives us a sale."

*Jeez, her sarcasm is mixed in with a dash of her humor*, thought Dan. "Good grief, dear," he exclaimed. "I didn't think your dental appointment would last all that long. I figured the store would be closed for only a matter of minutes at the most. What's going on with that tooth, the one that's been bothering you?"

"Gone! Rotten to the core," she declared, as she stood to accompany them. They walked around to the Dungeon door where Dan took out his keys and unlocked it for them to enter.

"The dentist had to take the tooth out. He left me with three choices: a nuisance bridge, an expensive implant, or walking around with another hole in my head. The missing tooth is in the back, so all three are a possibility. I can tell you right now I am not running around permanently with a missing tooth and I don't want to fool around with a messy bridge every night. So I'm going to have a proper implant. My only problem with this is that the implant procedure takes eight months and costs nearly $20,000!"

"Hmm, I guess you're worth it," drew out Dan, with a smirk on his face.

"You guess?" She playfully tried to whack him with her purse.

"I'm sure, I'm sure!" he said, blocking the symbolic blow with his forearm.

As they reached the main floor, Rivka turned to Ivy. "So what have you two accomplished this afternoon while I was being cruelly tortured." She settled on the stool behind the register to hear the answer.

"We saw the lovely outdoor layout and approved a menu," said Ivy. "I even signed a contract. I'll tell you more about everything later. What we're missing is a rabbi to marry us. Dan promised he would talk to Rabbi Moshe Goldfish for me."

Rivka looked over at her husband. "You're waiting for Godot, are you?"

"I guess I'd better get to it then," said Dan, as he picked up the phone and dialed a familiar number. "Hello, Rabbi Moshe?... This is Dan Sherman...Yes, we're fine...I'm calling to find out if you are available to officiate at the wedding of Ivy Cohen Reubens and Mark Schwartz...Sunday, May 24th...Yes, we know the sanctuary and social hall are booked all that day. No...They're planning an off-site wedding on the William Paca House lawn...Your other wedding is at noon?...Would two o'clock be a hardship for you?...Wonderful! They'll be pleased...I see...Yes...I'll make sure they understand...Fine... We'll see you on Friday night...Bye." He hung up the phone and reached under the counter for a book with worn white covers.

"Dan! Stop teasing and tell Ivy what the rabbi said," demanded Rivka.

"What *did* he say?" asked Ivy.

"Everything's all set," said Dan. "The rabbi agreed to two o'clock at Paca House. He does, however, want to see you and Mark beforehand and soon, too. I do believe he has some kind of pep talk and maybe some religious formula for a happy marriage. So call his office tomorrow morning and make an appointment."

"Thank you, Dan, and thank you, Rabbi Moshe, and thank *You, God!* My dreams are finally taking shape." Ivy sailed around the room in circles.

Rivka pointed to the book in Dan's hand. "Is that the missing one?" she asked.

Her question caught him just as he was heading into his favorite reading room, where he would sink into the old velvet recliner stashed in the corner.

"No. This is a book covering the Atkins family history from

1900 to 1968," said Dan. "I got it at the library this morning. It's by Regan, daughter of the original author. At first, I wasn't interested in this book, but there appears to be some overlap covering the period 1900 to 1934. It seems our thief wasn't interested in Regan's book. There must be some piece of information in the original Atkins family history that he doesn't want anyone else to learn. And you know what's really interesting, Rivvie? The librarian said it was not only checked out, but it has a whole bunch of overdue notices that were sent and returned to sender. And not only that, while I was standing there she checked the computer for the copy at Baltimore's Pratt Library. It's checked out and overdue, too."

"That is really strange, but you still don't know if any of the copies were actually stolen." reminded Rivka.

"Ah, but they were," Dan replied. "They had to be. Three copies of the original family history are unaccounted for. Our West Street library, the Pratt library, and our store copy are all missing. Doesn't that spell thievery?"

"I suppose so. Maybe," she answered. "But why would somebody want to prevent anyone else from seeing or using this crucial information?"

"The thief took three copies out of circulation, when one would have been sufficient to simply acquire that information," he replied.

"I see. So you think you're onto something. Supposing I tell you that I know something about the Atkins family, too."

"Tell me, girl. Out with it, or I'll tickle you in the ribs." He took a step closer to her.

"No, no," she pleaded with mock distress. "I'll tell."

"Ivy just told me that a woman by the name of Helen Margoles came in this afternoon, answering our *Journal-Gazette* ad. She wants to join our critique group. She explained that she and her husband are planning to move down here from Baltimore and they've purchased the Atkins home in West Annapolis. How's that, Mr. Detective?"

"Veddy interesting," he said. "Maybe we can enlist her help."

"I doubt that." she said. "A stranger just moving to town is unlikely to know much about a local family's history."

"That's two new members for the group," said Rivka.

"Two?" asked Ivy. "Who's the other one?"

"It's Tom Dwyer, one of our delivery men. He drives for Express Package. Dan talked him into attending on Thursday. He told Dan he wanted to do some writing—a unique personal experience story."

# Chapter 6
## New Faces
Thursday, April 9th, 2009

On the second floor of The Olde Victorian Bookstore, eleven members of the Mystery Writers' Critique Group sat chatting in a random assortment of straight-backed chairs, many of which were upholstered in faded red velveteen. These seasoned and wannabe writers were assembled around a grand banquet table—fifteen feet by five feet of dark, unpolished oak—worn instead to its own peculiar sheen. From above, an unmatched pair of antique crystal chandeliers bathed the table in solid reading light. All of this was central to the bookstore's largest reading room that was once the apartment's living room. The cream-colored walls were framed in travel-tour posters from around the world, an indication that they were accompanied by book stacks from the travel section. A few steps across a short hall led to Rivka's kitchen. The hall was occupied by the staircase and a tiny frail elevator marked FOR STAFF ONLY. The Shermans' bedroom and bath were accessed through a second door on the far end of the kitchen.

Rivka had been pouring hot beverages from a singing kettle and percolator on her stove. She turned off the gas burners, carried a tray of drinks to the center of the table, and set it down. She then took a chair at the head of the table next to her husband. At the last group meeting, an election had passed the chairmanship from Dan to her.

44

"Evening, everyone. I'm Rivka Sherman, bookseller extraordinaire, and I write about a lady deputy sheriff. I just published my novella, *Driven into the Woods,* A Deputy Glenda Glide Mystery. We are fortunate to have with us three new members tonight. In order to welcome them properly, I believe we should go around the table and introduce ourselves. Why don't we start on my left with you, Joel?"

"Hello, everyone," said the short, round-faced man with a nearly bald head. "I'm Joel Wise, attorney at law and the butt of far too many lawyer jokes. I dabble in legal-mystery short stories. If I'm allowed a plug, I just published a collection, *The Law and Mickey Mann, Esq.* Also, if you need a good lawyer, I put some business cards on the table."

"Hi, Frieda Fraume at your service—literally. I wait tables down at the Double T Diner." The plump woman in a bulky sweater grinned, pleased with her own witty introduction. "I write horse and farm stories. Last year I published a novel, *Ginger's Secret,* A Clara Taylor Horse Mystery."

"Hi, guys, I'm Katie Silver, wife, mother, and homemaker," said the attractive middle-aged lady with long ringlets in her glossy dark hair. An unbuttoned beige cardigan revealed a print dress. "I'm still trying to publish my book *On the Rails,* A Boxcar Bertie Mystery. Bertie is what you'd call a female hobo of the 1930s and she gets into all sorts of trouble."

"Hi, I'm Helen Margoles," said the fiftyish woman. Her shoulder-length light-brown hair, graying at the roots, was held firm in a headband. She wore a dark blue dress with a plunging neckline. "My husband, Leland, and I are in the process of moving down from Baltimore. We bought the former Atkins house in West Annapolis. I sure appreciate the warm welcome I've gotten from you folks. I'd like to try writing mystery short stories. I'm here to learn from the rest of you."

"Hello, I'm Ivy Cohen Reubens and I'm still trying to finish my book *Diary of My Murdered Mother,* A True-to-Life Mystery. I've tried to reorganize my mother's diary into a full-length mystery." Ivy was wearing her pink blouse and gray slacks, the same outfit she had on during the workday.

"Hi, I'm Cora Bacon—also a newbie to the group, but I've been an Annapolitan all my life," said the woman in a prim gray suit with her hair pulled back too severely. "Helen? What a coincidence. I actually grew up in the house you just bought. As for writing, I'm still experimenting. I hope to find my place in one of the mystery subgenres."

Rivka turned to her husband, tapped his knee under the table to get his attention, and gave him an approving nod. It was information she'd given him earlier—about the old Atkins house, a possible source of information.

*Cora was an Atkins,* Dan concluded with a sidelong wink to his wife. *Bacon is her married name. Ah, yes, I need to have a long talk with her.*

"Hi, everyone," said the clean-shaven man with a grayish face, an earnest expression, and deep-set eyes. "My name is Tom Dwyer, and I'm a union teamster. I'm afraid I'm new to all this writing stuff, but I do want to write about my real-life experiences as a truck driver—one experience in particular. It's sort of a mystery, anyway."

"Hi-yah, I'm Esther Reubens—an auntie to Ivy," offered the woman in the green turtleneck and faux-pearl necklace. "I've got a whole mess of started essays and short stories. I never seem to finish anything, except maybe the two Internet blogs I write. Maybe I'll put a bunch together one day and make a book of them."

"I'll bet most of you know me from the West Street public library," said the striking Nordic woman. "I'm Emma Rathbone, head librarian there. I've been a member of this illustrious group for the last year and a half. I write *The Petticoat Mysteries,* Lady P.I. Short Stories. My protagonist is Emma Robards, private investigator. I've got some queries out there, but no one has picked up on them yet."

"Well, I guess it's up to me to bring up the rear," said Dan. "It's one of those burdens that come with sitting next to the chair. I'm Daniel Sherman, husband of this lovely little lady, and writer of private detective mysteries. My latest is *Shadow of Fear,* A Kasper Brasse, P.I., Mystery.

Rivka chimed in. "Now that we know everyone, who will volunteer to read some of their recent work?" A few too many silent seconds passed, so she turned to the person sitting on her left. "How about you, Joel?"

"I'm in the middle of a story where Mickey Mann has a witness, Anita Birches, on the stand. He's defending Grover Fox, the accused murderer of Billy Danser. It's only a first draft, so take it easy on me, guys." He picked up a short stack of pages and began to read.

———

### Chapter 9, The Bookkeeper

Anita Birches, the prosecution's third witness, took the stand and was sworn to tell nothing but the truth just like those before her. Anita was buxom and leggy, with bottle blonde hair down her back to her waist—*not at all what you'd expect of a bookkeeper*, Mickey thought. In a tight skirt and equally form-fitting pink sweater, the woman didn't just sit on the stand, she slouched, she squirmed, constantly shifting her rear end as though she were sitting in the proverbial hot seat.

Her almost aggressively cheesy demeanor didn't seem to match the outright nervousness she displayed. It didn't jell with Mickey. *This woman has plenty to tell, but doesn't want to be asked about it.*

George Dulaney, the prosecutor, rose from his chair noisily and approached his witness. "Miss Birches, would you tell the court how you happened to be at Happy Hilda's Bar and Emporium on the night in question."

Anita cleared her throat. "I do the books for all of Hilda Kerr's businesses."

"Are you a certified public accountant?"

"No, sir, but I am good with numbers, so I'm a bookkeeper. Hilda doesn't have any problem with that."

"And exactly what did you see that night?"

"I saw...put a...in his..."

"Speak up, Ms. Birches, so the jury can hear you."

"I saw Grover Fox shove a kitchen knife into poor Billy

Danser's chest. When Billy fell on the floor, Grover just kept standing right there. Then he ran off. Out back, I think." She shouted her response louder than she intended to. But then she seemed somehow relieved to finally get it out.

"Tell the court—where in this establishment did this horrible event occur?"

"At the end of the bar...the far end...they were arguing...mean-like...both of 'em. I knew something bad was about to happen."

"And please tell the court—what time did all this happen?"

"Right at 11:35. I saw it on the big fancy clock over the bar."

"Ah-hah, said Dulaney. "Let me point out to the jury that 11:35 is well within the range of the time of death the medical examiner will testify to later." He turned back to his witness. "Where were you when all of this took place?"

"I...I'd just come in the front door," she replied. "Maybe ten minutes before. I sat down at the other end of the bar on one of the stools."

"So you had an excellent view of the knifing?"

"I suppose so."

"May I take that as a yes?"

"Yeah!"

"Thank you, Ms. Birches." Dulaney spun about to face the defense table. "Your witness."

Mickey Mann did a quick scan of his notes and approached the witness for his cross-examination. "Good morning, Ms. Birches. Are you comfortable?" *Let the jury see how shaky this witness is,* he thought.

"I suppose so. I'm not used to talking in front of so many people."

"Just a few simple questions for you—nothing to be nervous about. Now then, why is it necessary for the bookkeeper to be on demand and on location so close to midnight?"

"I come there sometimes to close out the cash register," she replied.

"But isn't the establishment open until 2:00 a.m.?" asked

Mickey.

"Yeah."

"Is this your customary routine?"

"Yes."

"What do you do until then?"

"I chat with everybody...maybe have a drink or two at one of the tables," she said.

"Did you have any alcohol that night?" Mickey pressed.

Ms. Birches hesitated. "I didn't ha...er, I downed a couple a beers at suppertime. And maybe I had a shot when I came in the door."

"How much of the argument did you hear?"

"A couple a minutes...maybe a few more."

"Did you hear any of the exchange...what it was all about... even some of what they were saying?"

"Sure I heard them...just nasty words, though...nothing that made any sense to me"

"Do you remember any of those words? Maybe the names they called each other?"

"No way," she answered. "They weren't loud enough to make any sense. And I don't think I could repeat those here in a courtroom anyway if I did make sense of them."

"I see. Just how far away were you from the two men when all this fighting happened?"

"I don't know, maybe from here to that door."

"Would you say that's about fifty or sixty feet?"

"I suppose so...If you say so."

Dulaney jumped up. "Objection, Your Honor. The defense is leading the witness."

"Sustained," said the judge. "Counselor Mann, ask a question."

"Yes, Your Honor." Mickey resumed. "Ms. Birches, was either one of the men facing you when the knifing occurred?"

"Yes, sir. But I could see Billy's chest with the knife stuck in it. Blood was comin' out all over. The killer, he musta drove it in hard and fast and then he ran off."

"Did you ever see the killer's face?"

"Not actually, but he had Grover Fox's build and he moved and talked like him. I'm sure it was him."

"But you never saw his face," Mickey reiterated.

"No, he ran off so fast through the back door."

"Did you recognize the weapon?"

"Yeah, it was one of those long carving knives from the kitchen."

"Exactly when did you first see the weapon that night?"

"I saw it sticking in poor Billy's chest when he was still falling and again when he was lying on the barroom floor."

"So you didn't see the actual knife *during* the stabbing?"

"Nope."

"Objection!" cried Delaney. "Defense is leading the witness."

"Sustained." ordered the judge. "The jury will disregard the last question and answer."

Mickey, in a grandstanding ploy, turned to face the jury while he continued to speak to the witness. "Let me get this straight. You just admitted you were at such a great distance that you could neither make sense of what the two men were yelling about, nor were you in a position to see enough to make a positive identification of the killer. Is that correct?"

"I suppose so."

"Objection!" cried Delaney a third time. "Defense is summarizing his case at this time."

"Sorry, Your Honor, I just wanted to clarify the witness's inability to clearly identify the defendant."

"Overruled." ordered the judge.

"Thank you, Ms. Birches. That will be all for now," said Mickey, as he returned to the defense table.

"The witness is excused. You may step down," said the judge.

———

Joel set his manuscript down and cleared his throat. "That's as far as I got, guys. What do you think?"

"Sounds pretty authentic to me," said Dan.

"Does Mickey win his case?" asked Esther.

"You'll have to read the book," answered Joel.

"How did you come up with the name Mickey Mann?" asked Dan. "Sounds a lot like the baseball player."

"That's exactly where it came from," replied Joel. "Mickey Mantle is one of my all-time favorite players. I had to alter the name a bit, of course. I mostly get my character names from the newspaper obits. You know, a first name from here and a last from there, but I wanted to honor the real Mickey this way."

"Thank you, Joel," said Rivka. "Well, folks, if that's the only reader we have tonight, we'll adjourn early."

Most of the members were on their way out when Frieda stopped Ivy. "Hey, I almost forgot," she started. "Ivy, I heard through the grapevine that you're actually gonna tie the big knot with Mark soon. *Mazel tov*! Have you set a date yet?" She pulled Ivy to her for a grand hug.

"Yes, Mark is getting his doctorate on Saturday, May 16th, and the invitations will go out this week. You and Garry certainly are on my list. Save Sunday afternoon, May 24th. Both the ceremony at two and the reception following will be in the William Paca House gardens."

"I wouldn't miss it for the world," said Frieda. "We're accepting right now."

Ivy waited to be the last one to head downstairs so she could lock up the bookstore as she always did on Thursday nights. "Good night, Rivka, Dan."

As the Shermans readied for bed, Rivka suddenly stopped in her tracks. "Dan, this is terrible. We haven't even thought of a wedding gift for Ivy yet."

"I don't know what's so terrible about it," declared Dan. "A young couple just starting out could always use cash."

"Don't be silly, Dan. You give them something attractive and useful, so as the years go by, they'll pick it up and fondly remember that Dan and Rivka Sherman gave it to them."

"Just like all those useless *tchotchkes* we got rid of when we moved from our old house to the store?"

"That was different, sweetheart."

"How was that different? You still have that list of gifts to remember who gave them, don't you?"

"Yes. We were pushed for space. There was no room here except for absolute essentials. We both agreed on every item on that get-rid-of list. Besides, we shipped whatever the kids wanted off to them. They were thrilled."

Dan grinned. "At least they pretended to be. So whenever you're feeling nostalgic, you can always take a peek at the list. We should have saved a few of those items for occasions like this. It's called re-gifting."

"Daniel Sherman, shame on you." She giggled.

# Chapter 7
## The Prodigal Son Returns
### Saturday, April 11th, 2009

Dr. Arthur Clement Atkins passed away the second week of January, 2009, at the ripe old age of eighty-nine. His death certificate read pneumonia, whereas the actual cause was a complicated conglomeration of illnesses one would normally group under the old-age label. His three daughters paid appropriate tribute to their father during the simple funeral and graveside service, though none of them chose to speak on either occasion. That was merely a reflection of his passiveness and disinterested attitude toward all of his progeny while he lived. His only son was at sea, on a commercial freighter returning from Lisbon to Baltimore when their father passed away, and he never knew of the January 14th funeral until April 10th when his ship finally made its way to a Baltimore quay.

Arthur Atkins left a considerable sum. His tenured employment at St. John's College in Annapolis as a professor of world history brought him some measure of esteem, but it could hardly account for the size of his current material wealth. Early on, a savvy stockbroker brilliantly turned him onto several budding firms that skyrocketed his moderate-sized inheritance to that most substantial sum he left behind.

The bulk of Arthur's estate, in the form of an investment portfolio, went to his eldest daughter, Cordelia Lear Atkins Bacon, age forty-nine, who preferred to be called by her childhood nickname, Cora. Her married name was Bacon, ever since linking up with banker Raphael Bacon eight years earlier. The cantankerous old man left the Atkins house and his precious literary collections to his unmarried middle daughter, Regan Lear Atkins, age forty-eight, who preferred the nickname Rae. Of the daughters, only Rae agreed to interrupt her teaching career and care for him in his declining years. One might say her inheritance depended upon it.

Professor Atkins wasn't particularly fond of his wayward youngest daughter, Goneril Lear Atkins. She had been a surprise birth twenty years after his son, their third child, was born. When Goneril was a sassy, rebellious fifteen-year-old, she got pregnant and ran off to West Virginia with her vagrant, pot-smoking, older lover. Keith Murdoc left her after twelve years of marriage when he learned that a second baby was coming. That was two years ago. It was five years after the loss of their first child.

Now twenty-seven, Goneril had, early on, adopted the name Gloria to avoid the obvious sound-alike references to gonorrhea and the terrible teasing that went with them at school and the workplace. An annual Christmas card between Gloria and her family comprised their entire communications for the last fourteen years. Arthur left her a sufficient amount in the form of a sustaining annuity. Three months after his death, she reconciled with her sisters and moved back into the house temporarily to help them pack up.

The naming of the three Atkins daughters was the handiwork of Arthur's late wife, the former Gillian Ann Lear, who had an eerie fascination with Shakespeare's *King Lear* and the coincidence of her own maiden name, Lear. She passed away in 2002 after a long period of stomach ailments and depression.

To Arthur's totally belligerent youngest, a son named Budreau Lear Atkins, who went by the name of Muddy, the father left the total sum of one solitary dollar. Arthur believed it to be justifiable retribution. Muddy had avoided the old man at all cost once he moved out of the house. His half-way decent career with the U.S. Merchant Marines didn't seem to make any difference to Arthur—the boy was completely intractable. These two never could get along.

Muddy struggled finding employment for years following the suspicious disappearance of his wife, Anne, in 1989. After a long investigation and a good deal of searching and harassment, the police finally accepted the theory that they were dealing with a disgruntled, runaway wife. They could easily see why a woman stuck with a husband of Muddy's personality might want to run away.

Whenever Muddy had occasion to be in a mid-Atlantic port, he would stay with his sisters at the Atkins home. On this Saturday morning, a day after tying up in port, Muddy put his key in the front door lock and stepped into the main parlor. He surprised all three sisters, who just happened to be sitting there conversing together.

"I'm home," he announced, as he dropped his sea-bag duffel on the faded oriental rug. The sisters' conversation came to a halt. All three stared at him with open mouths.

"Doesn't anybody care that I've come home to visit?"

One by one each of the sisters stood to give him a hug. Cora's was the most genuine; after all, he was her baby brother. Rae lent a dutiful hug, simply because he was family—he somehow belonged to them. Gloria only went through the motions with her brother. They had teased and taunted each other during their formative years. Gloria was the most vulnerable.

When the siblings were finished with the mixed reception, Muddy asked where their father was. The three sisters looked at one another, each hoping to avoid the explanation. Finally, Cora took the lead.

"Oh dear, Muddy, Daddy's dead. He passed away back in January. Rae found him on the kitchen floor in front of the refrigerator some time after midnight. He must have gotten out of bed to fix himself a snack. We didn't know how to contact you. We didn't even know the name of your ship."

"Was there a funeral, Cora?" he asked.

"Of course there was—on the fourteenth. At St. Anne's on Church Circle and then at Hilltop Cemetery off Forest Drive. Pastor Billingsley gave him a proper graveside service, too. Neither Rae nor I wanted to do a eulogy, and Gloria didn't arrive until later that same morning, so she wasn't prepared to say anything anyway."

"Was there a will?" he demanded.

The sisters looked at each other, anticipating the next question. Then each, in her own turn, nodded in the affirmative.

"Yessss," said Rae aloud after a period of prolonged silence.

"Well, did the old fart leave me anything?"

"One solitary dollar," said Gloria. "He said you'd know damn well why."

"That stingy old bastard," said Muddy. "He never did make the effort to understand me."

"What did you expect? All these years went by and you never once made any attempt to patch things up with him," said Cora.

"The old goat never even noticed me until I did something wrong. You can't imagine what it's like to feel invisible. As a boy, I did a lot of what I did because I wanted his attention. Maybe I did a little too much—he's disinherited me."

"If you're short on cash right now, I could give you some, Muddy," said Gloria.

"Thanks, but I'm not looking for any charity, Sis. In fact, I'm not in a bind at all. So who got the house?"

"Rae did," said Gloria. "Plus Daddy's fine literary collection."

Muddy turned toward Rae. "And you're going to go on living here just like nothing ever happened?"

"The only thing that's happened is that I have already sold the house," said Rae. "I got a good price, too. That money is my inheritance. It will allow me to pursue my writing career for some time before I have to go back to teaching."

"What?" cried Muddy. "But you can't do that—it's been the family home since colonial times, our damn roots even. Where would I come home to otherwise?"

In a calm yet firm voice, Rae said, "Daddy left the house to me, and I can do whatever I want with it. I don't want to live in a seven-bedroom house. It's far too big for one person, so I sold it. And there's nothing you can do about it now, Muddy. We went to settlement last week. We have two weeks to clear everything out of here."

56

"Where are you going?" he asked. "What do you plan to do?"

"Brother, I don't think that's any of your freakin' business," she replied. "You can't just barge in here once in a blue moon and dictate how we run our lives. You can stay in your room until the new people throw you out for all I care. The three of us will be out of here long before that."

"The new people?"

"The Margoles family. They're the ones that bought the place."

Muddy staggered down the hall to his room and fell on the bed, which had been stripped to a mere mattress. Rae's decision to sell had massive repercussions for him, but he was powerless. Or was he?

\* \* \* \*

It was a little after 2:30 when Ivy and Mark left the synagogue. The rabbi had purposely arranged their appointment to coincide with the end-of-the-morning *Shabbat* service. He felt it never hurt to beef up attendance that way. In his office afterward, Rabbi Moshe counseled the bridal couple on the age-old concepts of marriage.

They discussed what each of them wanted out of the union: making room for religion in both the home and synagogue; how their differing backgrounds would affect their marriage; the importance of forgiveness and atonement; how to resolve marital conflicts; how to prevent money from disrupting the marriage; how to keep the communication channels open; fitting intimacy, sex, and children into their marriage; and in-law considerations. They thanked the rabbi and agreed that they had some serious thinking to do. No, he hadn't said anything that would upset their nuptials.

Ivy and Mark were a striking couple as they walked down the synagogue steps to the street and beyond, holding hands. After strolling for a little over a block, Ivy stopped, disengaged her hand from his, popped opened her shoulder purse—probing—obviously looking for something.

"Ivy. What on earth are you looking for?"

"A photograph," she replied while she continued to search. "Ah, here it is." She pulled out a laminated picture and handed it to Mark.

He took a long look at the photo and said, "So, it's a black and white picture of you. I've already got a ton of pictures in glorious color. Why give me this one now?"

"First of all, it's not me. Second, I'm showing it to you—not giving it to you, because it's the only photo I have of my mother. Recently, my half-sister, Julie, found it hidden among our father's things and gave it to me. Even Julie thought it was a picture of me until I explained it was my mother."

"Your mother? That's amazing. You're the spitting image of her. You could be identical twins."

"Yes. I'm twenty-seven, the same age she was when that photo was taken. Apparently, we have the same petite build, coloring, and features."

Mark put his hands on both her cheeks and drew Ivy close. "Identical oval face and the most beautiful eyes—so large, dark, and sparkling. And your hair..."

"What about my hair? Mother's was black, loose, and straight."

"And she wore it draped over her left eye just like you do. Was that a conscious thing? Did you have any idea how she wore it?"

"I didn't know that was her preference until Julie gave me the photo. It's a fantastic coincidence. Maybe it was in the genes."

"Oh, I doubt that," said Mark. "More like the oval face shape dictated it, if you ask me."

"From her diary, I gathered she had a passive personality. I don't think I'm passive at all."

He handed the photo back to her, and she tucked it into her shoulder bag. They started to walk again.

"Passive, hah! I would describe you as a driven woman—not at all passive. And you've made quite a success of your job."

When they first started dating, Ivy told Mark how she ended up at the Shermans' bookstore. She was fresh out of college and without any teaching experience when she arrived in Annapolis four years ago. Unable to find a teaching job, she applied for a clerking job at The Olde Victorian Bookstore. Rivka and Dan not only hired her, but have always treated her like a member of their family.

"Do you remember how we met?" asked Mark.

"Of course I do, silly. It was at a party at my father's house. Herschel and Anna Reubens sure knew how to throw a backyard bash. I stumbled a few steps from the bottom of the veranda stairs leading to the backyard. I fell into the arms of a handsome young gentleman passing by. Do you even remember what you said?"

"I believe I said, 'All my life I've been praying for a beautiful woman like you. But I never expected you to arrive like manna from heaven, landing right in my arms.' I believe I tried to help you stand up again."

"Help me stand up? It was more like I struggled to get to my feet and free myself from your awesome grip. I was unhurt, but all a-fluster, as I straightened my dress. But thank God I only fell a few steps. It was pure chance that you were there to catch me. Right then I noticed your strong facial features and what a handsome hunk you were. A tad on the short side, but you appeared so intellectual-looking in your owl-like glasses. I found the sound of your words as inviting as their meaning."

"What do you mean—a tad on the short side? I'm five-foot-nine and a half. You're at least five or six inches less than me."

"It was just a first impression. You measure up fine to me now."

"Anyway, if I remember correctly, I replied, 'Supposing I choose not to believe in chance. I'd rather think it was our karma. May I interest you in a drink?' Perhaps I was a bit pushy, but wonder of wonders, you accepted. That was the beginning of one beautiful friendship."

Mark knew perfectly well that Ivy remembered their first meeting. He just liked rehashing the romance of it.

Mark Schwartz and his father, Leo Schwartz, saw each other only a few times each month. Mark was part of two fractured families. At age twenty-eight, he was all that was left of his father's first family. When he was two, his mother, Heddy, wasted away from tuberculosis after only three years of marriage. Several years later Leo remarried, but only for a short time. He and his second wife, Katie, had two daughters. Now in their late teens, they live in West Annapolis. with their mother, who remarried Mel Silver. Leo got to see his girls, Brenda and Barri, several times a week. Mark wasn't that close to his half-sisters because of the age differences and the fact that they grew up in different households.

Ivy and Mark continued to walk from the synagogue. Forty minutes later, they arrived at the three-story house Ivy had inherited from Irma Riley.

Once inside, the two made sandwiches from leftover rotisserie chicken. He sliced, and she spread mayo on multigrain bread. He added sweet pickles. Ivy brought out a bowl of cole slaw, then poured iced tea from a pitcher. They munched and drank while discussing the upcoming wedding details. After cleanup and with a cleared table, Ivy brought a carton in from the next room and set it on a chair beside the table. Mark slit it open with a paring knife and pulled out the first of 110 wedding invitation packets. Each elegant packet consisted of an outer envelope with an invitation and a second envelope inside containing an RSVP card.

"Wow! We have to address all of these?" gasped Mark. "We'll be here all night."

"We'll get it done in no time," she reassured.

Mark made a face. "We should have made computer labels, hon. It would go a lot faster."

"Shame on you, Mark, a handwritten invitation shows that you care enough to give them the personal touch. Calligraphy is the real classy way to go about it. Do you even know how?"

"No, and are you intimating that I don't have any class?"

"Mark Schwartz, don't you start with me. Take out your list and start addressing your batch."

"But your list is much shorter than mine and, besides, your penmanship is much neater than mine."

"Are you saying you want to shorten your list?"

"No way, my family would skin me alive if I eliminated any-one."

"On with it, then."

*Wow,* he wondered. *Where did all this bossiness come from all of a sudden?*

* * * *

The next morning Rivka was surprised to see Cora Bacon se-lecting oranges in the produce section of Food Fair. She pushed her cart into the next aisle to be sure it was her and then approached her. "Hi, Cora. I didn't know you shopped here."

"Hello," she greeted. "Yes. I started shopping here when Rafe and I moved to an apartment a few blocks over that way." She ges-tured with her left hand.

"Say, Cora, I've been meaning to ask you—does the family have any copies of your father's history of the Atkins family that my husband might borrow? Dan has been obsessed with missing cop-ies from the store and several libraries. He believes there's something in the book that the thief doesn't want anybody else to know about. Personally, I think he's going a bit overboard on this thing. But if you can help him, I'd appreciate it."

"Funny you should mention it," said Cora. "When I went over to the house to help Rae pack up Daddy's books, I did notice that the two copies he had on the shelf were also missing. I wonder if your husband isn't onto something. This is way more than a coinci-dence. I too wonder why."

"So no one else in the family would have a copy anymore?"

"Rae has all of Daddy's notes and literary collections. Per-haps there's a bunch of old manuscripts in the pile. It would have to be pure luck. Why don't you have Dan get in touch with Rae?"

"That's a great idea. I'll tell him. By the way, that orange has a brown spot on the other side."

"Oh, thank you. Bye."

Rivka whirled the basket around and headed back down the aisle toward boxed cereal.

# Chapter 8
## More Arrivals
### Monday, April 13th, 2009

Sunlight had already filled the Shermans' bedroom, when the routine garbage trucks invaded the bookstore's neighborhood and began to bash and thump the big green cans against metal, macadam, and concrete in a percussion chorus. Then, at two-minute intervals their brakes shrieked and screamed, just begging for new shoes. It was Monday pickup, and hardly anyone could sleep through the trashmen's medley. The Shermans were definitely awake now, but they remained inert, still lying there, denying the new morning's arrival. Rivka broke the silence.

"Dan?"

"Yes, Rivvie." He rolled over, throwing the heavy comforter off both of them. He was all ears.

"Don't be angry with me," she pleaded, sliding off her side of the bed.

"Why should I be angry with you, sweetheart? It's only Monday morning. We haven't had any time to irritate each other yet." He stood, scratched himself, and headed for the bathroom.

"I forgot to tell you something on Saturday," she called after him. "When I got home from shopping I meant to tell you what I found out from Cora Bacon."

"Oh? Where did you see her?" He stopped outside the bathroom doorway to listen.

"In produce at Food Fair, oranges, in fact."

"So tell me what she had to say. I'm not actually fluent in oranges."

Rivka giggled. "I asked her if her family had any copies of Arthur's book. And do you know what she answered?"

"No, what?" Now he was keenly interested.

"She said that while she was helping Rae and Gloria pack up to leave the house, she noticed that Arthur's two personal copies of the family history were missing from his office bookshelf. She thought that was really strange and said she wanted to help us if she can."

"But did she know if there were any more copies in the family?"

"Cora said that her sister Rae had all of Arthur Atkins' notes and literary collections and even some manuscripts. Perhaps the early family history is one of them. She also said you should connect with Rae to find out anything more on the subject."

"I'll be sure to call Rae this morning right after breakfast."

"Dan, you never did tell me where you were hiding on Saturday afternoon."

"I was in the Dungeon reading room, finishing up Rae's portion of the Atkins family history."

"Why would you expect to find anything in it?" Rivka asked. "Isn't it a totally different book?"

"Yes, it is different, but on the off-chance that there was some overlap, I felt that I had to read it."

"Did you learn anything of interest?"

"It was interesting, all right," said Dan, "but I couldn't find anything that would merit book thievery on this grand a scale. But your new information sounds promising, by George."

"Who's George, dear?"

"I don't know, but I'll Google it when I get downstairs."

After showers, breakfast, and various other morning routines, the Shermans descended to the main floor. While Rivka checked their voice mail for messages, Dan slid behind the store computer and logged on. Before he brought up the business program, he Googled "By George" and this is what he found:

"'By George' is a 'minced oath' that substitutes for 'By God,' for those who would regard the latter as blasphemy. And it's 'By George' because George and God are both G-words."

He called Rivka over after viewing the definition. "Now if I only knew what a 'minced oath' was."

"A minced oath is a word substitution to avoid either the profane or the offensive in writing," she answered.

"And how would you come to know this?"

"I was an English major, silly."

"I must have missed that class," Dan added.

"You going to call Rae?" she asked.

After flipping through the Annapolis phone directory, he dialed, and Rae answered on the fourth ring.

"Hi, Rae. My name is Daniel Sherman. My wife and I own The Olde Victorian Bookstore in town. Your sister Cora suggested I contact you. Do you happen to have either a bound or manuscript copy of your father's book, *The Atkins Family History, 1768 to 1934?*"

"What's this all about?" asked Rae. "This is a strange inquiry, considering there are several library copies available."

"That's just it," Dan replied. "All the library copies and our store copy have vanished into thin air. And Cora told my wife that the two personal copies your father had on his bookshelves are also missing. You're my last hope."

"I detect a tone of urgency," she said. "May I ask why this is so important to you?"

"Sorry if I came on a little strong, Rae. It's like this. When one nonfiction book goes missing, one assumes it's either for resale for its intrinsic value, or it's a simple case of theft to avoid paying for the book. Another reason might be to gain very specific information from its contents. When as many as five copies go missing at once, it's usually to prevent anyone else from gaining that specific information."

"But why *your* sudden interest in my father's book?"

"Our store copy sat on our shelf for several years with minimal interest. I asked myself, why would someone steal that particular book? I went to our local library to investigate and found their copies were gone, too. The librarian called the Pratt library in Baltimore and got the same answer. So you see, the mystery only deepened for me."

"Are you aware that my father is no longer with us?"

"Yes," admitted Dan in a humble and sincere voice. "I'm very sorry for your loss. He was an outstanding member of our community. I'm sure he will be missed."

"Thank you," returned Rae. "You may not be aware that our house has just been sold, and my two sisters and I are in the process of packing everything up and moving out. I'll be moving to an apartment in Eastport. I might add that this packing requires a great number of decisions on what to keep, what to sell, and what to throw away. Every bit of this has to be accomplished by the end of next week, the twenty-fifth to be exact."

"Ms. Atkins, I really hate to impose on you at a time like this, but can you at least tell me if you have a manuscript of your father's book?"

"I believe I do have his manuscript, but it probably wouldn't have all the last-minute editing."

"That's all right," said Dan. "All I'm interested in is the actual content. I want to read every available page of it—if you're willing to loan it to me for a week or two."

"I'm sorry to disappoint you, Mr. Sherman, but we have no time for searching forays, especially for something not essential to our move. All of my father's things that were worth saving have already been packed."

"If need be, I can come over and look for it myself," offered Dan in his most pleading voice. "I promise to keep out of your way and not disturb the moving effort."

"All I can tell you is that I think the manuscript is in one of three cartons sittings in our living room. You're welcome to come over here this afternoon and search through them, as long as you restore the cartons to their original order and seal them back up again for the movers. I don't like it when things get out of order."

"Thank you," said Dan. "That's extremely generous of you. Would one o'clock be okay?"

"That would be fine with me."

When Dan hung up, he found Rivka occupied with a customer who wanted to order a book she couldn't find on the shelves. Though he was bursting with his news, Dan started down the main aisle of stacks toward the back hall to feed Lord Byron and Lady Annabella. But when he got there, neither member of the royal feline family was in sight. Both of their bowls were empty, so he went to the utility closet where Rivka kept the bags of cat food. Dan found the door ajar about six inches. As soon as he opened the door all the way, the hall light streamed in over her ladyship. She was lying on her side in one corner with four little balls of fuzz suckling away. Lady Annabella lifted up her head proudly, as if to say. *Look what I've brought into this world.* Dan took out the bag of cat food, opened one corner of it, and dumped an extra ration into both royal bowls. He folded over the top of the bag before sliding it back into the closet. He stood for a moment admiring the feline scene before him. *I want Rivvie to see this, too. Get water and get Rivvie* were the thoughts running through his mind.

The proud owner of four brand-new grandkittens marched back up to the front of the store to find that Ivy had taken over the register. "Lady Annabella has had her kittens," Dan announced. "Four gorgeous little fuzzballs. They're in the hall closet. One of us must have left the door open and she took advantage of it for her birthing privacy."

"That's great," she said. "I can't wait to see them."

"You'll get your chance, Ivy, right after I show them to Rivka. By the way, do you know where she is right now?"

"She told me she was headed up to the kitchen to pay some household bills."

"Then she won't mind my disturbing her."

66

"What are you planning to do with the new kittens?"

"I suppose we'll have to give at least some of them away. We can't have so many cats roaming around the store. It might upset some of our customers."

"I'll take one home with me as soon as they're weaned," offered Ivy.

Dan headed upstairs to the kitchen and found Rivka writing and signing in their personal checkbook. She glanced up, acknowledging his arrival, but continued writing until she finished the current check. He waited and then announced, "I've got some great news."

"You mean you made some headway with Rae Atkins?"

"Yeah, that too. I'm going over there this afternoon to help Rae search for her father's manuscript. But that's not all."

"Something else is new?"

"How about I tell you we've got four new grandkittens downstairs in the hall closet."

Rivka laid down her pen, pushed back her chair, and jumped up. "This I've got to see for myself. Let's go."

Dan followed her down the stairs to the back hall. She stopped in front of the closet and, half in and half out, knelt down to get a better look.

"Oooh! They're sooo cute," she oozed. "I just want to pick one of them up and nuzzle it against my cheek."

"Wait! I don't think Lady Annabella would take kindly to that so soon after giving birth to them," cautioned Dan.

"I wonder if Lord Byron knows he's a father."

"I haven't seen him all morning, Rivvie. I wonder if he even came home last night."

Just then, the Shermans heard the pet flap on the back door squeak and, sure enough, his lordship squeezed through and bounded into the hall. Lady Annabella saw him and gave out a long, loud meow. The nearly all-black cat with four white bootie-like paws took one look in the closet and continued on to his lair in the poetry stack.

"The bounder doesn't seem to care that he's now a father," said Rivka.

"The way he figures it, his part of the work is done," said Dan with a smirk on his face.

"You men are all alike," she said, hoping to get a reaction from him. She got none. "Hey, what will we name them?"

"I've noticed that all four are a shiny jet black with different numbers of white boots just like the Laird," offered Dan.

"Three white ones, and that one on the end has two white ones," said Rivka.

"I count one and four boots on the opposite end," said Dan. "This is a real fluke of nature, but it sure is going to make naming them a lot easier than I thought."

"We're not going to name them One, Two, Three, and Four, are we?"

"We're not?" asked Dan. "Why not? It'll be easier to keep track of them."

"Then I guess we are."

"Know what, Rivvie? I believe we accomplished something this morning. If we get a bunch of sales today, it'll go down as a real good day."

"About your other good news, Dan—tell me what Rae Atkins had to say. Does she actually have the manuscript you were looking for?"

"The Atkins sisters are in the throes of packing, now that their house has been sold. All of their father's stuff has already been packed in three cartons. Rae thinks she remembers seeing it in one of the three. I'm going over there right after lunch to go through the cartons that might have the manuscript."

"You mean you're going to unpack what they've already packed? Isn't that a bit nervy of you, Dan?"

"I had to promise I'd restore each carton to its former self before she gave the okay."

"I'd say she was being quite generous."

"I agree."

\* \* \* \*

Meanwhile, up in a two-bedroom apartment in a blue-collar section of southeast Baltimore, Laura Dwyer regarded her husband slouching in his favorite recliner, staring off into nowhere. After twenty-nine years of a close marriage, she knew him pretty well. There were dark rings under his eyes, and his facial expression drooped. He hadn't said a word to her in hours and that was not like him.

"Tom, I know something's wrong, so don't put me off," she said. "You haven't moved from that chair in four hours and you keep staring out that window at nothing at all."

"I'm sorry, dear. I didn't sleep well last night—bad dreams and that sort of thing."

"You're having nightmares again, aren't you?"

"Yeah."

"The same ones as before?" she asked.

"Yeah, I'm scared to go to sleep. They'll haunt me the minute I shut my eyes."

"Come to think of it, I heard you calling out in your sleep last night. One time it was 'Stop' and another time it was 'No.' And you repeated both words several times. Then you woke yourself up."

"Sorry, I didn't mean to wake you, hon."

"That's okay. I went right back to sleep. But why, all of a sudden, are you getting these creepy nightmares again after so many years?"

"Laura, I think I know why," he confessed. "On the way home from the park yesterday, I stopped off for a beer at Murphy's Tavern-on-the-Avenue. I ran into Frank Mulhaney there. At first he seemed glad to see me. He even bought me a beer. Then he turned morose. I don't know what he was thinking, but he actually grabbed me by the collar and threatened me with his fists if I ever told anyone about his part in the hit-and-run. The guy is almost inhuman the way he acts about having taken a life. He worries more about someone finding out than having any honest emotion about her death. Frank has no idea how I feel. We never even learned the poor woman's name. There wasn't anything in the papers about it. Remember? You and

I scanned them for three weeks straight and nothing. That's what's *really* spooking me."

"Maybe it didn't happen the way you thought it did. Maybe she was just knocked out and unconscious and didn't die like you told me."

"No, Laura, you're grasping at straws. Frank felt her carotid artery and got nothing back. She's dead all right."

"In his excited state, Frank could have got it wrong, couldn't he?"

"I highly doubt it, woman. I saw the deep tire impression across her midsection. No way she could have recovered from that."

"Was there any blood around?" she asked.

"Come to think of it, I don't remember seeing any blood."

"I think it would be smart to stay away from Murphy's in the future," she cautioned.

(Tucked in the family history, a photo and history of the Atkins house.)

Lemule Wicks Atkins, a carpenter and builder, laid down the foundation for the house that stands on Prince Street today. In 1768 this master craftsman fashioned a wood rectangle, a two-story structure two rooms wide by two rooms deep, keeping to the colonial style: symmetry inside and out; two fireplaces with chimneys; multi-paned windows; and a decorative entry. Lemule built the house for his wife, Dora, and teenage son, Theodore Avram Atkins.

By the time Teddy Atkins reached his twentieth birthday, both his parents had succumbed to diphtheria, leaving the poor lad alone. His fortune changed after the Revolutionary War when he met his future bride, Priscilla Dawson. As a wedding present, her father, Horatio Dawson, a wealthy chandler, had the entire house reclad in stonework. Another two rooms were added to each story at the rear of the house.

More than a century later, the third story was added to accommodate the wishes of Debora Keen Atkins and her expanding family. A full-length widow's walk was included for the new roof. Debora could now see the harbor from there. A black wrought-iron fence surrounded the entire house.

The Lemule Wicks Atkins House (Circa 1768) as it appeared in 2009.

# Chapter 9
## The Manuscript
### The Same Day

At 12:55 the Shermans' 1996 champagne-colored Toyota pulled up to the curb in front of the Atkins' home. Dan noticed an object just inside the curb next to the car. He thought it might be a fire hydrant, so he pulled ahead to the next parking space. Stepping out of the car, he saw that the object was a dark-green hitching-post, a leftover from the horse-and-buggy days.

Dan swung back the black wrought-iron gate and followed a flagstone walk to a semblance of a mock Greek stoa entry with just two columns. He pushed the call bell, and a woman in a spinster-ish print dress answered the door. She was sturdy and plain-looking with no specific imperfections in her appearance. Perhaps a little too high a forehead, or too thin brows, or the lack of makeup led to his conclusion. A matching print bandana tied at the back of her neck covered her hair. She looked puzzled..

"Yes?" she said.

"Hi. Ms. Rae Atkins?"

"Yes, I'm Rae Atkins."

"I'm Dan Sherman. I spoke with you earlier about your father's manuscript."

"Oh, of course. You may call me Rae." She stepped back and swung the door wide for him. "Come right in."

Dan passed through a short entrance hall and, following her

to his right, he entered a large uncarpeted room he presumed had been some sort of parlor. Void of furnishings now and nearly full of cardboard cartons, the room displayed unfaded patches in the floral wallpaper where paintings or pictures had once hung. She led him through the sea of boxes, some sealed, some still open, until they arrived at the three sealed cartons she had set aside for him. A bridge table and single folding chair had also been provided for his convenience. A pair of scissors and a roll of sealing tape sat on the table as a reminder of his full-restoration promise.

"If it's anywhere, my father's manuscript should be in one of these three boxes. I'll leave you to your search now," said Rae. "I've got work to do upstairs." With that she turned and started to leave the room.

"Thank you. I really appreciate all this cooperation," he called after her.

Dan sat down at the table, picked up the scissors, and attacked the carton closest to him. Slitting the seals across the top and two edges, he folded the flaps back and began off-loading onto the card table: dozens and dozens of hard-bound green and brown journals; manila envelopes chock full of hand-written notes and photographs; and packets of bulging file folders wrapped in thick rubber bands. Then he examined everything he thought might be a possible precursor to Arthur's book. His perfunctory examination of the first carton's contents found only scraps of information, nothing that resembled a manuscript at all.

Dan was in the middle of repacking this carton, when he felt the presence of another pair of eyes on him. Looking up, he encountered an attractive young woman in a tight T-shirt and audaciously skimpy shorts—*all the rage, like hot pants,* he remembered. Her head was cocked to one side, and long dark-brown hair hung over that shoulder. Blue eye shadow and mascaraed lashes gave her a coquettish look.

"Who are *you?*" she asked. "What are you doing in here?" Her thick coat of makeup exaggerated her facial features when she spoke.

"I'm Daniel Sherman and I have Rae's permission to search for a manuscript in here. But who are *you*?"

"I'm Gloria Atkins, Rae and Cora's younger sister. I've been wrapping china for the barrels in the kitchen. Nice to meet ya, Dan."

"Glad to meet you, too, Gloria—nice name."

"Well, it sure isn't the name my mother gave me, but everyone calls me Gloria."

"Why? What did your mother name you?"

"Don't want to talk about that."

"Ooo-kaay." He drew out the two syllables.

"Do you need any help here?" Her offer seemed genuine.

"No thank you," he replied. "It's really a job for one person, and I've got that well in hand."

"I think I'll look in on Bunny, my baby. She's asleep upstairs." Goneril Atkins turned and flitted from the room in the same manner that she arrived.

When Dan finished repacking and resealing the first carton, he cut the seals and started unpacking the second one. About two-thirds of the way through it, he came across two well-worn, shiny-brown accordion envelopes, with flaps held in place by strings wound about two cardboard buttons. They looked so promising that he stopped his unpacking to open the first one. Dan slid out the pages contained in the first compartment, and a broad grin spread across his face. He found a title page, a table of contents, and at least the first three chapters of Arthur's book. Checking more of the folded compartments, he found an orderly succession of chapters, which continued into the second accordion envelope. He went back, studied the first pages, and saw the following.

———

### Chapter 1. Early Conflict and Heroism

Theodore Avram Atkins was only twenty-two in 1778, but he was already well aware of conflict going on in the colonies. In fact, he knew more than most of the individuals he met and even more about events in the other colonies, because this enterprising young man rode between the major coastal cities carrying the week's news to their leading print shops. This was ..."

———

Dan stopped. His search for the manuscript was over. *Now what?* he wondered. *I can't leave the carton open like it is—their moving day is imminent. I can't finish this much reading in less than two weeks. I know what I'll do. I'll promise to deliver the manuscript to their new address.* He repacked the carton using crushed newsprint to fill the space left by the two accordion envelopes. Then he resealed the carton. Everything was as he found it—well, nearly, anyway. *I wonder where Rae is.* He left the two manuscript envelopes on the bridge table while he went to find her.

At the foot of a grand staircase that curled gracefully through a full forty-five degrees, he called, "Rae? Rae?" No answer. Halfway up the stairs, he tried again, "Rae? Rae?" Still no answer. *Will I be intruding on their privacy if I go to the second-floor landing?* A few stairs shy of that landing, he attempted a shout. "Rae!" But Gloria appeared at the top to scold him.

"Shush, my little girl is sleeping in the next room."

"Sorry," he said. "Would you tell Rae that I..."

"Wait there, I'll get my sister, and you can tell her yourself."

Gloria disappeared, and shortly thereafter, Rae appeared in her place. "What do you need now?" There was a hint of annoyance in her voice.

"I just wanted to tell you I found the manuscript. I promise I'll take good care of it and return it to your new residence in three weeks. Would that be all right with you?"

"Yes, yes. I thought you said two weeks, though."

"It's the manuscript's length," he explained.

"Of course," she said. "But how do you know my new address?"

"How clumsy of me. I don't."

"I'll be staying at the Inn at Horn Point for the next six weeks, that is, until the renovations at my new place are finished. The inn is located at the end of Chesapeake Avenue over in Eastport. Think you can find it?"

"I know it very well. And thank you again." Dan turned, descended to the first floor, and picked up the two shiny manuscript envelopes from the bridge table.

Outside, as he started down the flagstone walk, he saw a man with a thick, dark beard approach the gate from the street. He was wearing an Irish tweed flat cap and leather jacket—someone Dan didn't recognize. The man even held the wrought-iron gate open for him as Dan continued to the Toyota. Dan stood in the street by the driver's door and watched this man enter the house using a key. *Wonder who he is. Looks like he belongs there, a brother, maybe.* He carefully laid the two envelopes on the passenger seat, started the car, and drove away.

* * * *

Stepping inside the Atkins' front door, Muddy waited for Rae while she descended the staircase. When she reached the bottom step, he confronted his sister. "Who was that tall stranger I saw leaving the house just now?"

"Oh, that was Mr. Sherman," she replied. *I wonder why he's asking.*

"What was *he* selling?" asked Muddy in a sarcastic tone.

"He wasn't selling anything."

"Then what in hell was he doing here?"

"He convinced me to loan him a manuscript," Rae replied. "And what's more, I don't like being interrogated this way."

"I don't care what you like and don't like. What manuscript is that?" He took a threatening pose.

"Daddy's book, the family history one, if you must know."

"Oh, hell no!" Muddy bellowed. "You didn't give it to him, did you?"

"I did and for three weeks, too—some research he's working on. It's only a loan. What's wrong? Besides, Daddy left it to *me*, so what are *you* carping about?"

"Nothin', never mind. Do you know who he is?"

"Of course. His name is Daniel Sherman. He and his wife own The Olde Victorian Bookstore over on Franklyn Lane."

"Ah, the bookshop. That's who he is. I thought he looked somewhat familiar."

"How do you know him?" she asked.

"I don't!"

"Then why are you so upset, Muddy?"

"I just think it's stupid to lend out Daddy's stuff." *Jeez, I've got to get it back before Mr. Nosy reads the whole damn thing and finds out about it.*

\* \* \* \*

On the drive home Dan couldn't wait to start reading the manuscript. With the two accordion envelopes under his arm, he rushed into the store past both Ivy at the register and Rivka at the computer. "Hi, ladies." he said as he headed straight toward the first-floor reading room. Before he got there he saw Rivka following him. "What?" he asked, as he turned to face her.

"I have a problem with the dumb computer," she replied. "It just won't behave."

"First of all, what are all the symptoms?" he asked.

"Well, I can't find the cursor anymore and I was in the middle of an important letter. I think the mouse died and don't tell me to bury the damn thing. I'm ready to bury the whole computer."

"I won't. Have you thought of putting new batteries in the mouse? You'll need two. There's a package of Double As in the bottom drawer of the counter." He laid the two precious envelopes on the counter because he anticipated what she was going to say next.

"Will you help me replace them, Sir Knight?" she asked in her humblest voice.

"Why sure, my fair maiden," he replied. "Just get two batteries out of the drawer while I press this little button on the bottom of the mouse to open the compartment and extract the dead ones, noting which way they face." Rivka handed him the two new ones. He inserted them, replaced the compartment cover, and said, "*Voilà!*"

Rivka wiggled the computer mouse and, sure enough, the cursor came to life once more. "My hero," she exclaimed and gave him a nuzzle on the back of his neck.

He picked up the two envelopes and started toward the reading room once more.

"I take it you found the Atkins' manuscript, and you'll be in isolation until you find what you're looking for."

"You got that right, dear," he replied.

Rivka watched him leave the room, thinking, *I'll get no more bookstore work out of him until he's finished perusing that infernal manuscript.*

Dan entered the reading room, aiming for the wing-back, upholstered recliner in the corner. Sitting down with the two accordion envelopes on his lap, he opened the top one to see whether it held the beginning of the book. It did, so he extracted the first few chapters and put both envelopes under the recliner—out of sight due to the antique gold fringe that hung down from the chair bottom. He then adjusted the recliner position and the proximity and angle of the reading lamp. Finally, he turned his full attention to his reading, starting the book from the very first line.

———

### Chapter 1. Early Conflict and Heroism

"Theodore Avram Atkins was only twenty-two in 1778, but he was already well aware of a war going on in the colonies. In fact, he knew more than most of the individuals he met and even more about the events of the other colonies, because this enterprising young man rode between the major coastal cities, carrying the week's news to their leading print shops. This was an often dangerous task as he was forced to cross battle lines between the loyal Tories and the rebelling colonists. For all of his bravery, Teddy received compensation of two pounds and ten shillings per month plus expenses. Being a frugal sort, he was able to save a considerable amount of his wages.

His outspoken uncle ran the local print shop in Annapolis, Maryland, and published the *Maryland Gazette*. The masthead read:

**"Annapolis, Printed by Jonas Green at his Printing Office on Charles Street; where all persons may be supplied with this *Gazette* at twelve shillings, six pence a year, and Advertisements of**

**moderate length are inserted for 5 shillings the First Week and 1
shilling each time thereafter: and long ones in proportion."**

The *Gazette* vehemently opposed the Royal Stamp Act, which
taxed the very enterprise Green ran. As a protest, he even suspended
operation for a short while, but his fervor for the ongoing struggle
moved him to reopen and publish again.

Teddy Atkins spent six days a week on his horse, and it took
nearly a month to complete one circuit, so he had no time for a wife
and certainly none for any brats. A couple years later he would change
his mind when he would meet Priscilla Dawson. For the most part,
the house he inherited from his deceased parents lay empty. Being a
zealous patriot, the young man allowed black powder and muskets
to be concealed there. He even devised improved ways to hide these
things from the Redcoats when they began their house-to-house
searches. They never found anything.

In October of 1781, during the Battle of Yorktown, Teddy
was wounded passing through the battle lines. The patriot had made
a bad decision in the interest of expediency, having neglected to cir-
cumvent the main fighting, and wound up in the thick of it. His but-
tocks wound meant he could no longer ride the news circuit, so Uncle Jonas hired Harrison Middlebury to take his place. It was during
this period of recovery that he met Priscilla at a town meeting. The
couple courted for about a year and then married on September 20th,
1782. Her parents, Horatio and Jennie, staked the newlyweds to the
purchase of a dry goods store on Fleet Street, and the two became
successful shopkeepers throughout the next forty years. The senior
Dawsons had made their considerable wealth in maritime shipping.

Teddy and Priscilla raised three children born a year apart—
Ted junior, Abel, and their sister, Isabel. Abel became a lawyer and
married Lena Johansen on June 15th, 1804. The younger Ted took
over the store for another twenty-three years. For some unknown
reason he never married. Thanks to Isabel and her diary, we know
much of what has been told up to now. A few letters from a Cousin
Rebecca Clay to her explained even more. Abel and Lena became key
progenitors of the present Atkins family with their two sons, Hiram

A. and Rudolph L. Atkins. Hiram became a general practitioner with a flourishing medical practice, and, though he married and divorced twice, he produced no heirs. Rudy, on the other hand, followed in his father's footsteps and became a successful lawyer even arguing a few cases before the U.S. Supreme Court. He married Lucile Bailey on July 8th, 1829, and that left their offspring, Jeffrey and Alice, to carry on the family line." ...

———

There was more, so much more, but Dan didn't want to miss anything of importance. However, it was far too much for him to digest in one sitting, so he tucked the manuscript chapters into their envelopes and stashed them under the upholstered chair. He had intended to close his eyes for only a few minutes, but dozed off until almost suppertime. The only reason he didn't sleep longer was that Lord Byron had entered the realm. The Laird circled the chair and then hopped up on Dan's lap, where he curled up and waited for Dan to rub him behind the ears. He purred to say he wasn't disappointed.

## Chapter 10
## The Break-in
Tuesday, April 14th, 2009

The morning proved to be eventful for the bookstore. One of the frequent tourist buses had stopped in the neighborhood around nine to view local Victorian and Georgian architecture. Those spouses in the party less interested in that subject just happened to wander into the bookstore to browse and buy. They kept Rivka and Ivy on their toes, constantly answering questions, finding books by title and author, checking out purchases, and keeping an eye out for sticky fingers. Of course, not all of their efforts turned into sales. At noon when the bus left, the store emptied like an uncorked sink. The two women were exhausted.

"Tell you what, Ivy," said Rivka. "I feel like we've already done a day's work. Why don't I treat you to lunch?"

"Sounds great to me," replied Ivy. "Can we go to the Double T Diner? I'd like to talk with them about a wedding cake. I wasn't impressed with the one my wedding planner dug up, nor the price she's charging."

"Sure. Let me see if Dan's free to tend to the register while we're gone. He won't mind getting away from our taxes for an hour or so."

The store's sales and business taxes, and even the personal taxes, were routinely handled by their accountant, George Hanery. Dan, who wanted desperately to continue reading the manuscript, had been meeting with George in the apartment kitchen, clearing up last-minute details; the mailing deadline was midnight the next day.

But Rivka had seen George leave ten minutes earlier. Approaching Dan in the kitchen, she asked, "Are you ready to take a little break from all these mind-boggling figures long enough to watch the register while we girls go out to lunch? Things are pretty slow now that the tour bus has left."

"Let me seal and put stamps on these envelopes first, and I'll come downstairs," said Dan. "You can leave then."

Rivka leaned over his shoulder and planted a kiss on his cheek. "Wonderful, I'll even bring you a corned beef on rye and a dill pickle as a reward. How's that for appreciation?"

* * * *

Rivka parked the old Toyota out in front of the Double T, and the two ladies were seated in a red vinyl booth, but not in Frieda Fraume's serving section. They received no more than a wave from her as the noon hour rush kept her on the go.

Their own waitress greeted them. "Hi, ladies, I'm Sal. What can I get you to drink?" A gray-haired motherly type stood there, resting on one hip with her order book in hand.

"Iced coffee for me," said Rivka.

"I'd like hot tea, Earl Grey, if you have it, " said Ivy.

"Coming right up." Sal disappeared behind the counter and reappeared a few minutes later with their drinks. "What'll ya have, ladies?"

Each of them ordered a bowl of matzoh-ball soup and a sandwich—an egg salad on pumpernickel for Rivka and a roast beef on a Kaiser roll for Ivy, chips included.

"Oh by the way we'll also need a corn beef on rye to go, plus a dill pickle," said Rivka.

While they waited for their orders, they noticed a woman standing in line just inside the door, waiting to be seated. She wore a beige jogging outfit and sneakers. A plastic clip held her hair off her very familiar face.

"Say, isn't that Helen Margoles over there?" asked Ivy.

"Sure is," replied Rivka, stretching to see. "Why don't you wave and ask her to join us?"

Ivy jumped up, got Helen's attention, and waved her to their booth.

"I never expected to see anyone I know in here," Helen said, sliding into the booth next to Ivy. "I'm waiting for my car to be serviced down the street, so I thought I'd treat myself to lunch. Say, have you folks ordered yet?"

"Only a couple of minutes ago," said Rivka. "I'll flag down a waitress for you." As it happened, the first one they saw was their own Sal, bringing their soup.

Two minutes later Helen ordered a Denver omelet, a side of fries, and hot coffee for herself. "Sometimes I like eating breakfast food when I'm out."

"How's the move going," asked Rivka between spoonfuls of soup.

"The hardest thing is all the decision-making. Deciding what to move, what to sell, and what to toss. We have so many pieces that won't be appropriate for a colonial décor and yet we have so many extra rooms to fill with furniture we don't own."

"Wow," said Rivka. "You hit the nail on the head. I know this because we had to get rid of nearly everything when we moved into the bookstore. It was neither physically nor financially feasible to keep our old home. It was hard parting with a lot of our things."

"Lee, my husband, had to make a floor plan for each of the four floors, so we can make those decisions more easily," Helen continued. "He's such a perfectionist that he measured every room and made his drawings to scale. Actually, we're pretty much ready, but we can't move in until the Atkins family is completely moved out on Saturday, the twenty-fifth. Our movers are coming on Monday the twenty-seventh."

"I guess you haven't had any time to do any writing then," said Ivy.

"That's about right," agreed Helen, with a deep sigh.

"Now, if you two will excuse me," said Ivy. "I need to talk

with the pastry chef about a wedding cake"

Helen slid out to allow Ivy to get to the aisle and on her way to the kitchen.

Sal dropped by with their checks and removed some of the dishes.

The conversation between Rivka and Helen continued throughout the rest of lunch and a little beyond. Then Helen looked at her watch and declared, "My car should be ready by now. I'll see you on Thursday."

"With all your tumult," Rivka said, "you'll still be willing to come to the critique group? You are one amazing woman."

Helen only smiled. She picked up her check, slid out of the booth, and left for the cashier.

A few minutes later Ivy returned to the table. "Where's Helen?" she asked.

"She went to pick up her car," said Rivka. "What about the cake?"

"It's going to be beautiful, if it's anything like the sample I just saw. I got to taste it, too. You can't beat their bakery stuff here."

"You better remember to have your wedding planner adjust your contract or you're going to wind up with two wedding cakes and paying for both."

They paid their checks and headed back to the store.

"We better not dally," said Rivka. "Dan will have a conniption fit if we keep him away from his precious manuscript too long."

\* \* \* \*

At 8:30 that evening Muddy Atkins approached The Olde Victorian Bookstore and waited outside for an opportunity to beat the burglar alarm system. His father's manuscript, the last path to learning his own deep, dark mystery, lay with this bookstore owner. That ugly secret had been well kept for more than twenty years, and he wasn't going to let a stupid move by his sister Rae spill the beans now.

*There was no reason for Rae to sell the family house,* Muddy brooded. *She could have done a little renovating and rented out rooms.*

*Hired help could do all the work. All she had to do was manage the place and the income would support her writing to kingdom come. It was a stupid thing to sell the house and an even dumber thing to loan out Daddy's book. Well, I can't do anything about those things now, but I do have a plan to get the manuscript out of circulation.*

Muddy could count on the bookstore's burglar alarm remaining off, at least during the nine-to-nine store hours printed on the window outside, and that left him thirty minutes to work with. When he'd observed the store's closing procedure on the previous night, he noticed that both the register and the front door were left unguarded while the lady owner turned off the lights in the other rooms. *She neither locks the door nor sets the burglar alarm until she returns from turning off the lights. I hope that procedure is a pattern and happens again tonight. My plan depends upon it. When the register and door are vacant long enough for me to enter, I'll sneak past the register and hide inside the store.*

Muddy kept looking at his watch as his time frame dwindled down to five minutes. From his vantage point, he observed Daniel Sherman removing the register cash and placing it in a vinyl pouch with a zipper. Then the man disappeared from view at the foot of the stairs. Next, he saw Sherman's wife leave the register and begin extinguishing store lights one by one. He quickly slipped inside and maneuvered among the stacks, using them as barriers between the woman and himself to avoid being seen. The woman returned to the register area, locked the front door, set the alarm, and turned off the last light at the foot of the stairs as she climbed to the floor above.

Muddy snuck into the main reading room and flopped into the recliner there to wait in the semidarkness for the owners to fall asleep. Ironically, he chose to sit over the top of the very same manuscript that he was searching for. Of course, he had no idea that Dan had left it under the chair. As his eyes grew more accustomed to the dark, they swept the room trying to contemplate where the man might have left it. One hour and thirty minutes into his wait, the lights were still on in the upper stairwell, and he could still hear voices. Another hour and, finally, all had turned both dark and silent on the next floor. It was time for him to start his search.

Muddy's logic led him to believe that the man had no reason to hide the manuscript, and that he would find it easily on top of some open surface. *It has to be someplace convenient to read, doesn't it?* At the very worst, he might find it stashed in some drawer. Using his flashlight, he scanned the Dungeon level and then the main level, finding nothing. He examined every surface, even the tops of all the book stacks. Then, he searched the three drawers behind the register. When that proved fruitless, he stared intently at the flight of stairs leading to the living area. *Is it too risky for me to consider getting that close to these owners? What if those old wood stairs squeak and give me away? What if I bump into or trip over something?*

*But maybe he took the manuscript to read in bed with him, and it's lying there on his nightstand, big as day, waiting for me to just pluck it away. I gotta take the risk, the stakes are too high not to. I can't have anyone poking around in my closet. No one's gonna believe me now, after all this time.*

Muddy gathered up his courage and put one foot following the other on one stair after another until he landed on the third level of the bookstore. On his immediate left the stairs continued upward. A right turn put him in a large room with a long table—some travel magazines lay on top. Although the intruder checked all the surfaces he could find, it was to no avail. He made a U-turn and strode into the kitchen, noting the open bedroom doorway to his right. Only an empty glass, flour and sugar bins, a cookie jar, and a top-loaded bread box stood on the counters. Then he found himself standing in the open doorway to the bedroom.

Shielding the flashlight with his hand, he controlled the beam he let into the room. He saw the mister and missus as two lumps of blankets in the king-sized bed. There was a nightstand on the far side where the smaller lump lay. He assumed it was her side of the bed. Atop her nightstand was a half-full glass of water, a pair of reading glasses, and an open copy of *Reader's Digest*, lying on its face. Underneath, on the open bottom shelf, there was a stack of magazines. The nightstand of interest to Muddy was the man's on the near side of the bed, but all he could find on top was a handkerchief and a few cough drops, plus a landline telephone. Underneath were four neatly stacked paperback books. He stepped closer and tried the lone drawer; it contained more handkerchiefs. He also tried the woman's nightstand drawer. Inside he found another pair of glasses, a small sewing kit, and a small flashlight. Silently closing the drawer inch by inch, he scanned the rest of the room. Next to a dresser, he saw a two-foot cube-shaped safe, but he had no idea how heavy it was or how to open it. Puzzled, Muddy carefully backed out of the room. He didn't know where else to look.

He climbed the stairs to the final floor only to find more stacks of books and a small table with an old newspaper on top of it. There were no other surfaces around, so he started down the stairs all the way to the main floor.

The booksellers had outwitted him, but he still had to leave the store without being detected. He lacked the combination to actually turn off the alarm, but he knew about the alarm's magnetic switch above the front door. He removed a strip of Scotch tape from the register counter and wrapped the alarm's two components together—the magnetic switch and the partner magnet—so they couldn't separate. Then, with the screwdriver blade of his penknife, Muddy unscrewed both components and bent their wires to put them out of the door's path. Next, he unlocked the deadbolts on the door from the inside and stepped outside. He closed the door behind him and, crushed with frustration, stared at the building for several minutes.

Muddy walked the neighborhood until he felt the stress of danger wear off and the stress of fear take its place. He had failed to recover the manuscript, but he survived the attempt without being discovered. His mind was a whirl, full of scenarios of being discovered and blame dropping like a wet blanket all over him. *What I need is a drink,* he told himself. *That'll drive the demons from my head. I need a clear head to figure out what I'm going to do next. I'll find a bar on West Street.* He started walking faster and in no time at all he found an open pub called Pinky's Place. He entered, approached the bar, and stared at the multitude of bottles on the shelves beyond his reach.

"You wanna beer?" asked the barkeep. "Or something stronger?"

"Something stronger is what I want—maybe some of *that.*" Muddy laid two crisp fifty-dollar bills on the bar and pointed to the bottle of Wild Turkey on the shelf. "I aim to get stinko, sir," he announced.

The barkeep eyed the serious bills and considered the customer's ultimate intent. Well, he'd pour until the bills were gone or the man became unmanageable. As soon as he filled a double shot glass to the line, his customer downed it like it was mere soda pop. Halfway into the second fifty, Muddy lost what sensibility he came with and picked a fight with a man two stools away. He didn't need to be in the right—he needed to punish or be punished, so insults turned to shoves and shoves became fists a-flying. Both wound up on the floor. Muddy hit the floor second and stayed down. His opponent got up and left the establishment, leaving the barkeep and Muddy as the only ones there.

Seeing that his customer was down and out for the night, the barkeep pocketed the bills on the bar, extracted another fifty from Muddy's wallet, and then called the police to pick up the drunk and disorderly. Twenty minutes later the paddy wagon carted him off to the police station, where he was introduced to the drunk tank. He spent the night there fighting with his demons, shouting epithets and thrashing about.

In the morning, Muddy didn't have enough cash left in his wallet to pay the drunk-and-disorderly fine. He called Gloria on the pay phone. She didn't have that much cash in the apartment and she couldn't get to the bank before noon. Next he tried calling Cora, but she didn't answer; he assumed she wasn't home. Finally, he called his least favorite sister, and Rae agreed to come down and pay the fine. But calling Rae meant he had to pay the price of enduring a venomous, never-ending scold from her. She dropped him off at his hotel, where he halfheartedly promised to reimburse her for the fine. But thanking her, showing any sense of gratitude, was beyond him.

Muddy spent the day visited by glimpses of his wrestle with the demons the night before. The most significant thing about these visits was that these demons bore the face and person of Daniel Sherman. *All my current problems are his doing, his fault. I'm going to make the SOB pay for digging up this whole mess after twenty years.*

There was a kind of sickness slowly taking hold of Muddy, an unfounded desire for revenge. *I can't go to sea again until I take care of this matter. I'll catch another ship when this is all over.*

## Chapter 11
## Alarming Discovery
Wednesday, April 15th, 2009

Dan didn't know what had awakened him, but he had this strange feeling, a feeling that someone else had been in the room with them. Turning toward the clock, he saw that it was 2:32, still the middle of the night. In the dark he quickly scanned the room and neither heard nor saw anything. He went into the bathroom with all his senses still attuned to his surroundings. Afterward, he slowly worked his way into the hall, listened at the head of the staircase, and concluded that it was all in his imagination. He went back to bed, but could not fall back asleep. He closed his eyes, yet even his lids were not dark enough to squelch his still-active mind. He tried to think of nothing—floating freely in space—counting sheep—but nothing worked. There were short snatches in the land of Nod where he wasn't quite sure whether it was actual sleep or not. Though fuzzy without his glasses, the glowing red numerals on the digital clock were always there—3:10, 3:55, 4:40, 5:20, and 5:45. When Dan saw that it was 5:58, he decided he'd had enough of trying. It was time to launch himself from the bedcovers onto his own two feet.

The alarm was set for the usual 6:45. He washed in the bathroom, dressed quietly, and slipped out of the bedroom, closing the common door to the kitchen so as not to wake Rivka. Dan had this bright idea to whip up a batch of batter and make banana pancakes for breakfast. There were even two overripe bananas in a basket on top of the fridge. He peeled both, mashed them with a fork, and dumped the result into the mixer. He followed the recipe on the flour box and added the remaining ingredients to the mixer. Of course, spills and splatters made their way onto the counter. He preheated the grill over the gas stove. There wasn't anything he could do to squelch the sound of the mixer, so he let 'er rip anyway. The grill also sizzled aloud with scoops of batter.

At 6:33 the bedroom door opened and Rivka marched out in her robe, nightie, and slippers. "What in heaven's name is going on in here?"

"Did the sound of the mixer wake you?" he asked. "I'm sorry."

"No, I believe it was the smell of burnt pancakes on the grill that did the trick," she kidded.

"Burnt? Oh crap...." He turned and flipped three overdone pancakes. Her early arrival had distracted him for a moment. "I'm still sorry I woke you," he said with his back to her.

Rivka set the table, poured the coffee, got out the butter and maple syrup, and sat down, waiting to be served. Dan turned off the burner beneath the grill and slid the last three of nine ovals onto a plate, which he put in the center of the table. He served a stack of three on his plate and two on hers.

Rivka added generous smears of butter and a large puddle of syrup to her stack. "What possessed you to make pancakes this morning?" she asked as she pushed a forkful into her mouth.

"I couldn't sleep any longer so I wanted to do something useful with my time," he replied after swallowing a mouthful. "Besides, I like pancakes, and we almost never have them anymore."

"Sweetheart, I really appreciate what you've done here, but I'll have to starve myself for days to get these delicious pancake pounds off." She grinned as she took a large bite dripping with syrup.

"Enjoy."

The Shermans finished their breakfast. While Rivka cleaned up Dan's messy counter and rinsed their plates for the dishwasher, Dan started downstairs to open the bookstore. He poked in the numbers to disable the store's alarm system and then went to open the front door to the street. That door was unlocked. *Strange,* he thought. *Why would Rivka set the alarm and forget to lock the door—both the keyed deadbolt and the blind deadbolt? That's not like her.* He brought up the register computer just as Rivka descended the stairs with the cash pouch. He stood next to her as she meted out the bills and coins into their proper bins within the cash drawer. He wondered, *Should I confront her with the screw-up and risk pissing her off? I guess I'd better get it over with.*

"Rivka, dear."

"What, hon?"

"When I came downstairs this morning, I found the alarm on and the door unlocked, both locks."

"That's impossible! I remember locking both of them. I even broke one of my nails while locking up. See!" She showed him the nail damage.

"Could your broken fingernail have distracted you?"

"Certainly not! You know me better than that." Her voice rose with a bit of ire.

"Okay, okay!" he said. "I believe you. Rivvie. But this is weird. There's no way a blind deadbolt can be unlocked from the outside, so whoever unlocked it did it from the inside some time after you had locked it. The alarm was still set this morning, so there's no way anyone could pass through any of our doors or windows without setting it off—unless the alarm wasn't or isn't working. Better call the alarm people and tell them I'm going to trip the alarm for a test."

Rivka dialed the number and explained that they were going to test the alarm system. Then she gave Dan the okay, and he opened the front door to trip the alarm, but to their surprise, they heard only street noise.

"Push the test button at the bottom of the box," he directed, "and be ready to punch in the shutdown code if it responds. Okay?"

"Yes, dear." She pushed the test button. The loud clanging noise filled their ears. It lasted only the half-minute it took her to key in the five-digit shutdown code.

Dan stared at the door and then, just above the door, he found his explanation. The door switch and its magnet were taped together—and both were unscrewed from the door and jamb, then bent away from the door's path. He pointed to the cause for Rivka to see and said, "We've been burgled. This was an inside job."

"Inside job? What do you mean, Dan? Lord Byron or Lady Annabella sure didn't plan this heist." Listening to herself, Rivka could hardly believe she was jesting at this moment.

"Yeah," said Dan. "Where was our trusty watch-cat when this nasty break-in went down? We're feeding and housing his whole family now. The least he could do is keep up his part of the bargain. I wonder where he was?"

"Probably in the cat closet with the mommy cat and her cute little litter," offered Rivka. "After all, he's a family cat now."

"More likely, he was out and about, carousing, if I know the Laird," said Dan.

"At any rate he wasn't on the job," agreed Rivka.

"Tell me," asked Dan, "was the register left unguarded at any time yesterday for more than a few minutes?"

"You mean the necessary time to unscrew those thingies up there? Well, if you remember the bunch of tourists from the bus yesterday morning, either Ivy or I was at the register until we left for lunch. When we got back, it was the same. You were at the register while we were gone."

"And I never left it—not even to pee."

"Ivy manned it during our supper hour," said Rivka.

"Then, you and I took over until you closed up, so when did the culprit manage to stage this break-in?"

"I can't imagine when," she said. "Oh, here comes Ivy now."

"What's going on?" asked Ivy. "The two of you look so grim."

"We had a break-in some time yesterday," said Dan, "and we're still trying to figure out when the culprit had time to defeat the alarm system."

"Wow, that is serious." said Ivy. "Is there anything that I can do?"

"No, Ivy," said Dan. "Rivka, can you run me through your nighttime closing routine?"

"Sure. First, while I'm still at the counter, I watch you empty the cash drawer and take the pouch upstairs with you. Then I go around and turn off all the lights. I leave the light on by the register so I can see my way. Then I lock the front door and set the alarm. Then I turn off the last light and head upstairs. By the time I get up to our room you've already put the cash pouch in the safe. That's about it."

"Wait," said Dan. "You mean you don't lock the door first and then do the other stuff?"

"No! It's the way I've always done it," said Rivka. "What's wrong with the way I do it?"

"First of all, someone could sneak in and hide during all that time you're away from the counter. Second, I think we should have the alarm people come out and either fix or upgrade the system so we're not as vulnerable."

"Dan, this morning I saw the cash pouch in the safe. It wasn't touched, so what do you suppose is missing?"

"Do we have to do a complete store inventory to find out what's missing?" asked Ivy.

"No, I think I know what the burglar was looking for," said Dan, as he rushed into the reading room to look under his wing-chair recliner. The other two followed him. "By golly, the two manuscript envelopes are still there—hidden from general view by the footrest and the fringe at the bottom." He sighed with relief. "But what if that's what the intruder was looking for? Maybe he or she gave up and left without any booty."

"I just knew that blasted manuscript was going to be more trouble that it was worth," declared Rivka. "What do you expect the intruder to try next? What grand mystery do you think you're going to solve by reading through it, anyway?"

"That's just it. I haven't the foggiest idea of an answer to either one of those questions. But I do know he or she must be getting pretty desperate to have broken into the bookstore like this."

"Oh, Dan, do you think he'll become violent? Are we in some kind of danger because of this? Because you're being so pig-headed about solving a problem when you don't even know what the problem is?"

"Perhaps you could return the manuscript to the bloody bounder and escape any real danger," offered Ivy.

"Ivy's right, Dan," pleaded Rivka. "Give it up. Take it back. I don't care about its dumb secrets. We don't need all this disruption. I feel so vulnerable and violated."

"But that way we'll never know what it is the culprit's trying to hide. And at this point, he may think we already know his secret, whatever that may be. Then we'd be completely defenseless."

"Dan, you're willing to put all our lives at risk to find out some silly miserable secret?"

"Of course not," defended Dan. "Maybe we're just over-thinking this thing. We don't know that this culprit is violent. We haven't received any threats."

"Not yet we haven't," said Rivka. "It's not fair."

"And just how do you propose I return this text to the culprit?"

"Give the damned thing back to Rae Atkins," said Rivka, "and let it haunt her instead. Make a big show of giving it back, so the whole world knows you gave it back."

"Rivka, trust me. You've been through a hell of a lot worse, so hang on."

"Oh, Dan, after my kidnapping, you promised me I'd never have to go through anything like that again."

"I guarantee you won't," he promised. "I'll return the manuscript, but first, I'm going to copy all 280 pages of it before I return it. Then I can probably return the original by early afternoon. The only problem I see is the culprit doesn't know how far I've already read and whether I now know his or her secret."

"Retaining a copy, hah! Daniel P. Sherman, I'm really pissed off at you. You can sleep in that old recliner all night if you pursue this any further." Rivka rushed out of the reading room back to the register, where Ivy was just hanging up the phone.

"Who was that, Ivy?" Rivka asked.

"The technician. He'll be here in ten minutes to restore the alarm system," Ivy said. "He told me the current system is over thirty years old. They could send out a salesperson next week if we wanted a system upgrade. In any case, today he'll fix the current version until we make a decision."

The technician arrived as promised, and took less than twenty minutes to restore the door's magnetic switch assembly.

Meanwhile, full of renewed determination, Dan retrieved the manuscript from under the chair and took it to the store's copy machine. He opened the machine with a key from his ring and slid the internal switch from "Credit Card" to "Admin." To avoid any damage to the originals by jamming, he ran the pages manually, one at a time. This took him nearly two hours. Then he carefully packed up the originals in a tote bag and paraded them past the register counter.

"See, Rivvie, I'm returning the manuscript. And it's only two hours later." With that, he and his tote bag disappeared out the front door.

"The alarm's fixed," she yelled after him, unsure whether he actually heard her.

\* \* \* \*

Knowing that the Atkins clan hadn't moved yet, Dan drove over and parked down the street from the family home in the first available parking spot. He walked a block and a half, then through the wrought-iron gate, up to the front door, and rang the bell.

Gloria Atkins answered. "Mr. Sherman, how nice, you've come back to visit."

"I'm afraid not, Ms. Gloria. I've come to return your father's manuscript to Rae. Is she available for a moment?"

"Sure thing, Mr. Sherman." She didn't invite him in. Instead, she walked to the foot of the stairs and yelled up, "Rae! Rae! You've got a visitor at the front door."

*Could the culprit be Rae, regretting her loaning him the book*

96

*in the first place?* Dan wondered. *Or was it one of the other sisters— or maybe the stranger he encountered on his last visit? Or...could the stranger be a brother?* He watched Rae closely as she appeared at the top landing and then slowly descended to greet her unexpected visitor.

"What's up, Mr. Sherman?" asked Rae as she approached the front door. "We're all so busy right now."

"I've come to return the manuscript."

"But you said you required weeks to accomplish your project. Why return it before you're finished?" she asked.

"I find I don't really have time for the project anymore. Besides, my wife has also lost interest in it. You know, running the store is a full-time job."

"I'm sorry it didn't work out," Rae said as she took the two shiny brown envelopes from him.

"Thank you again," said Dan. He retreated down the steps and through the gate to the sidewalk. All that while, he felt many eyes on him, giving him an uneasy feeling. He looked up into the front window of the living room to see the three sisters and the stranger all following his departure with interest. None had a smile. *Maybe they're looks of concern, but concern over what?* he wondered. *Could one of them be the intruder, the one with all the secrets? Or were they all complicit? No, I doubt Rae could be in on it. After all, she loaned me the original manuscript in the first place. But all the others knew about it, too. It's got to be a family thing if it's about their history, but that doesn't mean just the immediate family.* He hurried to the car and drove back to the store.

* * * *

"Well, it's done," he announced, so that Rivka could hear him as he came through the front door. He briskly brushed his hands together to demonstrate the fact he'd finished returning the so-called *evil* manuscript.

"But you're still gonna read the copy, aren't you?" she asked.

"Yeah. Of course I am. I didn't come this far just to drop it like a hot potato. I've put too much into this thing to give it up. Please

97

don't deny me this mystery. It's something I have to do. Otherwise, I'll spend the rest of my life regretting that I didn't follow through."

"Do what you must, but I've had enough of it."

"Then I'm forgiven?"

"No way, José." Rivka walked off in the other direction.

Dan shrugged, dragged himself into the reading room, and flopped into the recliner. He reached under the chair for the pile of copies he'd made. Thumbing through them for the place where he'd left off, he set the resulting two piles on the little table beside the chair and took a fresh page to read.

With the taxes in the mail, there were no more distractions. Dan could now devote all his time to binge-reading his copy of the manuscript, and he read for three hours straight before giving in to fatigue. He automatically shoved the manuscript copy onto the table beside him before adjusting his chair to the reclined position. His eyes fluttered some and then locked shut—never knowing sleep had won him over. He even slept through his supper.

Rivka discovered him there at mealtime and chose not to disturb him. *He'll raid the fridge when he wakes up*, she surmised. *There's some leftover tuna-noodle casserole inside.* She found him still asleep at closing time, so she covered him with a blanket and blew him a silent kiss. She went up to bed alone, wondering, *Was I too hard on Dan? After all, he has to be himself and try to solve all these problems, challenges, and mysteries that come his way. I guess I wouldn't have him any other way. He's always saying the same thing about me. I suppose that's a part of what love is all about. The truth is, the break-in was all my fault. If I had locked up first, there never would have been a break-in. I'm guilty and he didn't even yell at me.* She pulled back the covers, turned out the lamp, and slipped into the empty king-sized bed. She hadn't slept alone in a long time.

# Chapter 12
## Some Tales Hot and Some Not
Thursday, April 16th, 2009

Dan woke up on Thursday morning in the reading room, and yanked the recliner to a sitting position. Both shoeless heels hit the rug with a thud. A stiffness ran from the small of his back up and into his shoulders. He stretched and twisted until he heard a cracking sound, an unkinking of sorts, and then he stood to his full five-foot-eleven. Looking down at his feet, he noted that a blanket had been tucked around his legs and midsection. *Ah, Rivka's been here. Maybe she's not so pissed off at me anymore. Nah, if that were the case, she would've woken me up and had me come to bed with her. I can't understand why she's so rattled about my reading Arthur's manuscript. We've been through some pretty dangerous times together before. So it's nothing new for us to take a few measured risks.*

Looking at his watch he determined it was 6:30 a.m. Another fifteen minutes and the alarm clock would ring in their bedroom. Dan rubbed his hand over his stubbled face and let out a noisy yawn. He took a few steps before remembering the exposed manuscript on the end table. Turning back, he retrieved the two batches and stowed them under the recliner once more.

Dan headed for the staircase and the second-floor bathroom for his morning constitutional, a shower, and a shave. It was during the last stubble extraction that he heard the clock come alive. The Braun electric razor hadn't quite finished when Rivka, in a pink fuzzy

99

robe, pushed her way into the bathroom and nudged him aside from the mirror while she removed a bottle of prescription pills from the medicine cabinet. *Silence.* He just stood there watching her while she filled a half-glass of water, removed a pill, popped it in her mouth, and gulped some water down after it. *Not a word between us.* Her hand reached for the mouthwash in the blue bottle. A gargle or two later, the bottle went back into the cabinet, and the mirror returned to the fore. *Still not a word between us.*

Rivka started back to the bedroom and then stopped in her fuzzy mules. She turned to face him and then emitted an "Oh shit!" She raced back to bury her head in his hairy chest and throw her arms about his waist. "Why do you have to be such an obstinate mule with that wretched manuscript?"

Dan caught her up in his arms and replied, "There was only a two-hour lapse between the time you asked me to return Arthur's manuscript and when I actually did return it. I don't see why you're so upset. You know I love you too much to put you in any kind of danger."

"Then why do you insist on reading the copy?"

"Whoever it is doesn't know I've made a copy. If it means that much turmoil in the Sherman household, I'll stop now and burn the copy."

"You'd do that for me? You'd give up finding out what the break-in was all about?"

"Sure, I was miserable last night." It was a sizeable white lie, as he had really slept the night through just fine.

"Me too, but I wonder if you would ever forgive me or even yourself for abandoning this mystery. I suppose there would be no living with you afterward. I won't insist, dear. You can go on reading if you promise to be careful." She lifted her head and nuzzled the one clean-shaven cheek. "Besides, maybe I kinda like having a daring husband."

"Are you sure about that?"

"Yup! And you had better finish your shave. We open in less than an hour, and we haven't had breakfast yet."

"At least not a fancy pancake one like yesterday," he reminded her.

\* \* \* \*

Dan took the first tour at the register and turned it over to Ivy two hours later. Between customers he worked on some of the store's bookkeeping. Though he wanted to keep on reading the manuscript copy, he felt it would be less aggravating for Rivka if he moved out of plain sight down to the Dungeon reading room. There were tables and straight-back chairs in the room and a smaller chance of falling asleep there, so he collected the manuscript copy and made the move. He picked up the first page and began to read about the onset of the U.S. Civil War.

———

### Chapter 4. Born for a Cause

Emma Thornton Atkins (1832-1879) was a born activist and she became one of the first Annapolitans to take up the abolitionists' cause. Her brother, Henry Armstrong Thornton (1834-1881), no less an activist, signed with the Union Army, but returned from the Battle of Antietam (September, 1862) with only one arm. Having read the diary of Isobel Atkins (1784-1842), Emma was fully aware of the space Teddy Atkins (1756-1802) created in the house to hide weapons and ammunition during the Revolutionary War. She had her husband, Isaac Arthur Atkins (1829-1877), a carpenter and cabinetmaker, renovate the space and its access. In addition, Isaac installed a trapdoor to the crawl space beneath the house to facilitate an emergency escape route should that become necessary.

The Atkins home became a vital piece of the Underground Railroad, a means to deliver blacks from slavery in the South to freedom in the North and on to Canada. The risky part proved to be the transfer of slaves in and out of their home. In fact, Isaac was beaten twice and then released for his suspected participation. After four years it became so dangerous that it was necessary to redirect the railroad through another home in the city. The neighbors were as dangerous as the authorities. Emma and Isaac's two sons, Isaac Jr. (1850-1892) and Herman Peter Atkins (1852-1883), opened a woodworking shop along the Patapsco River in Ellicott City, Maryland, using the river's flow to drive their lathes, drills, and shapers. Unfortunately, Herman lost four fingers on one hand in a shop accident while adjusting one of the drive belts. His fingers were caught between the wheel and the belt as the belt moved around the wheel. The brothers returned to Annapolis when the shop burned to the ground in 1874.

Isaac Jr. married Deborah Keen (1854-1890), the sole daughter of a wealthy banker and entrepreneur. They had five daughters plus one son and sole heir, James Keen Atkins (1872-1910), who became a celebrated artist, painting portraits of local politicians and bigwigs...

———

Dan kept reading, reaching the turn of the century, and then broke for lunch. Afterward, he could hardly refuse Rivka when she asked him to unpack a shipment of incoming books; take two books to the post office for mailing; and assemble an order of office supplies. These and other errands consumed his entire afternoon. No sooner had the Shermans cleaned up after their evening meal when individuals began to trickle in for the Thursday evening critique group meeting.

By 7:30 everyone but Esther Reubens had arrived. She was staying home with a runny nose. Twenty minutes into the meeting Katie Silver took her turn to read more of her Great Depression-era, *Boxcar Bertie* story. First she brought her listeners up to speed.

"Here's where I left off last time. It's 1933 and Bertie Pachet has just dodged a railroad cop and hopped a freight train in New Haven, Connecticut; headed for Boston, Massachuseutts; and ultimately, Portsmouth, New Hampshire. It's mostly dark in the boxcar, even though the sliding door is only half closed."

———

### Chapter 5. Boxcar Surprise

*Was it a man's grunt or an animal's snort?* she wondered. *I can't tell if I'm sharing the car with a cow or a pig or a man. It sure smells like an animal and there's all this loose straw, or is it hay, on the floor? I'm not sure I even know the difference. I suppose animals eat hay and sleep on straw.* Bertie moved to the opposite end of the car, away from the strange sounds and whatever it was. She shivered with the cold and cowered against the car's front bulkhead. The weird sounds eventually abated, so that all she heard was the *clickity-clacking* track noise—more regular now as the train picked up speed. As her eyes became more accustomed to the available light, the form became more discernable. *It's a man*, she decided as she made out the dark shape curled in the fetal position against the opposite wall. *If I leave him alone, maybe he'll do the same for me.*

Bertie scratched together a fair amount of straw until the pile made a crude bed for her to sleep on. She lay down and tried to get comfortable. The straw was prickly and itchy, so it took a while for her to fall asleep, but when she finally did, she fell deep into dreamland.

Twenty-four-year-old Bertie Pachet grew up in a blue-collar family in the Hill section of New Haven. An alcoholic mother and abusive unemployed stepfather were the very things she wanted to flee from ever since she was old enough to consider escape. The best you could say for Bertie's looks was that she was tall and chunky with a square-ish, handsome face that was almost manly. But make no mistake, this urban tomboy was all woman inside and smart as a whip. With the help of a mentoring high-school teacher, she took advantage of a four-year scholarship to a Connecticut state normal school to become a teacher. As a scholarship recipient, she was able to find work in the school cafeteria. But a woman with a bachelor's sheepskin couldn't necessarily find employment in dire times like these.

Bertie wanted to keep sleeping, but something pulled and yanked at her foot. She opened one eye and rolled away from the wall to find a large figure of a man looming over her trying to get her shoe off her foot. She sat up quickly only to have the bearded figure shove her back down again.

"Gimme yer shoes," he bellowed as he moved to straddle her.

She managed to keep her shoe on during the struggle that followed. They rolled a few times as she fought him off. At one point, he backed into a kneeling position to gain leverage. Bertie took advantage of the momentary break to draw her feet up and kick out. The kick caught him squarely in the chest, throwing him backward against a vertical steel brace in the wooden bulkhead. The back of his head slammed into the brace hard enough to be heard, and he slipped sideways to the floor.

Bertie got to her feet and scanned quickly for any weapon she could find. A pitchfork sat in a metal clip on the adjacent wall. She grabbed it from its clip and stood over her would-be victim at the ready, but she soon learned that he was unconscious and bleeding seriously. Scanning to locate her knapsack, she saw that her assailant had dumped its contents onto the car floor, looking for booty. *He's a mean old bastard, but I can't let him bleed to death.*

She put down the pitchfork, and pushed around the few articles of clothing she had brought along until she located a woolen scarf. Several wraps around his head appeared to stifle the bleeding for the time being, but there really wasn't anything more that she could do. There wasn't any water to wash his wound. She sat cross-legged and rested his head gently in her lap. Examining his face more closely, looking beyond the beard, she determined that he was a lot younger than she originally thought. She sat there day-dreaming, listening to the rhythm of the tracks going *clickety-clack, clickety-clack.*

A half-hour later, his eyes fluttered open, and he stared at her. At first he was startled and then, "Hey! You're a girl." and then his hands went to his head. "Oooh!"

———

"Well, everyone, that's as far as I got this time," said Katie, shuffling the pages together.

"I like where you stopped," said Rivka. "You left me completely in suspense."

"That's hardly a compliment, liking where I stopped, but I know what you mean."

"It's a good story," offered Joel.

"I agree," said Dan. "Well written, too."

"We still have some time," said Rivka. "Is there anyone else who wants to read tonight?"

"I tried writing an opening chapter," said Tom Dwyer. "Be gentle, folks. I'm just a beginner at this."

"By all means, Tom, read on," said Rivka. "Let's hear what you have written."

Tom cleared his throat and began to read.

———

### Chapter 1. Ambition

Thomas Jerome Dwyer wants to write this confession to apologize for his wrongful behavior in a moment of great crisis many years ago. To this day, he has tried hard to put this terrible incident behind him. He feels that by telling his whole story now, it will somehow ease the burden that has plagued him for the past twenty years. To understand his story you have to know more about him and his personal ethics.

———

"Even though it's in the third person, this is about you, Tom, isn't it?" asked Dan.

"Yes," admitted Tom. He continued reading.

———

Tom was no stranger to work. Although he came from a loving family, his father and mother together barely eked out a living. As a six-foot-three, 200-pound junior in high school, he played varsity basketball and soccer, but as an eighteen-year-old senior, he obtained a work permit and had to wave goodbye to all sports. Although he possessed the brains and skills for college, he had other ambitions. The lad went to work bussing tables in a local diner. Even with the meager busboy's salary, he had to divide the paycheck three ways. As long as he lived at home, he felt he had to contribute a share to the family. Then a second share covered his personal expenses. The remaining share he saved to eventually take tractor-trailer driver training.

Tom's ambition was to travel the interstates driving the big rigs so that he might get to see the whole U. S. of A. He was proud of his country and wanted to see it all. The savings accumulated so slowly that he wondered whether he ever would be a big-rig driver.

Then one day the short-order cook spilled hot grease on himself and had to go to the hospital. This meant that the diner either had to shut down or someone had to step up. None of the servers or assistant managers were willing, and the owner, Mr. Metacropolis, was out of town for several days. Tom volunteered. When both his parents were working, he'd done a good deal of the cooking and frying at home. By the time the owner returned three days later, Tom had mastered the big grill and learned all the procedures and recipes needed to be a short-order cook. The owner was extremely pleased with him and immediately doubled his salary.

Tom's goals were now back on track. He could visualize the day when he might even receive the training he wanted. But two years later, during 1966, the Vietnam War accelerated, and he was drafted into the army. The army took one look at his background and made him a cook. But he never let go of his ambition. While on an eighteen-month deployment to 'Nam, he spent much of his spare time in the motor pool with his friend Tech. Sergeant Ralph Barkley, learning about trucks. Ralph even taught him to drive a pickup and let him practice some. During the time Tom served, he sent money home to help his family. By the time he had fulfilled his military obligation, he had earned his second stripe and had enough money saved to enter tractor-trailer training upon discharge. There was only one problem—he met Laura Bancroft in San Diego at a church party.

———

"That's all I got written so far," said Tom.

"It doesn't sound like a mystery to me," said Joel.

"Oh, I assure you it is," said Tom. "Don't you wonder what I want to apologize for?"

"Sure, you're right," replied Joel. "Good bio so far."

"It reads smoothly enough," said Dan. "Maybe it needs a little more day-to-day kind of detail during your stay in 'Nam."

"Maybe a little more on what it's like to be a short-order cook," said Katie.

"I may pick up on those things during my second draft," replied Tom.

"We have time for something shorter now," said Rivka. "Any takers? How about you, Joel?"

"I have an extremely short chapter on the medical examiner's testimony," offered Joel.

"You're up," confirmed Rivka.

Joel picked up his notes and began to read from his yellow, legal-sized pad.

———

### Chapter 8, The Medical Examiner

"The prosecution may call its next witness," said the judge.

"The prosecution calls Dr. Dereck Fuller to the stand," said ADA Dulaney.

From behind the defense table, Mickey watched as a stately man with white hair and wire-rimmed glasses came forward. He wore a serious look on his face and a tan, neatly tailored suit. It was someone Mickey didn't recognize, but apparently, Dulaney knew him well.

"Doctor, would you please tell the court your name, profession, and current position," directed Dulaney.

"Dereck Fuller, Doctor of Forensic Medicine. I'm an Assistant Medical Examiner for the state of Maryland in Anne Arundel County."

"And how long have you held that position?"

"I've been a practicing ME for twenty-six years—twenty-three years in Montgomery County and the last three years in Anne Arundel County."

"Have you had the opportunity to examine the deceased, William Billy Danser?"

"Yes, I have performed an autopsy and furnished samples for toxic screening. My full report, ME 3481920W.A.Danser, was turned over to the District Attorney's office on August 2nd."

"Doctor, have you determined the cause of death?"

"I have. The deceased displayed a flat, one-inch-wide knife puncture in the chest between the third and fourth rib an inch to the left of the sternum. Autopsy showed that the blade was serrated and at least eight inches in length in order to intersect with the aortic section of the heart. This trauma to the heart caused an immediate bleed-out, followed by functional stoppage. Presumably, death would have been within a few seconds."

"Was that all you found?" asked Dulaney.

"The screening showed high-level alcohol, no drugs, and little else of interest to this court."

"One more question, Doctor. Is this knife the likely murder weapon?" Dulaney showed him Exhibit A, a serrated kitchen knife.

"It fits the description all right, but there are millions of kitchen knives like that all over the world."

"Let me remind the jury that the knife with Billy Danser's blood yielded a bloody print that was a partial match to the defendant, Grover Fox."

"Objection!" cried Mickey Mann. "The prosecution is summarizing his case. Besides, his own witness, Sergeant Manfred, testified that partial was quite a bit on the lean side, only five points, if I remember correctly. And I don't believe anyone has connected the blood on the knife to Billy's blood."

"Sustained!" said the judge. "The jury will disregard the last statements from both the prosecution and defense."

"Your witness," said Dulaney.

Mickey stood and declared, "No questions at this time, Your Honor."

"Court will recess until tomorrow morning at ten o'clock sharp," ordered Judge Ira Hershfeld.

———

"Well, that's my short chapter," said Joel. "More to come."

"Nice work, Joel. It's getting late, folks, so we'll adjourn now," said Rivka, pushing her chair back. "See you next week."

## Chapter 13
## Brief Encounters
Five days, April 22nd through April 27th, 2009

Two damaged-in-printing books needed to be returned to the publisher for replacements. The Wednesday morning torrential showers had finally ceased, leaving the sidewalks wet, the trees dripping, and the clouds minimal and white. The warm sun had come to visit them for a day or more, so Dan decided to walk to the post office to mail these books with the crooked margins and uneven light and dark print. A few blocks along the way an uncomfortable feeling overtook him—he sensed someone falling into step behind him. He slowed, halted, and turned around to look several times, but although the streets were not entirely deserted, not one soul looked suspicious, nor did he recognize anyone he knew.

But two city blocks short of the post office, he stopped for a red-light crossing and, over his shoulder, saw a man looking in a store display window. He took a second, longer look and realized it was the same bearded man he saw at the Atkins' gate and in the window with the three sisters. The traffic light changed to green, and he crossed the street, but when he looked once more on the other side, that man was nowhere to be seen. *Maybe it's my imagination,* Dan thought. *Maybe it's working overtime these days. I don't think I'll mention this to Rivka because of the way she reacted the last time.*

A close encounter that Dan, ironically, wasn't privy to had taken place earlier on the same day he walked to the post office. While he sat in the Dungeon reading room, absorbing an hour's worth of the manuscript text, Muddy Atkins sat at a second table with his back to Dan, and with his face deep in C.S. Forester's *Hornblower and the Hotspur*, one of the Horatio Hornblower series. Muddy had already determined exactly what Dan was reading. Dan looked up a number of times during his reading, but he neither recognized nor even noticed the other occupant in the room. When Dan got up to leave for the post office, his stalker left *Hornblower* on the table, waited a minute or two, and followed Dan almost to his destination.

Two days later, on Friday morning, Dan again saw the same face. This time he had gone to a stationery shop on Fleet Street in downtown Annapolis to pick up business cards and shopping bags with the bookstore logo. When he came out of the shop, the same black-bearded man, in the same gray jacket and peaked cap, stood diagonally across the street from him—over six foot and lean of build. The stalker briefly regarded Dan with a disdainful expression, then hurried down Fleet Street toward the City Dock. Dan's eyes studied him and followed his form for several minutes. Then he returned to the car and drove back to the store. *It's not my imagination,* he reassured himself. *I recognize more than just his bearded face. Is this man stalking me? Why?* Again Dan kept the sighting from Rivka.

* * * *

On Saturday morning, moving day, the three Atkins sisters expected their movers to come to pick up the selected furniture and disburse it among their three separate apartments according to their pre-affixed labels. The ladies had either sold or thrown out everything in the house that wasn't wanted. However, Muddy was neither a party to the packing nor to the actual moving. He had rented a hotel room for the duration and long since denied any interest in acquiring anything from the house. He fully intended to resume his career with the Merchant Marines as soon as he took care of some loose ends. At least, that's what he told his siblings. The sisters wondered what those loose ends might be, but they knew better than to ask their devious brother. Still, strange as it seemed, he agreed to hang around for the movers to come, pack everything up, and cart it away. His volunteering to supervise the movers did free his sisters to retreat to the various mover destinations.

Gloria laid claim to a mere settee, two lamps, and a coffee table; she and her sometime husband and baby had an established, but limited, household. Rae was interested neither in cooking nor entertaining, so she declined most of what was in the kitchen and dining room. She earmarked a bedroom set, several place settings of china and silver-plate, plus a few pieces from the parlor. She had picked out a three-room first-floor apartment in the Eastport section of town, three blocks from Horn Point on Chesapeake Avenue. Cora held onto enough furnishings to outfit a luxury four-bedroom house overlooking the Severn River. All of her selections and her current furnishings would go into storage until her renovations were completed. Meanwhile, she would stay close to Rae in a two-room suite at the Horn Point Inn.

At 9:45 a.m. the moving van arrived and three burly men filled it in a little over two hours. Muddy signed the paperwork and watched the van pull away from the front of the house. His whole motive for volunteering to stay behind and supervise wasn't the helpful one he used on his sisters—it was far more devious than that.

With the van out of sight, Muddy went to his rental car and retrieved his toolbox. He carried the toolbox to his empty former bedroom and set it down just outside the closet. He turned on the overhead light and knelt down to work inside the closet. First, he drove a tiny woodscrew through the piece of molding he would normally use to release the rear wall of the closet. This screw disabled the release mechanism and denied access to the hidden room from the closet. He couldn't have the new owners prying into his secrets even if by accident. If need be, he could still access the room via the trapdoor from the crawl space under the house. That access was far less likely to be discovered. Next, he puttied the cracks in the molding and smoothed them over until they almost disappeared. Finally, he painted over the molding on the three sides of the closet with quick-dry paint to completely hide any anomaly in the woodwork.

When he was finished, Muddy packed up his things, locked

up the house, put the last of the keys in a preaddressed envelope, and mailed it to the new owners.

* * * *

Two days later, Dan took a spritz-bottle of window cleaner, a squeegee, and a roll of paper towels to the outside windows of the bookstore. While he dried one section, the reflection of the line of cars parked across the street became clearer in the plate-glass window in front of him. As he admired the clarity of his work, he saw someone move from car to car in the reflection. He spun about and saw a man's figure duck down behind an old Chevy Impala. Dan stood there looking at the Impala for several minutes, provoking the figure to delay making his escape for fear of being discovered. But Dan was persistent and waited. Tired of hiding, the figure suddenly emerged, darting up the street with his jacket collar turned up so Dan couldn't quite see his face. But Dan did recognize the gray jacket and cap, and the man's tall, lean build seemed to fit as well. *This is creepy. I'm pretty sure it's that same fellow who held the gate open for me at the Atkins house, and was looking out the window with the sisters. I wonder what the hell he's up to. Was he our intruder? If he was, what was he looking for? Does he suspect that I made a copy of the manuscript? How would he have found that out? And what's in it that's so all-fired important to him? I've simply gotta tell Rivvie now for her own safety.*

Dan gathered all his window cleaning paraphernalia, rushed into the store, and found Ivy at the register. He heard the register go *ka-ching* as she checked out a customer buying a trade paperback of Clive Cussler's *Treasure of Khan.*

She thanked the young man. "Enjoy your read." Then she noticed Dan standing and waiting. "Yes, Dan?"

"Where's Rivka?"

"She's in the back hall feeding the kitty-cats."

"What about the little ones," he said with a half-grin.

"Mamma cat's taking care of that." It was their little joke.

When Dan got to the back hall, he found Rivka sitting there on the floor with Four hanging on her shoulder and Two in her hands held to her face. One and Three were at the filling station while Lady

Annabella appeared to be sleeping. As long as he could see their paws, he could tell the kittens apart. He leaned over the lot of them and put the cleaning supplies on an upper shelf, supposedly out of their reach.

"They're so darling," she cooed.

"Rivka, when you're through here, we need to talk."

Rivka put the two kittens back on the pile of old rugs Lady Annabella had chosen for a bed and got to her feet. "Why so serious, Dan? Is something wrong?"

"I'm being stalked," he blurted out as they started up the main aisle to the front of the store. Dan explained that he'd seen the man for the first time at the Atkins' gate and then entering the house with a key; and another time looking out the window with the sisters. "It's that same fellow shadowing me. I have to find out if he's the Atkins' sisters' brother. If he is, that would explain a lot. It's weird. Wherever I go, he turns up like a bad penny. As soon as he's discovered, my shadow takes off and disappears. I have no idea what he's up to or what he expects to accomplish with these antics, but it's certainly nothing worthwhile." He went on to tell her of the three incidents when and where he noticed his stalker.

"How could he have found out about the manuscript being copied?" asked Rivka.

"That's just it. I don't know. He must be keeping a pretty close watch on me. Now don't go telling me 'I told you so.'"

"I won't. You've already done that for yourself. But why are you just telling me now? What do you expect me to do?"

"At first, I thought I was imagining him, but when it happened at least three times and who knows how many more, I figured I had better tell you, so that you can be careful wherever you go."

"Dan, you're making me nervous. Shouldn't we go to the police with this?"

"And tell them what? We haven't any proof. It would be just my word against his. And at this point, I can't even imagine what his word would be."

"Do you think he's dangerous, dear?"

"I don't know if or how dangerous he is, but the man seems pretty desperate to take all these steps to target me in particular. There's got to be something in that manuscript he wants to hide."

"What could possibly be worth hiding in the first place?" asked Rivka.

"Maybe heirloom jewelry or a treasure of some kind. Maybe some nefarious deed done by an ancestor, a family member, or even him. Or maybe the secret lies with the old dwelling itself."

"Or maybe you could bring him the manuscript copy as a gesture of goodwill?" suggested Rivka.

"That won't work anymore. He won't know how far I've already read, and whether I've figured out his secret or not."

\* \* \* \*

Up in Baltimore, a city known for the Ravens, the Orioles, its charm, and white marble stoops, Tom Dwyer wanted to stop for a beer and a little manly conversation on his way home from work. On that same Monday evening, he'd dropped off the delivery truck at the company garage and, once more heeding his wife's caution, he walked clear past Murphy's Tavern. Two blocks east of it and one block north, he stopped in the Blue and White Kettle. At first, he sat alone at the bar, but then a decent, no-name, working stiff on the next stool struck up a conversation with him. They talked Orioles baseball and Ravens football for a while and the intended one beer became two and then more until Tom felt a warm buzz.

Out of nowhere, he felt a serious nudging in the middle of his back. A spin around on the stool brought him to the stern face of Frank Mulhaney.

"You been trying to avoid yer old buddy?" muttered Frank, with a rough shove in Tom's side. The man Tom had been talking to slipped away, not wanting to be a party to this private confrontation. Frank grabbed his empty stool. "Trying to hide from me by changing yer watering hole, eh?"

"No, Frank. Honest, I'm not hiding from anybody, especially a friend I used to drive with."

"So, Tom, why don't you come to Murphy's anymore, huh?"

"Just a little variety now and then. I didn't know you preferred Murphy's."

"I do. Go there a couple times a week, but I missed you." Frank slapped him on the back. "Hell, let me buy you a beer 'cuz I was kinda rough on you."

"Aw, you don't have to do that. I understand," said Tom. His words came out slurry.

"Hey, bartender, two Bud drafts and a shot of rye."

It sounded to Tom like Frank had had a few more before this. The bartender set a pint mug down in front of each of them and set the shot glass down between them. Frank sucked in the foam and took a few sips off the top to make room. Then he dropped the shot of rye, glass and all, into his beer.

"It's a depth charge," Frank declared, as he whacked Tom another friendly one on his backside. "Bottoms up." He drank nearly half of it and set the mug down again. A few deep breaths and he finished his depth charge.

Tom, already feeling the effects, upended his mug and chugged it dry. "Say, Frank, you ever wonder why that day twenty years ago never hit the newspapers?"

"I told you never to bring that subject up again." Frank reached out to grab Tom by the shirt collar, but before he got there, Tom slipped off the stool and down onto the floor real slowly, seeing it like the world was moving in slow motion. Frank's voice sounded distant, like it came from someplace outside. Frank picked a very limp and pliable Tom Dwyer up off the floor and dragged him to one of the nearby green vinyl booths. "Bartender," he yelled again, "bring me a couple mugs of coffee. He's skunked—passed out on me."

An hour later, Tom was awake and rigid enough to make it home. Frank stayed with him until they reached the Dwyer front door. He sat Tom down on the marble stoop, rang the doorbell, and as soon as he heard someone coming, Mulhaney left the premises. He wasn't one to stick around for explanations. Laura answered the door and looked down at her immobile smiling husband. She silently helped him to bed.

# Chapter 14
## Connection
Wednesday, April 29th, 2009

Cora Atkins Bacon sat at the white enamel kitchen table reading a story in *Cosmopolitan* while overseeing her four-year-old grandson's lunch. Samuel Atkins Bacon sat to her left with a glass of milk and a peanut butter and jelly sandwich.

"Hi, I'm home." Her daughter, Daisy, had come in the front door and wound her way to the kitchen. She dropped a pile of mail on the table.

"Did you have a tough day over at Anne Arundel Medical Center?" asked Cora. She eyed Daisy with a mother's pride, her daughter looking so professional in her nurse's uniform, the short-sleeved pale blue shirt and matching pants.

"Yeah, the early morning nursing shift is always a bitch in any hospital," said Daisy. "Tomorrow should be easier. How's my little Sammy?"

"Hi, Mommy." He twisted and smiled up at her, one cheek smeared full of strawberry jam.

Daisy came around behind him and with two arms on her son's shoulders she kissed the top of his red-brown hair, a match to her own shoulder-length hair. The rest of his features resembled those of his father, but there was nothing she could do about that.

"Looks like some kind of invitation in that pile of mail I brought in," said Daisy as she slid into a captain's chair at the table.

116

"Oh," said Cora. She sorted through it until she found the decorative envelope and opened it.

"Who's it from?" asked Daisy.

"It's from Rivka Sherman," said Cora. "You know, that nice lady over at the bookstore. She runs the writers' critique group I belong to there. Ah, it's an invitation to a wedding shower for Ivy Cohen Reubens."

"Who's that?" asked Daisy.

"She's another member of the critique group, a lovely girl around your age, a bit older. She clerks for Rivka in the store."

"Why don't I know that name?" asked Daisy. "Did she grow up here?"

"No, she emigrated from England right after college—London, I think."

"When and where is this affair taking place?"

"At the bookstore on Sunday the tenth of May at one," Cora read from the invitation.

"She marrying anybody I know?"

"She talks about him quite a bit, Mark something. It'll come to me in a minute...Schwartz, yes, Mark Schwartz. That's it."

"Mark Schwartz?" Daisy repeated in a shrill voice.

"Why, do you know him?" asked Cora.

"I know *a* Mark Schwartz," claimed Daisy. "He was a student in the physics department at Hopkins a few years back. It couldn't be the same person. That would be too much of a coincidence."

"It must be the same person," returned Cora. "Ivy's Mark is about to receive his doctorate in physics at Hopkins."

"He is? Oh, no!"

"Yes, but why is this so important to *you*?" Cora stared hard at her daughter, trying to see beyond Daisy's evasions.

Daisy's green eyes welled up with tears. "Mom, are you ready for this? I can't hide it any longer. The truth be told, Mark Schwartz is Sammy's father."

"Oh my God! So you knew who the father was all along."

"Of course. Mark was the only one I let near me for more

than five years. He was only my second experience."

"So why didn't you confront him?" asked Cora. "And better yet, why didn't you tell me? Your father and I could have exerted some pressure on the young man to do the right thing." Cora's heart was beating faster now. "Your father isn't going to be very happy about this."

"I did confront him, Momma," Daisy whined, "and he pointed out how incompatible we were. Our backgrounds and our religions were so different that there was nothing left to build a marriage on. What more could I do?"

"Didn't you remind him that it takes two to make a baby?"

"I did, and he offered to help pay for an abortion."

"And what did you say to that?"

"I told him no. I wouldn't and couldn't abort. I'm Catholic and pro-life and an active protestor for life."

"And what was his response?"

"He said that marriage was out of the question, but he'd try to help financially if I needed anything besides a husband."

"Why didn't you insist?"

"I called him again after Sammy was born. He actually sounded ticked off. He told me he had no intention of becoming a father at that time and he even said I was harassing him. Mom, I hate to admit it, but I was the aggressor that night. We were at a bar and I was the one who suggested we go somewhere more private. We went back to his place and when I fell asleep on his couch, he covered me up with a blanket and slept in his own bed."

"I'm sure you didn't make a baby that way," said Cora in a sarcastic tone.

"Of course not. I woke up during the night, undressed, and shamelessly climbed into bed with him. So, being the aggressor, I could hardly insist on anything, could I?"

"What if this Mark wants to play some role in Sam's life? How would you feel about that?'

"I don't know," said Daisy. "Maybe I'd let him help pay for schooling. Something like that."

"Wouldn't he want something more in return?" asked Cora. "Say, going to a ball game together?"

Cora was trying hard to keep her voice on an even keel, not to betray her true feelings. She was heartsick. If only her daughter hadn't been so irresponsible. The pain she felt most was for little Sammy, now a smart four-year-old. Cora had overheard him talking to Daisy just a few days ago: "Mommy, why don't I have a Daddy like the other kids?"

And Daddy was about to be married—to someone else.

## Chapter 15
## Enough Already
The Same Day

Although credit cards accounted for most sales at the bookstore, cash transactions still had a way of disrupting the day-to-day balance in cash register drawers. Perhaps the number of bills was too large for a typical register section. Or the surplus of twenties, tens, or coinage exceeded the practical amount needed for making change. Of course, any shortages had to be considered as well. In an attempt to restore today's imbalance Dan had prepared a deposit for the bank. He tucked the excess bills, coinage, and deposit slip into a night deposit bag and zipped it up. Squeezing past Rivka at the register, he kissed her on the cheek, and headed for the front door.

Outside, the clear air and warm sun set the day's mood for him. It was one of those days when Dan realized he had an extra spring in his step. He left the Toyota behind in favor of his size-twelve shoes.

When he reached West Street, the unpleasant memory of being followed earlier in the week kicked in. He kept looking over his shoulder, but found no one there. He had to laugh to himself. *Do I really want someone to be there? Am I getting paranoid?*

He arrived at the M&T bank and stood in line waiting for an available teller. He looked up at the bank's logo on the window and wondered about the curious choice of initials that sounded so much like "empty bank." He scanned the large open room and noticed Esther Reubens waiting in an adjacent line. He waved and mouthed a silent "Hi" to her, and she returned the greeting. He continued looking about and recognized another one of the bookstore's frequent patrons. Then it was his turn.

"Hi, Mr. Sherman. What can I do for you today?" asked the familiar face behind the teller window.

"Hi, Gladys. Just an exchange of bills, and a deposit this morning." He passed the bank deposit bag under the glass shield to the smiling teller. He watched as she counted and meted out the bills into their respective slots. She recorded the exchange, counted out the smaller bills and coinage, and placed them in the bag along with the deposit receipt and withdrawal slip. Dan had counted with her and always found her to be accurate, so when she passed the bag back to him, he thanked her and turned to walk away. He zipped the bag up inside his warm-up jacket. When he looked up again, he saw another familiar figure, standing at the blank-forms counter—a familiar yet dreaded face. The bearded fellow had again made a strange and unwanted appearance. He seemed intent on filling out a form. The man looked up and grinned, as though sending Dan some kind of message.

Dan decided to confront him and walked straight toward him. As soon as the man realized he was being targeted, he dropped the pen and headed for the door and outside. Dan followed and closed the distance between them. The man hurried into a trot. When he saw that Dan was serious and closing, he shifted into a full run. Noting that the guy was probably ten years younger than himself, Dan decided further pursuit would be fruitless. He stopped and, with hands on his hips, watched the guy disappear behind St. Anne's at Church Circle.

Dan's pace as he returned to the bookstore reflected his increasing anger—each step quickened and purposeful. His teeth gripped his lower lip. *Why?*

Dan made no attempt to hide his pissed-off attitude as he barged through the front door of the bookstore, stomped past the register counter, and mumbled under his breath.

Rivka noticed his mood right away. "What's going on, Dan? You look like you're ready to strangle someone."

"I just had another go-round with that bearded creep, inside the bank, no less. I'm getting more and more convinced that he's a member of the Atkins family."

"What did he do this time?"

"That's just it. He didn't do anything. I've got nothing to take to the police. I can't prove a damn thing. He's just always there, no matter where or when I look. I even tried to confront the crud, but he literally ran off before I could get to him. I can't figure out what he expects to gain from all this stalking."

"I still think you'd better take this to the police. Maybe we can get a restraining order or something."

"And tell them what?" asked a totally frustrated Dan.

"At least tell them what he's doing, so if he takes it to another level, they'll know all about it already."

"I think I've got a better idea," said Dan. "Cora Bacon. She seemed pretty level-headed to me when she introduced herself at the critique group. Maybe she'll tell me whether the fellow I've seen at their house in her brother, and if he is, why he's acting so odd."

"Do you think she'd open up more to me? You know, a woman-to-woman connection."

"I didn't think you wanted to get involved in this thing."

"How can I *not* get involved?"

"Maybe we both should be there," offered Dan.

"No, no, she'll feel we're ganging up on her. Let me call her for a sit-down somewhere friendly-like."

"I'll await your pleasure, my dear."

Rivka looked up Cora's number on the access list for the critique group, picked up the landline phone, and called. She answered on the third ring. "Hi, Cora, this is Rivka Sherman from the bookstore....Yes, I'm fine....And you?...I'm calling because I have a certain family problem that I believe only you can help me with....No, no, there's no special expertise required....What? No. It's sort of personal. I'm not sure, but I think it's about your brother....Oh! I'd like to sit down with you over a cup of coffee somewhere where we can talk. We could meet here or perhaps at Chick & Ruth's Delly on Main Street....Yes, 3:30 would be fine. See you then." Rivka hung up.

"How did that go?" asked Dan.

"Cora seemed amenable to the idea of a meeting, though she was a little taken aback when I said that her brother might be the subject."

"I hope you know what you're walking into," said Dan. "It's a sticky thing getting someone to talk about a member of their family."

\* \* \* \*

Getting a parking space on Main Street always seemed next to impossible, so Rivka headed for the Hillman parking garage a half-block away. From there it was a short walk to Chick & Ruth's, where many of the notable state legislators had their favorite sandwiches named after them. Mid-afternoons were quiet and slow, so it was easy to find Cora seated at one of the tables toward the rear of the long, narrow establishment. The two greeted each other as Rivka took a seat facing Cora.

Rivka ordered a warm apple fritter with a scoop of vanilla ice cream and coffee with milk and artificial sweetener. Dan sometimes teased her about her concession to the zero-calorie sweetener accompanying a sumptuous dessert. Cora chose a brownie and iced tea.

They chatted easily while they waited for their food. Although it was tough for Rivka to broach the subject, she plunged ahead.

"First, Cora, I need to know if your brother has a black beard and usually wears a cap and gray jacket."

"Yes, that's Muddy." Cora shifted uneasily in her chair. "Now will you tell me what this is about?"

"Of course. It's about your brother. May I ask you a personal question?" Without waiting for permission, she asked, "Can you tell me anything about him?"

"That *is* a rather personal question," replied Cora, "but I don't mind answering it. Yes, he's our brother. I suppose I love him as a dutiful sister should, but I have to say he's a first-class pain in the ass.

Muddy—he's called Muddy rather than Buddy. Our father stuck him with that name for the obvious reason—the trouble he causes those around him. He spends most of his time at sea. In fact, while ashore, he stayed at our house until our move. He's in the Merchant Marines, so he pops into town every once in a blue moon, expecting the great welcome-home treatment. The best he gets is mere tolerance. The only one he actually exchanges hugs with is my sister Gloria." Cora smiled. "I've given you a long answer to a short question, probably more than you want to know. Now may I ask what this is all about?"

"My sole purpose here today is to see if I can gain some insight into a serious situation we have. Your brother is stalking my husband."

"Stalking?" repeated Cora. "I don't understand."

"Yes, stalking. On at least a half-dozen occasions Dan has encountered Muddy following him or watching him closely. When Dan tries to approach him, he runs off."

"But why would Muddy do such a thing? Are you absolutely sure it's him?"

"There's no doubt about it," assured Rivka. "We believe it has something to do with your father's manuscript, the Atkins family history. We think there's something in the book that Muddy doesn't want made public. Dan got interested when our bookstore copy vanished from its shelf. His interest peaked when he found out that all the public libraries' copies had also disappeared—and your father's personal copies as well. The actual stalking began when Dan borrowed your father's original manuscript from your sister Rae. I have to believe Muddy is trying to scare Dan into not reading any further. Dan even returned the manuscript early so that Muddy would stop the stalking. I can tell you right now that didn't stop him."

"I don't know what to tell you," said Cora. "It sounds a lot like Muddy, the way he acts and does things. Growing up, my sisters and I teased him a lot, and he came up with all these elaborate schemes to retaliate. Muddy is a compulsive prankster and a vindictive retaliator. Often he takes these things to extremes. Rae and I don't believe there's an emotional bone in his body—he's incapable of feeling anything."

"On another subject—have you actually read your father's book?" asked Rivka.

"Why, yes, some time ago. I'm not sure I can remember that much about it. All about our ancestors, who married whom, who begat whom, and such. Nothing of interest to anyone else. That's why he didn't sell all that many copies."

"Was there anything in it that *you* wouldn't want the world to know about, say a murderer or a horse thief?"

"I suppose the family history contains our share of heroes, villains, and wastrels, but I don't think there's anything the current family needs to be ashamed of. I haven't the foggiest notion of what Muddy is trying to hide. I could ask him, but he'd only tell me to mind my own business."

Rivka drained the last sip of coffee from her cup. "I have to thank you for being so frank with me. I guess we'll just have to let this drama play itself out."

"Rivka, I feel awful about this. If I find out anything, I'll let you know," said Cora.

The two women stood to leave, walked outside together, and went their separate directions. Rivka maneuvered her car out of the garage and drove back to the bookstore. Cora had found a space at the foot of Main Street. She drove over the Eastport bridge on her way to her sister Rae's new apartment at Horn Point.

Cora guided her Mercedes into a guest parking space at the side of the brick and stone apartment building, a unit of the Oceanic apartment complex. Upon entering the building, she stopped at the mailboxes to check Rae's apartment number. Deliberately neglecting to use the bell, she pounded on the door. Rae opened it, attired in a pale-blue terry robe and a hair turban.

"Oh, I like your outfit," said Cora.

"If you wanted fancy-schmancy, you should have called ahead and made an official appointment."

"Next time, dear," said Cora as she gave the rooms a once-over. "No kidding, I really do like the layout of this apartment and what you've done with it."

"Thanks," said Rae, "but there's still a bunch of cartons to be unpacked. So what brings you to my doorstep this time of day?"

Rae gestured Cora to a chair at the kitchen table, while she poured leftover coffee into two mugs and stuck them in the microwave. She set the timer and pushed START.

"I'm not sure whether I'm looking for advice or information," Cora said.

When the microwave stopped its whirring sound and *dinged,* Rae removed the mugs and set them on the table. She plopped into a chair across from her sister. "Since when have I been appointed your adviser or informer? That's a new one for me."

"All kidding aside," said Cora, "I'm strongly concerned about Muddy's recent behavior."

"What's he done now?" asked Rae as she stirred sweetener into her cup. She took a cautious sip of the hot liquid.

"He's been stalking Dan Sherman for several weeks, and his wife has come to me to complain about it."

"Why her, Cora?" Rae asked. "Shouldn't her bookseller husband be talking directly to you?"

"Rivka and Dan Sherman are good friends and colleagues of mine in a mystery critique group the Shermans hold at their house. She wanted to talk woman-to-woman with me. Rivka told me Dan's tried unsuccessfully several times to approach him, but Muddy always manages to evade him. In fact, he runs off whenever Dan gets too close. All Dan wants is a simple explanation."

"Then why doesn't he go to the police?" asked Rae. "Stalking is still a crime, isn't it?"

"I believe it's purely out of respect for us," replied Cora. "Besides, that won't give him the explanation he's looking for."

"I'm not sure why you're involving *me* in this. I don't know how I can help," said Rae.

"Because stalking is only part of the problem. Dan believes that Muddy is trying to hide something connected with Daddy's book. He thinks Muddy is responsible for all the missing copies of it.

That's why Dan borrowed the manuscript from you."

"But Dan brought the manuscript back to me, saying he no longer had time for his writing project."

"He brought it back, thinking Muddy would stop annoying him if he did, but Muddy must have assumed that Dan had made a copy of the manuscript."

"Cora, you still haven't explained why you're involving me in Muddy's continuing transgressions. I've given up trying to reform or even understand the sonofabitch."

"Rae, you have literally spent years with Daddy, working with him on his book and writing yours. So I figure there's no one better informed on the Atkins family history than you. Dan Sherman's suspicion has triggered my curiosity. I want to know exactly what's in the book that Muddy wants to keep hidden and why he's going to such extremes to protect it."

Rae thought for a couple of minutes before replying. "First of all, Muddy has never given a damn about our family, let alone its history, so I don't think his secret would be about either a person or an event. I'm positive Daddy left no secret codes, keys, treasure maps, or riddles to be resolved. The only thing left is a place and that would support his vehement objection to my selling the house. A secret place might indicate the house's hidden room. Daddy mentions the hidden room three times, but never locates it for the reader. I'm not even sure *he* knew the location or its access. In a way, you have to admit that Daddy was a bit on the lazy side. If he couldn't find what he was looking for in a book, a map, or research paper, it wasn't worth looking for."

"Could Muddy have stumbled across this hidden room?" asked Cora.

"That's entirely possible," replied Rae. "Don't you remember how he liked to play hide and seek as a youngster? It's a terribly big house with plenty of nooks and crannies, but Muddy knew it better than any of us. He liked to explore the place, too. He could disappear whenever he wanted to, especially when he got on the wrong side of Daddy, and that was pretty often, right?"

"Right," said Cora. "You might have uncovered Daddy's secret with the hidden room, but not *why* it was so very important to him."

"The *why* would depend on what he intended to use it for," said Rae. "It wouldn't be the first time it was used to store contraband. During the Revolutionary War it was arms and powder. During the Civil War it was slaves, During Prohibition it was liquor. God only knows what Muddy's trying to hide there now."

"You don't suppose he's into stealing or smuggling or slavery, do you?" asked Cora. "Oh God, even dealing drugs."

"I wouldn't put it past him," said Rae.

"One more thing," said Cora. "What do you think Muddy expects to accomplish by stalking Dan Sherman?"

"I would have to believe Muddy is stalking the bookseller to dissuade him from pursuing the project any further. Instilling fear is a strange and drawn-out strategy, but then again, he's never been known to follow the norm."

"Have you ever wondered why that is?" asked Cora. "The three of us girls have always been rational enough, but he's always taken the unpredictable path."

"I'm not about to analyze our brother," replied Rae. "I hate to admit it, but in my opinion he's hopeless."

## Chapter 16
## Flashbacks
Wednesday through Saturday, November 7th through 9th, 1973

On Wednesday, Budreau Lear Atkins reached exactly eleven years and three months old, but more than that, it was the same day his father dubbed him "Muddy." This was not to say he hadn't earned that title long before then. He certainly was no stranger to trouble, nor all the misleading lies that went with getting into and out of those murky and even "muddy" situations. He didn't mind the title, for it meant he had gotten noticed by his father, an accomplishment in itself.

Oddly enough, each time the lad strayed from decent behavior or even skirmished with the law, his mother, Gillian Ann Lear Atkins, took his side, saying: "Forgive the boy, he's still young and can't see his way clearly yet."

After hearing his wife's "clearly" plea so many times, his father, Arthur Clement Atkins, dropped his son's nickname Buddy and began to call him Muddy. It was his form of sarcasm, a defense mechanism he often used in dealing with his wife. Theirs was a trying marriage. When Muddy's young friends heard the new nickname, there was no calling it off; it would stick with him for life.

On that particular Wednesday morning Muddy found himself involved in multiple crimes and misdemeanors. In the morning, while his two older sisters were at cotillion, he went into their closets and randomly exchanged dresses and shoes among them. Usually, he just mixed up their toothbrushes or messed with their homework, but with the two of them gone at the same time, it was too perfect an opportunity to miss. He didn't need an excuse—being older, they naturally picked on him mercilessly. His bedroom was the only one on the first floor, but it was situated directly beneath and overlapping the girls' bedrooms on the second floor. He could safely listen to the brunt of his folly because the heating registers were in the floor and ceiling.

The prank results were predictable and satisfying. Cora would scream bloody murder, stamp her feet, and call her brother a few choice words. And Rae would run squealing to a sympathetic yet defensive Gillian. She usually meted out only mild and meager punishments to her only son.

Muddy especially enjoyed eliciting Arthur's wrath. When successful, it meant his father actually knew the boy existed and couldn't be ignored. The boy would endure any sort of punishment to achieve that end. And Muddy was certainly creative.

Arthur always used wooden matches to light his pipes. Muddy sought out any box of loose matches he could find—first soaking them in water and then drying them out so the residual dampness and ultimate lack of effectiveness couldn't be detected. His father would go through more than a half-dozen matches trying to light up with dud ones before realizing he'd been had by Muddy. After the third such incident, he kept his matchboxes locked up in his top desk drawer. But the lad was resourceful; he knew his father kept the key under the desk blotter.

Another favorite prank of Muddy's was to reshuffle the pages of any new manuscript on his father's desk, annoying Arthur to the point of chasing his son through a loop of first-floor rooms, including the study, the parlor, the dining room, the main hall, and the study again. As he never caught up with Muddy in the heat of his anger, he was never quite sure what he'd do with the rolled-up magazine or newspaper he held during the chase.

Sometimes Muddy would lie awake at night, restless and just itching to drive another family member up a wall. He had been warned many times to restrain these urges, but the compulsion was always too strong, too enjoyable. For the most part, his shenanigans could be classified as fun-loving misdemeanors. But this left some remaining part; there had to be an underlying mean streak in there somewhere. Punishments only made it worse, another reason to strike back. On some very rare occasions an explosive temper might erupt out of a perfectly good-natured conversation. Even Muddy couldn't tell what triggered it. The reports from the psychologist were full of psychobabble his parents didn't take the time to decipher. But some experts would label it a bipolar personality. His two previous run-ins with the Annapolis police involved shoplifting and defacing public property. In each case, Arthur used his prominence and influence in the community to get the charges dropped in return for sizeable donations to local politicians.

A little past midnight on this Saturday morning, Muddy lay awake in his bed while the other members of the Atkins family lay fast asleep. Here he plotted his most devious shenanigan yet. The previous afternoon, he'd witnessed his father sharing alcoholic drinks with two literary friends in the study. Muddy noted that these three men wore pleasurable smiles as Arthur boasted of the quality, taste, source, and cost of these potables, especially his fine collection of brandies. Muddy got to thinking, *If these drinks are all that good, shouldn't I be sampling them? Why should I miss out on all the fun?*

From his first-floor bedroom Muddy slipped across the hall into Arthur's study. As he passed the big oak writing desk, he grabbed two sizes of paper clips and a stainless-steel letter opener—and knelt in front of the black-lacquered liquor cabinet, decorated with Chinese figures, sampans, and mountains. Bending the ends of the two paper clips into ells that just fit the skeletal single-tumbler lock, he tried the smaller one first, but it merely bent, lacking the leverage to turn the heavy tumbler. Next, he tried the larger clip and had more success. He heard the lock click. The double doors sprang ajar. There was no need for the letter opener and the more forceful access.

Swinging both doors wide, he surveyed his trove of colorful and shapely bottles. *If I take sips from just the open bottles, Father will never know I've been here.* His father's boasting came to mind again as he viewed the brandies on the top shelf. His first taste came from the open bottle of Hämmerle Apricot Brandy. *Oooh, sweet, hot, strong, and yummy,* he admitted. Setting it down next to him, he reached for the next open bottle, a Gölles Elderberry brandy, and took a swallow too much; a good deal of it spurted out onto the carpet. But the flavor lingered. *Yum, I like that, but I better take smaller sips.* He waited until his tongue and throat settled and then took smaller sips, before moving on to the remaining open bottles: Reisetbauer Carrot Brandy, Hämmerle Quince Brandy, and Hämmerle Williams Pear Brandy. There were more brandies, but he'd have to break the seals on those. Having a child's taste rather than an acquired adult taste, Muddy reverted to the sweeter, fruitier brandies that he had started with.

By 4:00 a.m., he'd consumed a half-bottle of the elderberry and two-thirds of a bottle of the apricot. He lay sleeping there on the floor in front of the cabinet, totally smashed amid a circle of mixed brandy bottles. The uncorked pear bottle lay open on its side, most of its contents having been spilt on the oriental carpet.

By 6:00 a.m., Muddy had twice regurgitated his stomach's solids on his pants, shoes, and carpet, but he was too drunk to do anything about it. He was immobile.

At 6:30 a.m. Gillian went to the front door to retrieve Arthur's *Journal-Gazette* from the front stoop. On her way back to the kitchen, she passed the open door to the study and got a major whiff of the fermented, distilled, and concentrated fruit as well as the by-products coming from Muddy's gut. She stepped into the study and found the revolting source and its accompanying mess. Leaving the newspaper at the breakfast table with her husband, Gillian went to get help from Cora, her eldest, and together they dragged Muddy into the nearest shower.

By the time Arthur finished his paper and left the breakfast table, Muddy had been scrubbed clean and duly deposited in his bed. Despite the rough handling and the dousing, he'd fallen fast asleep again. When Arthur started down the hall toward the study, Gillian fell in behind him, hoping to soften the imminent explosion. But the stench had permeated the hall and was even more intense than she had predicted. Reaching his destination, Arthur turned purple with rage. The verbal fallout, epithets she never ever heard coming from her husband's mouth, came in aftershocks lasting several minutes and culminating in one great resolve.

"Let me at him!" The raging bull spun around, lowered his head, and charged for Muddy's bedroom door across the hall.

Gillian stood her ground and blocked the boy's doorway like a matador with cape, redirecting his charge. "Keep in mind, this boy that you've called a 'wild destructive fiend' is your only son—our only son, and he's only eleven years old. Remember, excessive alcohol in general and especially your fine brandy has its *own* way of punishing. Muddy will be asleep for hours and when he awakens he'll have a headache, bellyache, and hangover to match his deeds."

"I don't care!" Arthur bellowed. "The money, the ugly mess, the very audacity of him. He actually went on a bender in our house."

"Calm down now, Arthur," she said, in a soft voice just above a whisper. "It's all said and done and paid for. Nothing we can do about it now. Calm down. Remember what the doctor said about your heart. Don't worry about the mess. The girls and I will have everything shipshape in two shakes of a lamb's tail." Gillian had a charming way of mixing a metaphor or two.

"What...what about next time...when he burns down the house? What are you going to tell me then?"

* * * *

Muddy did awaken several hours later with a monster headache, a raw, churning stomach, and a monumental case of the dry heaves. It wasn't guilt that he felt. It was more like anger over botching the whole episode—that and the real fear of his father's wrath. He remained in his room for as long as he could. When his need for food and his mother's embrace exceeded the fear of running into his father, he ventured a trip to the kitchen. Gillian welcomed and coddled him and fed him as a mother should. But when he stepped into the hall again, he faced his father coming from the opposite direction. He darted into the dining room to begin the usual loop escape. As expected, Arthur took the bait and followed. Once around and neither could continue. His father stopped to catch his breath and Muddy hid in his bedroom closet.

He sat down next to the shoe boxes lined up behind the clothes with his knees propped up under his chin. He supported his knees by wrapping his arms about his lower legs. When that became tiresome, he rested his hands on the white colonial baseboard molding that girded three sides of the closet.

Some time later, he idly reached out with his right-hand index finger and traced the groove at the top of the molding, first toward him, then around the corner behind him. There was nothing he could see with the door closed, but in the middle of the wall he felt a two-inch anomaly in the continuity of the molding. Frustrated, with absolutely nothing else to do in the closet, he turned toward the rear wall and played with that short section until he pressed upward on its groove.

The entire rear wall suddenly moved, giving Muddy quite a start. He scooted backward, got to his feet, and slowly opened the closet's outer door, checking first for his father's presence. When he saw that the coast was clear, he stole across the floor to his bureau, where he kept his flashlights. He didn't want to turn on the overhead light and tip off his father that he was hiding in his own bedroom. He put the smaller of the two flashlights into his pocket and turned on the long one with the three D-sized batteries as he headed back into the closet.

Muddy pushed through his clothes, stepped over the shoe boxes, and leaned on the rear wall, tilting it inward and upward. He found himself in a hidden room full of cobwebs.

He wound the cobwebs around the long flashlight so he could see in front of him. There was even a bit of competing light coming from above. When he looked up, he found a fake heating grate set in the floor above. The more Muddy explored the ell-shaped space, the more fascinated he became. The long walls were at least ten feet apart. The short ones were a good six feet apart. An on-end barrel with a dusty gingham covering and two short nail kegs sat at the turn.

After exploring his hidden room for the next half-hour, he returned to his bedroom, pulling the rear wall of the closet shut behind him. He lay back on his bed contemplating how he would upgrade the room and turn it into some kind of personal clubhouse. He never told anyone of his discovery. It was his secret—his personal place of refuge.

## Chapter 17
## The Stories Continue
Thursday, April 30th, 2009

Thursday evenings were special at the Olde Victorian Bookstore. The store closed earlier than usual so that the Mystery Writers' Critique Group could meet upstairs in the grand reading room, where the travel books and maps were displayed and the imagination expanded. Whenever attrition took its toll on membership, other writers, some seasoned authors, some wannabes, stepped in to take their place. Each left an inkling of their skills and wisdom at the long table and the others benefited. Each meeting brought story parts and bits to be read and criticism in the form of kindness to be dispensed, so that learning for all prevailed.

On this Thursday evening Chairperson Rivka put out some light refreshments and called the meeting to order. When she asked for readers, Joel said he'd added another witness to his trial scenes in *Mickey Mann, The Billy Danser Case.* He picked up his text and began reading.

——

### Chapter 9. The Barkeep

"The prosecution may call its next witness," said Judge Ira Hershfeld.

"The prosecution calls Leo Wilkey to the stand," said ADA George Dulaney.

A middle-aged man with a potbelly and a scruffy, salt-and-peppered beard took the stand and was sworn in.

"State your name and occupation," ordered Dulaney.

"Leo G. Wilkey and I'm a barkeep—you know, a bartender." He wiped his rimless glasses on the tails of his checkered flannel shirt and slipped them back on his wrinkled face.

"And where do you work?" asked Dulaney.

"At Happy Hilda's place on 19th and Elm," said Leo, turning toward the judge to make sure he heard the response.

"Were you at work on the night in question?"

"Yeah, I'm there most nights 'cept Mondays."

"Were you there *that* night, the night in question?"

"Yeah."

"Did you see the two men fighting?"

"Naw, but I heared 'em well enough, I was away from the bar, wiping down tables when it happened. I turned when I heared Billy yell."

"Did you see the faces of either man?"

"Yup, I saw Billy Danser well enough."

"What about the other man?"

"Naw, but it had to be Grover 'cuz he was the only other person at the bar."

"What happened then?"

"Well, Grover let go of the knife and run out the back door through the kitchen."

"Objection!" cried Mickey. "The witness has not properly established the identity of the killer as the defendant."

"Sustained," declared the judge. "The jury will disregard the defendant's name in the previous statement."

"Was there anyone in the kitchen who could identify the killer?" continued Dulaney.

"Nope. The kitchen closes at nine and there ain't nobody in there after that. Even the lights are out."

"No further questions. Your witness," said Dulaney.

Mickey glanced down at the lined yellow pad in front of him for a half-minute, stood up, and strode toward the witness.

"Good morning, Mr Wilkey," started Mickey.

"Yeah, g'morning, and it's Leo." The witness ran a hand

through his straggly beard.

"Okay, Leo, then," repeated Mickey. "Were you and the two men fighting the only ones in the establishment at that time?"

"Naw. There was a couple at one table and three young guys at another and I think a couple of singles around somewhere. And Effie was in the end booth."

"Effie?"

"Yeah, Effie, she's my barmaid. Only she was on break."

"Couldn't any one of those people have knifed Billy Danser?"

"I suppose so, but none of them was sitting at the bar."

"Wasn't there someone else sitting at the bar at that time?"

"Nope, nobody."

"What about Ms. Birches? Wasn't she at the bar?"

"Yeah, but she ain't no man."

"What's that got to do with anything?"

"It were two men's voices doin' the fighting."

"About how long would you say your back was turned away from the bar?"

"Maybe five minutes or so, while I wiped down the six tables along the wall."

"Didn't you turn around when the argument got started?"

"Nope. The guys are always arguing about somethin'. Ain't nothin' new or unusual to make me pay any mind. Only when I heared Billy a-yellin'."

"Then it's possible that any one of the persons you've indicated could have knifed Billy."

"I suppose so."

"How well do you know Grover Fox?"

"I don't. Never saw him before. I just served him a couple Jack Daniels on the rocks."

"Was there any conversation involved?"

"Naw, just him askin' for the two JDs."

"So on the basis of those few words you were able to identify his voice as that of the killer?"

"I'd like to think I'm pretty good with voices. A barkeep talks and listens all day long."

"Would you bet your life or another man's life on that identification?"

"Maybe not."

"Thank you, Leo. That's all for now, Your Honor."

"The witness may step down," said Judge Hershfeld.

———

"That's all I wrote for this witness," said Joel.

"That's great," said Frieda. "I felt I was in the courtroom the whole time. Only thing I wondered about was whether the others in the establishment should be called as witnesses, too."

"I have to agree with Frieda," said Katie. "One of them must have seen or heard something."

"I get to deal with all of them later," replied Joel. "Some are reluctant witnesses, others didn't see or hear anything, and one surprising witness for the defense will reveal something very important to the trial."

"I like the part where Mickey gets to tear down the identification in front of the jury," offered Emma.

"Who wants to read next?" asked Rivka.

"I suppose I could read a little more of my story," offered Tom. "I've written a couple new chapters."

"Sure, go ahead, Tom," said Rivka. "We're all anxious to hear more."

"We're all ears," said Dan.

Tom began to read.

———

### Chapter 2. A Free Man At Last

June 3rd, 1969. Tom Dwyer walked out the gates of Oakland Army Base in California a free man. Having served his country for thirty-six months, he received an honorable discharge. Tom and two friends he'd met at the transit base had nearly twelve hours to kill before their train left for the East Coast. One of those friends suggested they use some of the time to go to a church social he'd noticed on the base's bulletin board.

"There will be single girls there," he said. "Besides, the church is only a block and a half from the Jack London railroad station." They checked their duffels with the baggage master and walked to the church. There was a welcome sign over a door leading to the basement recreation hall. They could hear recorded music there from the street. Upon entering, a matronly woman welcomed the three newcomers to the church social and reminded them to come for Sunday worship.

"Thank you, ma'am," said Tom, "but all three of us are headed home on the East Coast. We're just killing time before the train leaves. Is it okay that we're here?"

"Of course. You're welcome, young man," she replied.

While speaking with the woman, Tom looked over her shoulder and noticed a group of girls sitting all by themselves at one edge of the dance floor. There didn't seem to be enough male partners at the social. One girl in particular seemed to stand out. As he approached her, she made eye contact. He smiled, and she did the same.

"Would you like to have the next dance with me?" Tom asked.

"I'd love to. My name is Laura Bancroft," she offered, extending her hand.

"I'm Tom Dwyer," he responded, accepting it. "I was about to say Corporal Tom, but that's all over with now. I'm out of the army."

"Congratulations, Tom."

They danced and chatted together the entire evening and, of course, he obtained her telephone number and home address. He learned that nineteen-year-old Laura lived with her widowed mother in a four-room apartment not far from the church. She worked as a sales clerk at Toni's Knitting Shop in downtown Oakland. Her light brown hair was cropped, curling around her ears. Her eyes were big, round, hazel, and sparkling bright. Laura's voice was soft and mellow like a mother telling a fairy tale to a tot. On her tiptoes, her head came to the top of his chest.

Their conversation never lagged the whole evening and, when the social ended, he walked her home. Tom told his buddies that he'd meet them at Jack London station at midnight. Their train wasn't leaving until 12:37. Tom and Laura had their goodnight peck, perhaps a lingering bit more, and promised to write to each other.

On the way to the rail station Tom made the biggest decision of his life. As soon as he met with his friends, he told them, "I've just met the girl I'm going to marry. I'm not going with you guys. I'm going to cash in my ticket and stay here until I convince her to marry me and come to Baltimore with me." And that's just what Tom did. He rented a local hotel room for that night and spent the next day looking for a rooming house. He found a room not six blocks from the Bancrofts' apartment and set a two-week goal for his mission.

That second night Tom shocked her with his call. She had been a little down, having found and lost him in the course of three hours. She was pleased to hear from him again. They made a date for after work the next evening and that was the beginning of a succession of dates and activities that culminated in his proposal by Wednesday in the middle of the second week. The ring was only a half-karat diamond, but she not only accepted it but the proposal as well.

They were married the following Sunday afternoon, June 15th, 1969, in the same church where they met—with her mother Rose Bancroft as matron of honor and her Uncle Ben Thacher who took her down the aisle. Cousin Erwin Thacher stood up for Tom as best man, as all his buddies had gone home. The bride and groom were off on their Baltimore honeymoon that very same night.

Tom and Laura spent four lovely honeymoon days in a modest Baltimore hotel. Tom's mustering-out pay only went so far, so he had to find work as soon as possible afterward. The ring and honeymoon cost plenty. He did not want to touch any more of his savings, which were earmarked for his tractor-trailer training. A driver friend, whom Tom went to high school with, recommended a school called Interstate Standard. Tom was accepted there, starting Monday, the 23rd of June.

——

"Aah! Don't you just love a romance?" declared Rivka.

"Yeah, I love it when it has a happy ending," said Esther.

"Me too," said Cora.

"I think you're a natural-born yarn teller," said Dan. "I know it's a true story, but I wonder if those precise dates are all that important to the story. Somehow, I got the notion you wanted to write it like fiction, but it's sounding more like nonfiction."

"You're right, Dan, I seem to be straddling the two."

"I think we have time for one more reading," said Rivka. "How about you, Katie? Have you got any more on *Boxcar Bertie?*"

"Sure," said Katie as she shuffled through a pile of loose pages. She began to read.

——

### Chapter 6. Discovery

"Hey, you're a girl!" he repeated.

"Yep, a real live girl just like my mama," returned Bertie, with a dash of intended sarcasm. "And no doubt you're a boy under all that fuzz."

He tried to sit up, but couldn't, and landed with his head back in her lap. His hand automatically went to the side of his head. He moaned several times, while his whole body rolled back and forth several more times and continued squirming with discomfort.

"But you're a boy with a nasty bump on your head. You need some serious medical attention. I think I've stopped the bleeding for the time being, but maybe you require some stitches."

A long, deep-throated whistle and the *clickity-clacking* of the rails had reached a constant rhythm, reminding them that they were on a train that wasn't going to stop any time soon.

"How long was I out of it?" he asked.

"'bout fifteen minutes," she replied.

"How'd it happen?"

"You don't remember?"

"No, I don't. I wouldn't ask otherwise." He rose up on one elbow, so he could get a better look at her.

142

"You tried to steal my shoes while I was asleep, and we fought until you hit your head. You can't just go around taking anything you want. Besides, there's no way my woman's shoes would fit you."

"I apologize for everything I did. I didn't know you were a woman at the time. I still don't remember doing anything like that. I must have been desperate. Did I hurt you at all?"

"A few minor bumps and bruises," she answered. "I'll survive, but my being a woman shouldn't have mattered—you shouldn't steal from anyone."

"Sorry. I guess I failed my very first attempt at thievery." He sounded down-in-the-mouth.

"First timer, eh?"

"Yeah, I've never done anything like that."

"What's your name?" She needed to change the subject.

"Stanford Milhouse, but mostly I'm called Stan. What's yours?"

"Bertie, Bertie Pachet."

"Where you headed, Bertie?"

"Greener pastures, I guess. Any place I can land a job. What about you?"

"I thought I'd try Boston. I got a cousin there that works on one of them big old estates. I'm kinda handy at a lot of things. Maybe they can take me on."

"Yeah, Boston for me, too. I thought I might wait tables or clean rooms or cook for somebody. Nobody's got the patience for a sweet little voice anymore."

"You a singer?"

"More like, *was* a singer. But yeah," she answered.

"You any good?"

"Some people thought so. I even paid good money to take some lessons."

"Hey, the train is slowing down," he said. "We must be coming to a station."

"Probably Saybrook," she said. "There must be some passenger cars up front. Can you stand up yet?"

"I think so," he replied, struggling to his feet. "But why?"

"The rail yard cops will be searching all the empty boxcars, looking for freebee riders like us."

"Couldn't we just shut the door?"

"Nope," she replied. "Then they would know we're here for sure."

"Then what can we do?"

"We hug the outside wall and make ourselves as skinny as possible, hoping they don't look too closely."

The train slowed to a full stop and reverberated a few time as the individual cars bumped together to their final stop. For a while, all they heard were the normal outside noises—street traffic, other trains in the distance, a few birds, and a voice here and there. Then they heard the clunking of hardwood on metal as the rail yard cop made his rounds with his billy club, making as much racket as he could. The clunking got louder and louder as the billy club got closer—the next car, then theirs. He hesitated at their car a little longer, seeing an object at the opposite end of the boxcar. He scanned the far end with a long flashlight.

*Is the rail yard cop suspicious?* wondered Bertie. *His flashlight is lingering there longer than necessary. He must have seen something of interest. Will he come inside and drag us off and beat us like that rail cop did in Bridgeport last month?*

——

"I've got another chapter written, but I'd like to go over it one more time before I read it to the group," said Katie.

"Wow. How are you going to get them out of that one?" asked Frieda.

"Tune in next time," said Katie. "Same time, same station, as they used to say on the old radio shows."

"Now you're dating yourself, Katie," declared Esther.

"I love the suspense you've built up," said Ivy. "That's something I have to work on."

"I don't remember you reading us anything about the Bridgeport rail cop before," said Dan. "Did I miss a chapter?"

"No," replied Katie. "I planned for that incident to have happened before my story started."

"It sounds to me like you're missing a good action scene," offered Dan.

"You may be right. I'll take it under advisement." Katie smiled at her exaggerated officious tone.

Rivka brought out chocolate chip cookies, coffee and tea as the group chatted more about each other's work. She finally declared the critique meeting adjourned.

## Chapter 18
## Emotion and Emotionless
Friday, May 1st, 2009

It seems as though people spend most of their lives waiting for this or that. On this particular morning, activity in the bookstore seemed pretty routine until Ivy received a welcome phone call she had been anticipating for weeks. Her long-awaited wedding dress had finally arrived at Muriel's Bridal Boutique, and the seamstress there wanted her to come in for a final fitting. Ivy surrendered the bookstore cash register to Rivka and happily prepared to leave for the bridal shop on Main Street. She had been waiting for this day ever since she had picked this particular dress out from the array of bridal catalogues. She encountered Dan on her way out, and he offered to drive her there, even though it was well within her usual walking distance.

She replied, "I'll walk slowly enough, so I won't work up a sweat."

"No, no. We can't have you trying on your dress of a lifetime without being absolutely fresh, now can we?"

"I suppose not. I'll have to accept."

Dan dropped her off in front of the shop. She told him she was perfectly able and willing to walk back to the bookstore after her fitting, and he agreed. Dan drove back to the bookstore and when he came through the front door, he stopped at the register to consult with Rivka. "You never did finish telling me what happened at your meeting with Cora Bacon," he said.

Rivka eagerly straightened up. "Cora was very forthcoming, Dan. Just as you suspected, the stalker is the Atkins sisters' brother. His nickname is Muddy because of his obnoxious personality. Apparently, there's no love lost between Cora and Muddy. The two older sisters have a long history of mutually teasing their only brother and of his reciprocating with pranks that go back to their grade-school days. She said Muddy is a compulsive prankster and a vindictive retaliator, and he's often been known to take things to great extremes. She thinks he derives a sadistic pleasure in carrying out these ridiculous vendettas. To quote Cora: 'I don't believe there's an emotional bone in his body—he's either unable or unwilling to express his emotions.' Dan, I looked up emotionless personality, and it's a psychological disorder called alexithymia."

"Wow, that's a mouthful," said Dan. "But it doesn't tell us why he's stalking me, or what's in his father's book that he's trying to hide from the world."

"I asked her outright whether there was anything in the book that she or the family would be ashamed of or want to hide. She couldn't think of anything and hadn't any idea why Muddy would want to stalk you."

"I guess Cora wasn't all that much help then," said Dan.

"Yes she was. After all, she identified your stalker. Now we have an idea who, or maybe what, we are dealing with in Muddy Atkins."

"I really wonder if we do know enough, if she says he's all that unpredictable."

\* \* \* \*

Cora drove her bright green Mercedes SL Class convertible up to the Annapolis Waterfront Hotel entrance and turned the car over to a young, good-looking valet parker, who tried unsuccessfully to flirt with her. Inside the lobby, she ignored the reception desk and headed straight for the elevator. Dressed in a navy business suit, she made her way directly to room 233. She knocked rapidly four times and waited.

"Who's there?" a deep male voice answered.

"Your sister."

Muddy opened the door and blinked twice. "What the hell are you doing here?"

"That's no way to greet your sister. Aren't you going to invite me in?"

"Sister schmister. What the hell are you up to? You're not one to make social calls, especially not to me. Out with it, woman. You must want something from me."

"Of course not, dear brother. It's just that I hadn't heard from you in several days, and I wanted to thank you for handling the movers at the old house. It sure made our lives a lot easier on moving day. At first I wondered why you volunteered, but then I realized that you were just being nice."

"Meaning you thought I was acting out of character?" he asked. His sarcastic tone was not missed.

"Don't get me wrong, Muddy. Motive aside, you were appreciated. Now, if you don't mind, I'd like to come in and sit down."

"Of course, my manners seem to be malfunctioning today." His hand swept through a healthy arc, showing her the way in.

Cora took a seat in front of the wide glass sliding doors. The expanse revealed a view of the Annapolis City Dock and its famous Ego Alley, a tiny harbor inlet where boat owners paraded their floating prides and joys during the summer season. Muddy sat down on the bed opposite her and tried to analyze her real reason for coming.

"Yeah, I was just being nice." He sounded as though even he wasn't convinced of his own generosity. Her gratitude didn't sound right to him. *She hasn't any idea that I really needed time in the empty house to seal off the secret room from the new owners.*

"Muddy, I know you were opposed to Rae selling the house, but Daddy left it to her, and she should be free to do with it as she pleases. I believe she sold it for money to support her writing career."

"Rae should've asked each of us whether we wanted to buy it beforehand," he complained. "She never asked me. That's why I'm so pissed at her." *The old buzzard could have left something for his only son.*

148

*The house would have been nice—even a partnership, so I could have blocked any sale.*

"I didn't know you wanted to buy the house," said Cora. "Were you able to save that much dough serving in the Merchant Marines all this time?" *The Merchant Marines pays well, but not that well,* she thought.

"No, but one of you sisters might have wanted to keep it— maybe turn it into a bed and breakfast or something." He admitted to himself, *No way I could I have saved that much, even if I'd behaved and avoided spending the lion's share on whisky, waste, and whores.*

"I have no interest in that sort of thing, and Gloria certainly couldn't handle a project like that. No, Rae did the right thing in selling it. There are far too many rooms to clean and take care of without maintaining an expensive household staff."

"But our house has been in the family since colonial times," he protested, "and I don't want to see strangers living in it." *Ordinarily, I wouldn't give a crap.*

"I didn't know you felt that way," she said. "You've never taken any interest in the family history before." *The sonofabitch is lying. What's his motive?*

"There're a lot of things you don't know about me," declared Muddy.

"I'm sure there are, but one thing is nagging at me."

"What's that?"

"Why are you so suddenly interested in Daddy's book?"

"Who says I am?"

"It's kind of obvious. I hear you've been following Dan Sherman, that bookseller, all over the place ever since he borrowed Daddy's manuscript from Rae."

"Damn it. You've been talking to that Sherman guy, haven't you?"

"Maybe," she admitted. "But why are you following him around otherwise?"

"That's my business—and you'd better stay out of it if you know what's good for you." He hadn't meant to voice an ugly threat;

it just spilled out.

"What are you trying to hide, little brother?" *Now I've got him,* she thought.

"That also is my business, not yours." *The bitch is getting too close.*

"I'll bet dollars to donuts it has something to do with the house. Doesn't it, Muddy dear?"

"You're all wrong, Cora. You couldn't be more wrong." *Too damn close.*

"Ah! Perhaps you protest way too much, little brother."

"Now you're getting much too obnoxious, I think you ought to leave."

"Why, Muddy? Am I getting too close to the truth?"

"You wouldn't know the truth if you stepped in it. Now get the hell out of here before I throw you out."

Cora stood and walked toward the door. As she passed him, he reached out and pinched her hard on the rump. It was his way of curbing his frustration—a way of having the last word. She spun around and slapped him—a stinging blow across the face in one swinging action. Stunned for only a few seconds, he returned an even stronger slap. She ran out the door in tears, the left side of her face wearing a red mark half the size of his hand. It smarted now, but later, it would turn sore, black and blue. She had failed to get Muddy to admit to anything, but she thought she knew what he might be hiding.

* * * *

Ivy burst through the front door of the bookstore in a magnificent mood. She kissed Dan on the top of his head, hugged Rivka thoroughly, and whirled around in the immediate space on her tiptoes. "The dress is so beautiful, far more beautiful than its catalogue pictures, and it looks so terrific on me. A tuck here and a nip there, and it'll be finished. I'm so very happy." She whirled around once more and plopped a plastic bag full of letters down on the counter.

"What's all this?" asked Dan.

"Oh, I stopped by the house to pick up my mail," replied Ivy.

"From the looks of it, a bunch of the invitation responses have started to arrive," said Rivka.

"It sure looks like it," declared Ivy.

"When will the dress be ready?" asked Rivka.

"The bridal shop said they'd have it here on Monday afternoon, sometime after one. Everything is going so smoothly."

Dan looked at Rivka, and she looked back. The same thought coursed through both minds. It was one of those things you never say out loud or it won't be or stay true unless you add a magical phrase like "Knock on wood" after it.

"*Kine-ahora,*" said Rivka almost in a whisper. "It's what my grandmother used to say in Yiddish: 'You shouldn't tempt the evil spirits. Enjoy the fact that things are going smoothly, but don't say it aloud for the spirits to hear.'"

Ivy shrugged and took over the register. Because business was slow, she dumped the pile of letters from the plastic bag onto the counter. She began to open them and check the RSVPs against a list she had taken from her purse. About two-thirds of the way through the pile, Ivy stopped and began to cry. Rivka had gone upstairs to their apartment to start supper, but Dan heard Ivy sniffling and came in from the reading room. "Ivy, what's your problem? Why are you crying?"

"I'm full of emotional chills. Here, look for yourself." She showed him the response card with a note tucked inside its fold. Dan noted the return address on the envelope. It was W. Sachs, 103 Devon Court, #4B, London, EC1Y8SY, U.K. He took the note from her and studied it. "Why, it's from your foster parents."

"Yes, and they've accepted. They're coming to our wedding. Isn't it wonderful? Janice and Wayne Sachs took me in when I was only three months old. They raised me and educated me like I was one of their own. We still keep in touch—at least one letter every other week. Janice does all the writing for them. I sent them an invitation, but I never expected them to accept. They're coming, all right, but my foster brother, Ollie, can't come because his wife, Beatrix, is expecting their second child any day now. I'm so proud of what Ollie has accomplished. He's managing a Marks and Spencer department store in York now."

"Then your tears are tears of happiness," said a relieved Dan.

"Oh yes. I couldn't be happier." She wiped her eyes with a tissue.

"Hey" said Dan. "You've got a little visitor down there. He came to console you."

Three, the kitten with three white paws, had succumbed to wanderlust and meandered out into the front of the store by himself. Ivy reached down, picked him off the floor, and hugged him to her cheek. Then she held him out in front of her so they could see each other eye to eye.

"Oooh, you must have known that I intended to pick one of the litter when you guys were all weaned. Instead, you've come all the way out here to pick me. Okay, so it's love at first sight, but I can't take you home until Mark and I come back from our honeymoon. For now, it's best for you to return to your mamma. Lady Annabella will be missing you. Dan, can you watch the register for just a minute while I return Three to her mamma?"

"Sure, go ahead, Ivy. I don't mind."

Ivy and Three headed for the rear of the store and the back hall closet to join her feline siblings. Ivy chatted to her newfound friend all the way to her destination. When she got to the back hall, she found Lady Annabella gone and the other three kittens wandering about the hall looking for their mamma. She set Three down among his siblings, concerned where Her Ladyship had gone. *Is it temporary or final?* she wondered. *Has she tired of nursing and just taken off and abandoned her litter?* She opened the rear door and scanned the yard for any signs of the neglectful mother. There were none. She shut the door again. *I wonder if Lord Byron is aware of this.*

On her way back to the cash register, Ivy stopped by the poetry stacks to see if the Laird was in. Lord Byron jumped from his tartan loft to the floor. He stopped as soon as he saw Ivy coming and, not knowing what else to do, began to wash himself.

"Lord Byron did you know that Lady Annabella has abandoned her kittens?" declared Ivy. "So it's back to bachelorhood for you, M'lord—as if you really cared."

The Laird stopped for a few seconds and tilted his head to one side as though he actually was listening, but not understanding. She knelt momentarily, rubbed him behind the ears, and continued on to the cash register.

"Dan, did you know that Lady Annabella has up and left us? Left her little ones as well."

"Yes, Ivy, I believe she left some time last night. That's the way with alley cats. They attach themselves to no one." *It's that way with some humans, too,* he thought. *They act without emotion. It's the making of a psychopath in some cases."*

"But the kittens, they're not even weaned yet. What will they do?" pleaded Ivy.

"Lady Annabella must have determined they're old enough to survive on their own." Dan explained. "Who's a better judge of that than the mamma?"

"Without Annabella, how are we going to keep the little ones in the back hall, Dan?"

"I'll get one of those gates they use for children at the tops of staircases," said Dan.

"But the holes in those things are so large, the kittens will squeeze through," she replied.

"You're right. Maybe one of those expandable window screens will do the job," said Dan. "I'll pick one up first thing in the morning." *I wish the problem with the psychopath was as simple to solve.*

## Chapter 19
## The Scream
Monday, May 4th, 2009

As a voracious reader and bookstore owner, Dan knew that once a reader commits to the content of a book, there's a drive, a need to arrive at an ending that reveals whodunit or, at the very least, how things turn out for the protagonist. As the reader approaches the last chapter, there is an apprehension that the sought-after answers might not be there.

Dan was getting close to the end of the Atkins manuscript. He was anxious about starting the last chapter of Arthur's book. That anxiety had taken hold of him. Had he missed what he was looking for? The bookstore chores had kept him overly busy, and he'd been too tired at the end of the day to read continuously. But now the opportunity was here. He picked up the top page and dove in.

——

### Chapter 23. Beating Prohibition

James Keen Atkins (1872-1910) had two sons: Edgar Aaron Atkins (1892-1948) and James Keen Atkins II (1894-1918). In 1916, during his sophomore year at Duke University, James II was suspended for cheating on an exam. He then had the immediate misfortune of being drafted into the army and wound up at Belleau Wood in France. It was May of 1918 when General Pershing ordered a counteroffensive to stop the German advance under General Ludendorff. Unfortunately, a direct artillery hit tore poor James to pieces. He was one of the 10,000 fatalities in that battle. Nevertheless, his remains were sent home for an Arlington National Cemetery burial.

Edgar's asthma helped him to avoid military service altogether. He completed college near the bottom of his class with a degree in business. Edgar Atkins entered the business world of shipping and trucking and rose quickly, acquiring a fleet of more than twenty trucks. The aggressive upstart liked to call himself an entrepreneur; however, his competitors had labeled him a cut-throat thief, and the authorities minced no words in calling him a local crime boss. But none of these tags were ever substantiated by hard evidence.

During Prohibition (Eighteenth Amendment to the Constitution, 1919-1933), Dirty Ed, as he was known to his crew of eleven, smuggled illegal hard liquor in from Canada and distributed it to local speakeasies, which were private clubs that sold liquor both by the bottle and by the glass at great profit. His lavish parties for the enabling Annapolis elite were often held at the Atkins home; for those events, the alcohol was conveniently stored in the same hidden room used by Emma Thornton Atkins and her abolitionist friends. A neighbor lady, who was a staunch member of the Women's Christian Temperance Union, sent Federal agents to the house after one of these affairs. Six agents were unable to find any trace of the liquor after a three-hour search. Edgar amassed a great deal of wealth during this period, even though he lost the use of his left arm in a shoot-out with a competitor. It was said that Dirty Ed left a trail of at least nine murders, which were never quite pinned on him.

After the Twenty-First Amendment repealed Prohibition, Edgar and his wife, Mary, sold the trucking business for several millions and opened a discount liquor store on Main Street. Mary gave birth to Arthur Clement Atkins on August 4th, 1932 and Roland Thomas Atkins on May 12th, 1934.

———

The typing ended here and Dan found the following handwritten notes that he assumed had never made it to the the final book because of the title dates, 1768 to 1934.

———

Roland never married. Edgar met his maker in June of 1948 when a pickup truck struck him crossing Compromise Street in town. Some said that it was an intentional hit by another of his competitors, but that assumption was never proven.

Arthur Atkins married Gillian Ann Lear on September 12th, 1958. They had three daughters: Cordelia Lear Atkins (February 8th, 1960), Regan Lear Atkins (March 22nd, 1961), and Goneril Lear Atkins (November 3rd, 1982), plus one son: Budreau Lear Atkins (August 8th, 1962).

———

Dan took a deep breath and put the book in his lap. He remained for a time in the recliner just thinking about what he had read. *There's nothing in Arthur's book that anyone would be ashamed of. Sure, there were criminals and individuals who weren't exactly pillars of the community. On the other hand, there were also some heroes and major contributors to society. Nowhere did I detect any obvious attempt at coded or otherwise hidden messaging. So I have to believe Muddy is trying to hide the fact that the house contains a hidden room. That's it! But why? So what? For what illegal purpose is he using this room? Drugs, stolen goods, family heirlooms he's kept from his sisters? It could be anything. Do I really want to know more? Do I really want to get more involved? How dangerous is this Muddy Atkins?* Dan's train of thought was suddenly interrupted by a ruckus out by the register counter.

"It's here! It's here," cried an excited Ivy. "My wedding gown is here at last."

As Dan approached, he heard the bridal shop delivery truck pull away from the bookstore curb. Ivy was dancing around with a huge box.

Rivka came running. "What's all the commotion?"

"My wedding gown is here," said Ivy at the end of her twirl.

"Oh! I couldn't imagine what happened. Let's go upstairs and try it on."

Rivka put her hand on Ivy's back and hustled her toward the stairs, while Dan plopped down on the stool behind the register.

In the Shermans' bedroom, Ivy shed her slacks and blouse and laid them on the bed. She undid the elastic strings securing the box, removed the cover, lifted out the wedding gown, and pressed the satin smoothness to her cheek. Rivka helped her slip it on over her head. When all of the zipping, twisting, and adjustments were finished, Rivka led her to the full-length mirror behind the bedroom door.

"It's absolutely beautiful and fits perfectly." said Rivka. "You can't gain a pound between now and the wedding. With your hair up and heels, you'll look downright gorgeous for Mark. Now we have to be very careful taking it off." Rivka lifted and Ivy wriggled her way out of it. Rivka hung the gown on the heavily padded hanger included in the bridal shop box. Then she slipped the thin plastic garment bag over it and zipped it up.

"Do you want me to hang it up here until you leave tonight?" asked Rivka, indicating the back of her closet door.

"No, I'd like it downstairs, so I won't forget it," replied Ivy.

"Oh, I don't think there's any danger of that," said an amused Rivka.

"There're some hooks in the back hall. I can hang it there," said Ivy, while getting back into her blouse and slacks. As she sat down at the foot of the bed, a sudden rush of sadness washed across her face.

"What's wrong, Ivy?" asked Rivka. "You were so happy just a moment ago."

"I was just thinking that my real father won't be walking me down the aisle and giving me away."

"No, Herschel and Anna Reubens are both gone now," said Rivka "At least you got to find your father, spend some time with him, and learn that it was his wife, Anna, not him who was responsible for your mother's death." Conflicting thoughts flashed through Rivka's mind. *Ivy's father could hardly be called blameless, but I'm not about to bring that up here.* She forced her voice to sound perky. "Hey, Ivy, there's always your Uncle Meyer Reubens to walk you down the aisle. I bet your Aunt Esther would make a fine matron of honor. I'm sure they'd both approve."

"I had two other persons in mind, Rivka, but I haven't asked them yet."

"And who might they be?"

"I'd love to have Dan walk me down the aisle and give me away. And I'd love *you* to be my matron of honor. The both of you have taken me in, protected me, and have been like parents to me ever since I arrived on your doorstep four years ago."

"Of course, I'd be proud to be your matron of honor." Rivka gave Ivy a big motherly hug. "And, I'm sure Dan would be honored as well. But I'll bet he'd rather hear you ask him yourself."

"Oh my goodness," declared Rivka, looking at her watch. "We've been up here for over an hour. Dan will wonder what happened to us." She headed for the stairs.

Ivy carried the gown downstairs and hung it on a hook by the back door. The three of them met at the register a few minutes later, where Dan was ringing up a sale, a Robert Ludlum book entitled *The Lazarus Vendetta*.

When the customer left the store, Dan turned to the ladies and said, "It looks as though the two of you are getting ready to gang up on me."

"Not really," said Rivka. "It's just that Ivy has something important to ask you."

"Something important, you say? Well, out with it already."

"I would love to have my favorite gentleman give me away at the wedding. I want you to walk me down the aisle."

"Now how could I refuse an offer like that? I would be happy and proud to walk you down the aisle, young lady. You realize I'm no amateur at this—I walked our Jenny down the aisle almost six years ago."

"And he did a fine job of it, too," added Rivka.

Ivy rushed at Dan, threw her arms about him, and buried her head in his chest for a long squeezing hug. "Thank you. I do love you both so much."

"Before I forget, there was an email for you from your foster parents in Great Britain. It's their flight plans as far as I can see." He handed the two-page email to her.

Ivy read it aloud with all the specifics. "...We have reservations to stay at Annapolis Waterfront Hotel. Looking forward to seeing you. Love, Janice and Wayne."

"It's for real," cried Ivy. "I can actually believe they're coming now. I'm so excited."

"You've had one big emotional day," said Dan. "You've never really told us much about your foster family."

"That's true," added Rivka.

Neither one of them expected Ivy to provide the full-blown details that followed.

"Well, Wayne is truly a dear, loving man. He was a solicitor working for the law offices of Bleak and Fullbrite. He's retired, probably seventy-three by now. Wayne's about your weight and size, Dan, with lots of curly brown hair. Janice is a wonderful, stay-at-home mom, a short straw blonde, who fills her time with volunteer work now that Ollie and me are all grown up. She's probably seventy-one now. Ollie must be about thirty-six, somewhat athletic and looks a lot like his dad. He's a department store manager up in York. They're all big football fans. Chelsea Football Club is their team."

"Thank you, I feel I know them already," said Dan, suppressing a yawn. Maybe we can arrange to pick them up at BWI airport when they come in."

"Is that today's mail piled up there on the counter?" asked Rivka.

"Yeah, but I haven't had a chance to look at it yet," said Dan.

Rivka dove into the pile, mumbling the Yiddish word *shnorer* [beggar] for each of the charities deemed either unworthy or already donated to. Those envelopes were destined for the wastebasket under the counter. The bills wound up in the 'IN' basket. Two popular magazines ended up on the wall side of the counter to be read between customers. "Oh, here's one addressed to you, Dan."

He took the envelope from her and turned it over to read the return address. "It's from Stewart Reubens. Isn't he the late Herschel and Anna Reubens' son?"

"Yes," said Ivy.

"Stewart is your half-brother, or is that stepbrother?" asked Rivka. "I can never remember which."

"Half-brother is right, dear." offered Dan. "The half refers to when kids biologically have one parent in common, but you're step-related when kids biologically have neither parent in common, as with a child of a former union."

"So open it already, Dan," said Rivka. "The suspense is killing me."

"You're acting like I never receive any mail," murmured Dan as he ripped off the end of the envelope and slipped out the contents. "It's an invitation to a bachelor party for Mark at Stewart's place on the sixteenth. That's a Saturday night at seven. There's an RSVP card inside. I might as well send it off now before I forget."

Ivy pushed a metal cart full of books collected from the reading rooms into the rickety elevator, reached inside, and pushed the DOWN button. The doors closed, and Ivy started down the stairs to meet the elevator on the floor below.

When Ivy was out of earshot, Rivka said, "That reminds me. I'd better arrange a wedding shower for Ivy. Let's see, there's Frieda Fraume, Esther Reubens, Katie Silver, Alice Zimmer, Helen Margoles, and maybe Cora Bacon. I'll have to ask Mark if they want any of their friends invited." She wandered off so Dan couldn't hear her any longer.

Some forty minutes later, Ivy came up the stairs from the Dungeon level and wanted to have another look at her wedding gown on its hanger. *The whole idea of marriage seems so much like a dream, another peek might even make it real.* At the top step she turned toward the back hall. One look and she let out a banshee-like scream that echoed through the whole bookstore.

## Chapter 20
## More Stories Told
### The Same Day

Dan and Rivka rushed toward the source of the scream and found Ivy holding two of the newborn kittens. Tears were streaming down her cheeks.

"The kittens did it, Rivka. One and Three were climbing up the garment bag covering my gown. Their tiny claws were ripping into the plastic and tearing it to shreds. I can see one small area where they even damaged the satin. What am I going to do?"

Rivka took a closer look. "Oh, that's not so terrible. It's right on the seam. I'll bet the bridal shop can fix that in a jiffy. They're professionals and know how to hide imperfections. Maybe they'll even move a few pearls there."

Dan handed Ivy a box of Kleenex, and she wiped away the tears. "Come on, when you're ready, I'll run you and the gown over to the bridal shop, and we'll see what they have to say."

"Thank God," said Ivy. "I don't know what I'd do without you guys."

"By the way, where were Two and Four?" asked Dan.

"I don't know," replied Ivy. "Roaming the store, for all I know."

"Go," said Rivka. "I'll track them down."

\* \* \* \*

Another Thursday evening arrived and the regular meeting of the Mystery Writers' Critique Group gathered in the reading room upstairs. There were more stories to be told and discussions to be held, as well as friendships to be developed and nurtured. And if by listening a lesson is learned, all's well that ends well with the group each week.

Rivka set a tray down on the banquet table with a pitcher of iced tea, another of water, a stack of red Dixie cups, and another of Styrofoam cups for the hot drinks. She went back to the kitchen and brought out two store-bought packages of cookies—Oreos and oatmeal-raisin.

Frieda, Helen, and Joel were already there and engaged in a conversation involving local politics. Dan remained at the store's front door, acting as doorman until the last of the members arrived. Then he locked only the door's access from the outside before climbing the stairs and joining the meeting. Fire laws prevented locking any exits from the inside when the store was occupied. As soon as he took his seat, Rivka called the meeting to order.

"Does anyone have anything to read tonight? Ah, Katie, I suppose you have another chapter of *Boxcar Bertie*."

"I do," she answered. "Bertie's in a boxcar stopped in a rail yard and hears the rail cop banging his nightstick on each car. Closer and closer he comes. At their boxcar he spots something at the far end and hesitates." She picked up a bunch of pages and began to read.

———

### Chapter 7. Close Call

Fortunately, the rail yard cop proved to be too lazy to bother climbing into the boxcar to inspect. He continued past them. Some minutes later the train whistle blew a warning blast. The string of boxcars stretched from one to another until every last one strained and then moved, allowing the whole train to roll as one. It gathered speed, closing in on its normal *clickity-clack* rhythm.

"Whew, that was close," said Stan.

"What's down at the other end that the rail cop was so interested in?" asked Bertie.

"Just my duffel and my guitar," said Stan. "I didn't think he could see that far in the dark."

"A flashlight covers a lot of ground. If he'd taken more time to examine your stuff, he would have had a reason to come in. I don't think he recognized anything."

"That's all I got in this world, every stitch." He strode to the other end and picked up his belongings.

"You said a guitar. Do you play?" she asked.

"Yeah, you wanna hear something?"

"Sure, we got nothing else to kill the time with," she replied.

Stan already had the instrument half out of its canvas case.

"Or maybe not," she said. "It's only twenty minutes to New London, and I think we should get off there and get your head gash taken care of."

Stan unraveled the scarf for her to see. "I think the bleeding's stopped. How's it look to you?"

"It's a mean-looking gash, but you're right, the bleeding's stopped. Still, I think we ought to get that wound cleaned out before infection sets in. Maybe it needs iodine or something stronger. I don't know whether you need stitches or not, but it's sure going to leave one hell of a nasty scar."

"I guess you're right, Bertie," said Stan. "I don't know why you're so caring for me when I treated you so badly. I was actually gonna steal your shoes from your feet."

"Maybe it's the mothering instinct in me. Better put that scarf back on. You'll need it when we jump."

The time to New London passed quickly, and Bertie prepared them for a pre-station debarking. As soon as the train slowed to a reasonable speed, they positioned themselves at the door. First, they flung their belongings out the door. Then Stan leaped out, and Bertie followed, both landing on the rough ground and rolling to a final stop in the sooty gravel a few hundred feet from their tossed gear.

They had crossed a number of tracks when Bertie noticed a rail yard workshed. "Look, a building over there." She pointed. There was a black rubber hose coiled up next to the shed. As they got closer, they saw a spigot on the end of a pipe coming out of the ground. She dove into her backpack and retrieved a spare clean sock. She went to turn on the water and discovered the wheel handle to turn it on was missing.

"I don't think we can turn the valve on." said Bertie.

"Isn't that the handle up there on the nail?" asked Stan.

"Right on," said Bertie. "Just what the doctor ordered." She grabbed the handle, fitted it to the valve, and turned until the water flowed. Soaking the sock, she dabbed at the dried bloody mess at the back of his head, cleaning it as she went. When she finished, she told him, "It's the best I can do for you. Any more and I'm afraid I'll start the bleeding again." They each slurped a drink before she reached over him to turn off the water.

"Thanks. Say, there's a patch of thick green grass behind that shed that looks like it might make a great bed," said Stan.

"I guess we both could use a little sleep, especially under that shade tree," agreed the twenty-three-year-old tomboy.

That's exactly where they headed. Stan fell asleep first, while Bertie lay there thinking, staring up at the crab apples in the tree. They were almost ripe, she noted, before dozing off. The sun was warm and the breeze cooling. They slept for hours, making up for much needed rest and taking advantage of the soft bed of grass. When they awoke, the sun had gone down, and there were at least three small flickering lights along the grassy knoll that lay along the tracks. The two got to their feet and gathered their gear before strolling toward the flickering lights.

Bertie soon realized that they had stumbled across one of many hobo camps and that the lights were actually cooking fires. Large tin cans hung suspended over the fire. Perhaps some were filled with weak coffee and some with a makeshift soup or the rare hobo stew if the ingredients had been pilfered or begged from local gardens. Four men huddled close to the nearest fire to get warm and chat.

"May we?" asked Stan.

The man wearing a black watch cap motioned silently to an

open spot, so they put down their gear and sat in a ring around the fire. Minutes passed, and then he looked up at them. "Do you have anything to contribute?"

Bertie fumbled through her things and came up with a Baby Ruth candy bar. Stan cut it into six equal pieces with his pocket knife. It didn't take long for every one of those pieces to disappear. After a time, the bald man, stirring the tin can with a large hunting knife, declared: "It's done." Each one of the men dipped into the can for a half-fill with their own tin cup. Then the man in the watch cap looked to Bertie. She dipped with her own cup and then she looked to Stan, who merely shrugged—he had no cup. Bertie drained her cup and passed it to Stan, who dipped and ate his meager share.

Stan unpacked his guitar and strummed a few odd bars before moving on to "She'll be Coming Round the Mountain." Bertie hummed a few bars and then started to sing the words. Before long everyone sang the lyrics they could remember to "You Are My Sunshine" and "I've Been Working on the Railroad." All the music put everyone in a good mood, except when they were finished, a few of the men were overtaken by nostalgia.

A train whistle blew several short blasts and most in the group knew it was the next freight north and east. By the time it came to pass them, it was still moving slowly enough for boarding. The man in the watch cap ran alongside, grabbed a bar, and swung inside. Stan and Bertie ran together hoping to land in the same car. First Bertie and, close behind, Stan made it inside. No sooner had they safely landed, than they regretted their choice of boxcar.

———

"You know, I'm enjoying the story, Katie," said Dan. "Especially the growing relationship between the two main characters, but I'm having trouble visualizing what they look like. I think a good description is in order."

"Good point, Dan," she answered. "I'll pick up on that the next time around."

"I think it's pretty exciting," said Frieda.

"Me too," said Helen.

"Tom, I believe I saw your hand up before. Do you want to read next?" asked Rivka.

"Sure," he replied. Tom began.

——

## Chapter 3. Big Rig Training

It was a rigorous 165-hour course approved by the Federal Motor Carrier Safety Administration. It included classroom work, simulator training, one-on-one instructor training, and practice on a driving course and backing-up range. Students needed to qualify on six- and ten-speed manual transmission semis and with weighted trailers up to fifty-three feet in length. Tom was a pretty quick learner, acquiring and honing all the necessary skills to obtain his Class A Truck/Trailer Commercial Driver's License. During the thirty-some days it took him to complete the course, Laura managed to get an hourly sales job at Bobbins, a dry goods store in the heart of the city.

For the short term, the time it took for Tom to complete his training, they lived with his mom and dad. Upon graduation, there appeared to be a shortage of long-haul, cross-country drivers, so once Tom joined the Teamsters Union he had no trouble finding work. Usually, but not always, there were two drivers taking four-hour shifts at the wheel for days on end. It depended on the destination mileage. At last, he was realizing his ambition—seeing the open country, but he valued the time at home with his bride even more.

After three cross-country trips, the newlywed couple moved to their own apartment not too far from Tom's parents. They could afford the extra rent now that he was making good money. Tessie, his mother, passed away the following year from a pulmonary embolism, a fatal blood clot, and Ned, his father, was never the same after that. Alzheimer's slowly destroyed what was left of Ned Dwyer, and he died three years later in a nursing home. Other than the fact that Laura could not conceive, regardless of the efforts of medical science, and the fact that Tom spent an excessive amount of time away, the couple had a relatively unstrained marriage.

In the fall of 1988 with their savings now substantial, Laura put her foot down and insisted that Tom consider driving short haul or even local runs, so that he might come home most nights after work like in regular families. Even Tom had to admit the long hauls were getting old hat and pretty tiresome after nearly twenty long years. He applied at four different firms and accepted the best offer at Express Package Delivery Service, a firm that delivered anything under one-hundred pounds throughout the Baltimore, Washington, and Northern Virginia area. It meant driving the much smaller over-the-cab box truck. He could start right away, but he'd have to spend two weeks learning the most efficient delivery routes and some unique parking skills. He would be paired with an experienced route driver for that learning period at the regular driver pay level.

———

"Wow," said Dan. "You sure have had an interesting life."

"I agree, but I still don't see the mystery you promised," said Joel.

"You'll see it in the next chapter," said Tom.

"Any more readers tonight?" asked Rivka. "No? Then the meeting's adjourned."

\* \* \* \*

The drive back up to Baltimore that Thursday seemed longer than most nights. Sure, the heavy downpour and wet roads could have been a factor, but more likely, Tom's mind was divided between the driving and the meeting he had just left. He read well enough, and the group seemed to like what he'd written. He wondered what the group would think of him after he read his last and most shocking chapter.

Tom turned into his street and then backed into a parking space fifty feet from the door of his row house. The rain was still unyielding, so holding his thin vinyl briefcase over his head, he made a mad dash for his front door. The marble stoop offered no skyward shelter, so holding his home key at the ready, he unlocked the front door and darted inside the warm, dry living room as quickly as he could. He stomped his feet several times on the mat just inside the door and yelled for his wife.

"Laura, honeybunch! Quick, bring me a towel before I drip

all over your fine carpet."

In a matter of seconds she rushed out of the kitchen and into the bathroom, emerging with a large, fluffy towel. "And you'd better take off those shoes."

He dried himself and the vinyl briefcase before kicking off both shoes and carrying them through the kitchen to the back hall where he tossed them on the floor. Back in the kitchen, he sat down at the table across from Laura.

"So how did it go tonight?" she asked.

"Not bad. In fact, I think they liked what I read. I got some nice comments, but what I'm really worried about is what I'm going to read next week. It's my last chapter and it's all about the accident and my confession."

"You don't have to do it, you know," she said. "You told me that writing about it would be sufficient to calm your conscience. You don't have to tell the world." She laid her hand across the table on his and squeezed his fingers affectionately.

"No. I feel I must tell someone about it," he said. "I've carried all this guilt around with me long enough."

"Aren't I someone?" she asked. "You've told me all about it so many times. Don't I count?"

"Sure you do, honeybunches," he replied. "It's just that you're so quick to forgive. You're prejudiced because you're my wife and my love. These are nice solid people with open minds in the critique group. They're a cross-section of different occupations and even some different religions—the Shermans and some of the others are Jewish. I want to know what they all think."

"What about Frank Mulhaney?" she asked. "Won't he be upset when he hears that you blabbed the whole thing to the world? Didn't he threaten you recently about that?"

"Sure, but how's he gonna hear about it?"

"When you publish the story, of course."

"Who says I'm going to publish it?" he replied. "I have no intention of publishing my confession."

"What if he hears about it via the grapevine?" she asked.

"You're confessing to an awful lot of people in that group. Can you trust every single one of them to keep your secret?"

"I don't know," he answered. "It's a chance I'll have to take."

"It's a chance I don't want you to take, honey, but I'll stand by you no matter what happens."

"Thank you, honeybunches. That means a lot to me."

# Chapter 21
## Surprise Shower
Sunday, May 10th, 2009

One would have to go back to sixteenth-century Holland and Victorian-era England to find the origins of the bridal shower. It started in Holland as a parade of small practical gifts for enabling the bride-to-be to begin a household, and served in lieu of a dowry either denied because of parental disapproval or simply not available due to the family's finances. The Victorian era added the party aspect and, possibly, the "shower" name, as the many gifts of family and friends were often laid out on paper parasols, symbolic of the rain shower. In planning a bridal shower, it isn't quite clear when or where secrecy from the bride, the surprise, became a part.

Rivka had gone well out of her way to keep Ivy from learning about her upcoming bridal shower. The diligent planner addressed and signed all the invitations after Ivy had gone home from work and made all her follow-up phone calls after Ivy's working hours as well. The guests included the females from two generations of the Reubens and Schwartz families and those from the critique group, plus a few friends the couple had cultivated during their dating. The guests were instructed to be at the bookstore no later than 1:30 p.m. Sunday, May 10th. The purchased decorations were stored in the apartment upstairs, so nothing could prematurely reveal the surprise event to Ivy.

Sunday was usually Ivy's day off. Rivka needed a ruse to get her to the Sunday 2:00 p.m. shower venue without spoiling the surprise. She asked Ivy to fill in at the store between 2:00 and 5:00 p.m.

on Sunday, while the Shermans attended a special film showing at the Orthodox synagogue in town. Ivy accepted the extra assignment in stride without a hint of suspicion.

Dan, Rivka, and Frieda spent all Sunday morning putting up the decorations in the main floor reading room. The upstairs refrigerator held mini sandwiches, pastries, and other treats Frieda had brought from the Double T Diner. An empty folding table along one wall was reserved for the food.

Rivka set her wrapped gift next to Frieda's on the long reading table. Two rows of folding chairs surrounded the table. Peanuts, chips, fruit, and candy were on folding trays placed among the chairs.

At 12:55 the first guests, Esther and Julie Reubens, arrived. Then Katie Silver, Mark's stepmom, came with Mark's half-sisters, Brenda and Barri Schwartz. Cora Bacon and Helen Margoles walked in together about ten minutes later. Others trickled in. With only five minutes to spare, Alice Zimmer, Leo Schwartz's live-in girlfriend, arrived. By then, the gifts were piled high on the table.

Over the past few weeks Rivka and Dan had mulled over the choice of gifts for both the shower and the wedding. Ivy deserved a well-thought-out gift. The wedding registry at Macy's gave some hints for a wedding present. Of course, every other guest faced a similar quandary.

The deeper problem with shower gift selection was that Ivy had been fortunate enough to be living alone in an established, well-equipped, fully furnished household—a four-story house that she inherited from Irma Riley, her former landlady. It had been a token of Irma's gratitude for Ivy's loving kindness and care-giving when the poor old lady had no one else to turn to. Ivy and Mark looked forward to making that same house their permanent family home.

At 1:55 Ivy came through the storefront door and immediately heard a dozen ladies shrilly screaming "Surprise! Surprise!" It took a minute or so for her to realize what was happening. The party kicked off with clapping and hugs as each of them came forward to embrace Ivy. Esther affixed a paper bridal crown and veil atop her head with a hairpin. After a half-hour of general chatting, the group settled down to listen to Julie read a welcoming poem she had written for the occasion. Then Rivka suggested that one by one, everyone take a turn with something funny, clever, or flattering to say about Ivy.

"I'll start," said Rivka. "I first met Ivy Cohen when she answered our newspaper ad for a retail clerk. She was a young and inexperienced British transplant, fresh out of King's College. Right from the start, I saw something in Ivy. I knew she would become more than just an employee. Dan and I soon learned that she had a story to tell and a mission to fulfill. She had emigrated to the U.S. to find her father and the murderer of her mother. Somehow, we became willingly involved in this difficult search and wound up accepting her as a member of our family. She eventually found what she was looking for and so much more, her very own loving family."

"Oh, Rivka, I love you and Dan so much," said Ivy.

"That loving part didn't happen right away," said Esther. "The entire Reubens family had become suspicious of Ivy, when she claimed to be the illegitimate offspring of one of our wandering husbands. My brother-in-law Herschel admitted on his deathbed that he fathered Ivy, and that his wife, Anna, had murdered Ivy's mother, Lainee Cohen. After that, we accepted Ivy as the real victim, one of us, and not a fortune-hunting intruder. We love her dearly now."

"Love you too," said Ivy.

"It wasn't always easy for Ivy," said Julie. "Stewart and Josh both showed an interest in her, but at first she had no idea which one was her half-brother, so she had the problem of keeping her distance from both. It's a good thing Mark entered the picture and saved the day. As it turned out, Stewart is Ivy's half-brother, and she is my half-sister and, going forward, I intend to improve on that relationship."

"Me too," said Ivy.

"Stepmother-in-law?" offered Alice Zimmer. "It's sure not an official title, and I suppose it never will be as long as Mark's father, Leo, remains gun-shy of a third marriage. We certainly love each other, and I'd be happy to have you, Ivy, as a daughter any day."

"Thank you, Alice," said Ivy.

"I think I don't have to share any mother-in-law titles with you, Alice," said Katie. "After all, I'm actually Mark's mother. I raised him and nurtured him after Leo's first wife, Heddy, passed. Just because I divorced Leo and married Mel Silver doesn't mean I gave up any of my grown children. I know you mean well and, surely you love him, too, but I'm Mark's mother and I look forward to being your mother and not just a mother-in-law."

"I look forward to calling you Mom," said Ivy.

"Mark has always been our big brother," said Brenda Schwartz, and I've always been the big sister to Barri. Now Ivy's going to be *our* big sister. I think that's going to be a lot of fun. I look forward to it."

"Me too," said Barri Schwartz. "I've been demoted again. I guess there's no hope for me, the sister at the bottom of the totem pole. Welcome to the family, Ivy."

"Thank you, girls," said Ivy. "You're both at the top of my totem pole."

"I know Ivy through the Mystery Writer's Critique Group," said Frieda. I've listened to her reading her mother's diary at the meetings, and through her mother's words, I learned a lot about who Ivy is and where she came from. I love everything about you, kid, and I wish you all the best things in life. Mark too."

"Thanks, Frieda, you've been a real friend," said Ivy.

"I also know Ivy through the critique group," said Cora Bacon, "but I must confess, I'm a newcomer to the group. So all I can say is: May your marriage to Mark be all that you want it to be and so much more."

*Her words convey all the right sentiments, but somehow they lack sincerity*, thought Ivy. *I wonder why.* "That's so nice of you, Cora," she said.

"I'm afraid I fall into the same newcomer category," said Helen Margoles, "so I hope your marriage is blessed with all kinds of love and happiness."

"All I can say is thank you," said Ivy.

"Anyone else want to have their say?" asked Rivka.

Combinations of love, happiness, and best wishes were the

responses from the three remaining ladies.

"Love and kisses to all of you. You've all been so kind," said Ivy.

"Let's open some presents," said Rivka. "Ivy, don't be bashful now."

Ivy reached for the box closest to her. She picked it up and shook it, but nothing in the sound of it revealed anything. She started to meticulously un-tape the white wrapping when Frieda chided her about being so careful.

"Rip it open or you'll be all day about it," suggested Frieda.

"I really don't care how long it takes," said Ivy as she grabbed one edge of the wrapping and boldly tore across anyway. "I'm going to enjoy every bit of this shower. Ooh! It's an eight-place setting of Corelle dinnerware. Ooh! And the bright, blue-on-white floral pattern is so pretty." She slid the card from the envelope. "It's from Rivka. She wrote, 'Now you can get rid of that awful collection of mismatched dishes that Irma, of blessed memory, left you.'" Ivy chuckled. "Perfect, Rivka, Thank you so much."

Ivy gave her a big hug and reached for the next closest gift on the table. This time she was so excited, she needed no encouragement to rip away the wrapping, which revealed a plain-white, department-store gift box. Removing the cover, she found a dual set of terry towels and washcloths. The hand towels were embroidered with His and Hers. The card said it was from Esther, and that gift rated another hug.

The next gift was a pair of super-sized, monogrammed coffee mugs from Frieda. Her card read, "Think of me whenever you relax with a cuppa."

When the outer wrapping came off the next box, there were oohs and ahs from nearly everyone. The white gift box was labeled Victoria's Secret. Opened, it contained a pale, pink, filmy negligee, a gift from Katie. Ivy held it up against the front of her. A similar Victoria's Secret box yielded two very short, sheer, and revealing nighties. These violet and blue teddies were from Mark's half-sisters, Brenda and Barri.

"Oh, I just adore the purple one," said Helen. "It's my favorite color."

"Ivy, aren't you going to model those gorgeous teddies for us?" asked a teasing Frieda.

Ivy held up one of the teddies close to her shoulders and demonstrated that it would not cover all that much and, what it did cover, still revealed all. "Is that better?" she replied with a pronounced hip wiggle. Smiles, titters, snickers, and laughs emanated from the ladies. The pile of paper wrappings on the floor next to Ivy grew as more and more gifts were unveiled. The pile began to spread under the recliner where Ivy had been sitting. Brenda, sitting next to the recliner, leaned over to gather in the spreading trash and noticed a neat stack of papers secreted beneath the recliner. She slid the stack into view and saw the title: *The Atkins Family History, 1768 to 1934.*

"The Atkins family...Hey, this looks like some sort of historical manuscript," said Brenda, picking the stack up off the floor and holding it in her lap.

"The recliner is Dan's favorite relaxation spot," said Rivka. "Oh, that's something he's been reading. He often stores his current reading under the chair."

"So, Rivka," said Cora. "Your husband really did make a copy of my father's manuscript. You do know that's illegal. The manuscript is copyrighted, protected material."

"What can I say?" admitted Rivka. "Guilty as charged."

"I'm not sure how Rae will react when she hears there's a copy," said Cora.

"Does she really need to know about it?" asked Rivka. "Anyway, I'm sure Dan will either destroy the copy or give it to Rae when he's finished with it."

"We'll see," answered Cora. "You know why he's so interested in it."

"Really," replied Rivka. "When Dan finds a mystery, he obsesses over it."

"Sorry about the distraction," said Brenda. "Shall I put it back?"

"Yes, please," replied Rivka. "Dan will be looking for it there."

"I've got a few more presents to open," said Ivy as she reached for the next gift-wrapped package. It stood taller than the rest and with the wrapping removed, the color picture and writing on the box previewed the two-cup, espresso coffeemaker. The gift card revealed that it came from Helen and Cora jointly.

The remaining gifts included a paisley silk scarf, a six-pack of twelve-ounce iced-tea tumblers with pitcher, a blanket in a Southwest pattern, and a small tool box with a few essential household tools. These were gifted by aunts, cousins, and two of Ivy and Mark's friends. Frieda and Rivka slipped out of the room and upstairs to the apartment to remove the food from the refrigerator and carry everything down to the reading room—mini sandwiches, petit fours, cookies, and Neapolitan ice cream. Ivy couldn't eat but a bite here and a sip there as she wandered among the guests thanking them and chatting with everyone. Soon the party shrank in size until just Rivka, Ivy, and Frieda were left behind.

Dan joined the ladies in cleanup and they had the reading room restored to normal in about fifty minutes. Ivy's gifts were conveyed to the Toyota. Dan drove her home and helped carry them inside. When he returned, Rivka had a question for him.

"Why did you leave the manuscript copy under the recliner where just anyone could find it? Brenda accidentally dragged it out when she was gathering up the gift wrappings. Now Cora knows you scanned a copy. She cited the copyright laws to me, but she wasn't sure whether she would tell Rae or not."

"Oh shit!" said Dan. "My bad. I'll destroy it now that I'm done."

# Chapter 22
## Revelation
### Tuesday, May 12th

Two days after the shower Cora walked into the bookstore and stopped at the counter. "Hi, Rivka. How are you?"

"I'm fine. What brings you in so bright and early this morning—a new book, perhaps?"

"Great party you threw for Ivy on Sunday," said Cora, intentionally changing the subject.

"Thank you. Everyone seemed to have enjoyed themselves."

"I know I did," said Cora.

Rivka thought she detected something insincere in Cora's response and manner. "Can I help you with anything?"

"No, Rivka. Actually, I have some information to pass on to Ivy, something she really needs to know."

"Ivy is busy with a customer upstairs right now. I can pass on whatever you have to say or you can wait for her in the reading room over there."

"Thank you, Rivka, I'll wait." Cora raised her right arm in a half-wave as she strolled into the next room and took a seat. She picked up a magazine someone had left behind on the table and began to read.

Dan, working on a book display at the end of a nearby aisle, overheard Cora's conversation, turned to Rivka and whispered, "Sounds pretty ominous to me."

Ten minutes later Ivy and a customer came down the stairs from the travel section. Ivy brought the customer to the counter to ring up a book, *Fourteen Months in Japan*. Rivka took the book from Ivy and pointed to Cora in the next room.

"Cora says she has some important information for you."

Ivy stepped into the reading room and took a chair next to Cora. "Hi. I understand that you have some gems of wisdom that you want to pass on to me."

"I do, my dear," said Cora. "I do." Cora cleared her throat. "Well, not exactly gems, Ivy. I hope you'll understand why I'm telling you this in the first place. It's not at all my intention to rain on your parade. I just thought you ought to know the kind of man you're marrying."

"You mean Mark?"

"Yes, Mark Schwartz," said Cora. "He's not the Mr. Innocence you think he is."

"I don't understand," said Ivy. "Why would you be telling me disparaging information about Mark? I can't conceive that he's done anything that bad. In fact, I refuse to hear of it."

"What would you say if I told you your young man has already fathered a child?"

"That's not true," said Ivy. "I don't believe it. He would have told me. We don't have any secrets."

"It is true. He's the father of my grandchild, Samuel Atkins Bacon. The boy is four years old now and my pride and joy."

"How do you know Mark is the father of this child?" asked Ivy.

"My daughter, Daisy, is the mother and she recently told me that Mark is the father."

"So it's just her word?" Ivy retorted.

"No, he's already admitted his complicity in the matter. In fact, he offered to pay for an abortion. But as a Catholic in good conscience, Daisy couldn't have any part of that."

"Were they married?" asked Ivy.

"No, the cad outright refused to marry her and has no interest in being a part of the boy's life."

"Does your daughter know you're here talking to me about

this?"

"No. The poor girl wants to forgive and forget him now. She's determined to raise the boy on her own. I will be there to help her, of course."

"This is not at all like Mark. I think you're making all of this up," said Ivy with tears running down her face.

"You think?" replied Cora. "Maybe you'd better have a nice long talk with that young man of yours."

Cora stood and walked toward the front of the bookstore. Ivy's eyes followed her through the front door to the street. Then Ivy pulled her feet up into the chair and began to sob like a baby—aloud, shaking, and uncontrolled.

Rivka heard the sobbing and came running into the reading room. "What's wrong, dear? What did Cora tell you?"

"I don't know what to believe. Cora told me that Mark has a child by her daughter and refused to marry her. He has never said a word about this to me. It can't be true, can it?"

"Until you talk to Mark you can't be sure of anything. I do know that Cora is a grandmother. I've seen her pushing a stroller at the supermarket. So a three- or four-year-old toddler does exist."

"But is it his?" sobbed Ivy.

"Only Mark can clear that part up."

"Why would she tell me something like that?" asked Ivy. "It's pure meanness."

"I agree, but if it's true, I suppose she's striking out more at Mark than at you. I think she's trying to spoil his marriage."

"But Rivka, it's my marriage, too. What do I do now?"

"Before Cora shot off her big mouth, you loved Mark unconditionally. Be honest now: would you still love him if you absolutely knew he had this child by another woman?"

Rivka's question hit Ivy by surprise and her "Y--yes" response was slow in coming. "But he sure would have a lot of explaining to do. I don't know why Mark hasn't said anything to me."

"No matter how heroic we make our men out to be, there's a tiny bit of cowardliness that stands between the truth and their past sexual transgressions. It's all about how they perceive our judgment of them. The sooner you confront Mark and get all this out in the open, the sooner you'll get your marriage back on track."

"Do I simply forgive him for having sex with another woman?"

"Why not?" said Rivka. "It all happened long before he met you. Besides, he chose you to marry, not her. Your only fault with him, really, is about why he didn't inform you about his past baggage. And you can lay into him all you want on that front."

"What about the child?"

"Ivy, you yourself are the product of an illicit affair. Should Lainee and Herschel's guilt been passed on to you, their daughter? Of course not. The child is innocent."

"That's not what I meant—of course the child is innocent. What I'm curious about is what part, if any, will Mark and I play in the child's life?"

"There's no way of telling that until, if, and when the two families begin to communicate," offered Rivka. "Now I think you had better dry your tears, and we both should get back to selling books. You'll get to confront Mark tonight. Tread carefully. You are both extremely sensitive people and your whole future is on the line. I'm sure you'll work everything out."

* * * *

**I**vy hadn't quite made up her mind how or even when she should bring up the subject of fatherhood with Mark, when she heard his key in the front door of her home. *I don't want to pounce on him as he comes through the door. Maybe we'll talk while he sits at the kitchen table as I make dinner, or perhaps it'll be best waiting until after we've both been fed.* Ivy remained cool, offered a quick smooch on the cheek at the door, and waited, but when the last dish had been dried and put in the cabinet, the two of them settled on one end of the living room couch. Ivy then slid over one cushion apart and shifted her hips to face him.

"Is there something wrong, sweetheart?" asked Mark.

"Let's just say I learned a little about your sordid past this morning," Ivy began with an emotionless expression.

Mark smiled. "Sordid past? My father telling nasty tales about me again?"

"No, sir, it was a grandmother in her mid-fifties."

"Whose grandmother? What's this all about, honey?"

"Your son's grandmother, Sam's, of course."

"Oh-oh! How much do you know? Sweetheart, I can explain everything."

"Don't you sweetheart me! You had better start explaining. Didn't you think it was important for me to know you have a child?"

"But all that happened before I even met you. A lot more than that happened before I met you. I just thought you didn't need to know all the details. I dated quite a number of girls in high school and during my undergrad college days and went to bed with a few of them. You knew I wasn't a virgin."

"So now you're telling me you've fathered a whole kindergarten full of kids running around out there?"

"No, no, nothing like that. Sam is the only child, and I have had absolutely no contact with him. I feel a little guilty about that, but *we* both thought that total separation was for the best. It's only her old lady who keeps meddling in our affairs."

"*We?*"

"Yeah, Daisy and I," said Mark.

"Ah, Daisy. How did you meet? Was she a barroom pickup?"

"Not quite. We first met when I was hospitalized with pneumonia. She was my nurse for a time. However, she did run into me at a bar one night a few months later and came to my table."

"Is she pretty?"

"She's not hard to look at, if that's what you mean. But she's really not my type."

"Your type?" repeated Ivy. "She must have had some attraction for you to hop into bed with her."

"I didn't. Daisy climbed into bed with me, not the other way around."

"That's a pretty fine distinction, if I ever heard one. I should think who got in first wouldn't have mattered."

"No, no, you've got it all wrong, Ivy. Daisy had a little too much to drink that night and fell asleep on my couch in the front room while I was making coffee. I actually went to sleep in my own bed all alone that night. Hours later, she woke me and hopped into bed with me. I wasn't about to refuse what she had to offer. My big mistake was that I didn't challenge her on protection. How could I have known that she was Catholic and couldn't use The Pill or any other intervening device?"

"Did you ever go back for more?"

"No. Even if I had wanted to, I didn't know how to get in touch with her, but she sure knew how to reach me. The next time I heard from her was a phone call four months later, saying she was pregnant and wanted me to marry her."

"Did you ever consider marrying Daisy?"

"Of course not. We had absolutely nothing in common but the child."

"Speaking of the child, you said you regretted not having a role in the boy's life. Would you like that to change?"

"I wouldn't mind teaching him to throw a football with a spiral sometime or taking him to an Orioles game. Of course, you would have to agree to let him into our lives and just how much."

"Me?" asked Ivy. "Why me—he's your son. You would have to accept him first and so far you haven't. If the magic is there, I would accept him, too."

"Jeez," said Mark. "Are we through with the cross-examination yet?"

"I suppose so," replied Ivy, "but don't think you are off the hook yet. I'm still pissed at you for not telling me about this. I'm so upset that I think it would be best for you not to stay over tonight."

"You're punishing me?"

"Yeah."

"You mean this is goodnight?"

"Yup."

Mark leaned in to give her a goodnight kiss, but she leaned

away from him with a determined expression on her face. He got up from the couch slowly, hoping Ivy would change her mind, but she remained silent. He headed for the front door, put on his baseball cap, and left the house, dejected and confused. *Is the marriage off?* he wondered.

**\* \* \* \***

On the following Friday, Dan and Rivka drove Ivy to BWI Thurgood Marshall Airport to meet Janice and Wayne Sachs, who were scheduled at 10:10 p.m. via the airport shuttle service from D.C.'s Ronald Reagan Airport. The shuttle pulled into the terminal at exactly 10:13 p.m.

Janice spotted Ivy immediately and began to screech with joy. She couldn't wait for the vehicle to stop. Her door wouldn't open until the driver parked and released the locks. Once it was open, she flew the fifteen feet to Ivy, and the two embraced for several minutes with Janice's high-pitched voice still screeching.

"I've missed you so much," she said, "and I've loved all your monthly letters. Thank you for staying in touch."

"I feel the same way about you two and Ollie, too, of course," said Ivy.

As mother and her foster daughter talked nonstop trying to shrink three-and-a-half years of separation into mere minutes, Rivka and Dan stood by waiting to be introduced. Looking over Ivy's shoulder, Janice suddenly broke away and turned to hug Rivka.

"I would have known you anywhere, Rivka," said Janice. "I want to thank you for being so good to Ivy, for taking her in, and treating her like family. The hard part is I don't think she'll ever return to London."

"I agree," said Rivka. "Ivy will follow Mark to wherever his career and their marriage take them."

As the shuttle driver emptied the trunk full of baggage onto the sidewalk, Wayne approached Dan and held out a hand to be shaken.

"I'm Wayne Sachs, Ivy's foster father and I'm quite sure you are Daniel Sherman."

"It's Dan, and you're absolutely correct. I'm pleased to finally meet you in person. Ivy has done a marvelous job of describing you both. I feel like I've known you for years. Shall we gather up your baggage?"

"I believe I will let the other passengers pick through the luggage first," said Wayne. "What's left should belong to us."

"Sounds about right," cautioned Dan. "But a bit risky if you ask me. Accidentally, or on purpose, someone else could run off with your baggage."

"Maybe you're right, Dan." Wayne walked to the cluster of luggage on the sidewalk and picked out two large suitcases, a garment bag, and one overnight case. A small carry-on stood at Janice's feet where Wayne had left it.

"Everyone, wait here while I bring the car around."

Ten minutes later, Dan drove up to the spot where he left them and popped the trunk lid on the Toyota. Wayne took one look at the space and shook his head.

"I don't think we'll be able to get all our luggage in that size boot, Dan."

"Let's see what we can do anyway," said Dan. He managed to put the two large suitcases side-by-side with the clothes bag lying on top. The trunk lid had to be squashed down to hear the closed click. "The rest can be lap luggage. Why don't we pile in and get going—you guys must be tuckered out by now."

"You know you don't have to stay at a hotel," offered Ivy. "I've got plenty of room at the house—three extra bedrooms and your own bath."

"No thank you. That Annapolis Waterfront Hotel is fine with us," said Wayne. "We're privacy freaks. We like living by ourselves."

"Besides," said Janice, "you two have a lot going on, so you don't want us underfoot the whole time. Oh, and we plan to rent a car and do some sightseeing over in Washington."

"Okay, then, the hotel it is," announced Dan, as he turned the engine over and pulled out into a stream of traffic. Forty minutes later he drove up the ramp to the Annapolis Waterfront Hotel. The bell captain took over the luggage while the Sachses registered at the desk.

Dan, Rivka, and Ivy said their goodnights and left for home.

## Chapter 23
## A Questionable Bachelor Party
### Saturday, May 16th

One would have to venture way back in history—1,200 years before bridal showers began—to capture the origins of the bachelor or stag or buck's party. Fifth-century Spartan soldiers celebrated the groom's last night as a single man with a formal meal and toasts to honor him. As the tradition evolved, it centered on the unmarried male, and instead of merely honoring him, the custom grew to include roasting, humiliation, and, in some cases, temptation and wickedness. The modern version includes alcohol and sometimes even strippers.

Mark's status as a groom was still in question as Ivy had not yet informed him of a reprieve. He was also banned from her bedroom for the time being. It wasn't so much that he had had a child out of wedlock, rather that he hadn't told her about it—a serious lie of omission in her mind. But she hadn't called off the wedding either, and those in charge of revelry were totally unaware of any change of intent, so they brought the bachelor party to fruition. This was the night.

\* \* \* \*

Dan was not looking forward to the bachelor event. First, he didn't know what to expect; he had never attended a stag party before. Also, he was nervous, believing he would feel awkward, the obvious senior among the group of twenty-somethings. Dan even wondered why he'd been included. Rivka had reassured him that he would get along just fine with the group and mentioned that his contemporaries, Meyer Reubens and Leo Schwartz, would be there. Josh Reubens' invitation included the instructions to the home of Esther and Meyer Reubens. Josh was the older of their two sons, a first cousin to Ivy, and a close contemporary of Mark Schwartz.

The warm breeze rustling the blossoms in the dogwood trees soothed Dan as he strolled from his car to the Schwartzes' house. He heard recorded music as he approached the front door. Just as he reached out to press the bell, the door swung open, and Julie Reubens, Ivy's half-sister (Herschel and Anna's daughter), rushed through it onto the porch, almost bowling Dan over.

"Oh, I'm so sorry, Mr. Sherman. In my carelessness I could have hurt you all over again."

"No harm done, dear Julie. Please call me Dan. And three years ago you were a bit out of sorts when you shot me in the arm for siding with Ivy. That was a long time ago and everyone, including me, has completely forgiven you."

"Oh, I know that, Dan, and I've gotten over those awful guilt feelings. My therapist has helped me to understand the sins of my parents. Actually, I've tried to forgive their terrible actions in London, but some deeds are just not forgivable. Anyway, Stewart and I have grown to love Ivy as our newfound sister."

"That's wonderful," said Dan. "I saw in the newspaper where you sold the house you grew up in."

"Yes, after my parents were gone, Auntie Esther thought it was best that I move in here with them. I agreed, and with Stewart practicing law in a Baltimore firm, we had no need for such a big house."

"Where are you off to now in such a hurry?"

"I'm headed for the movies with a friend. There's no room for the female of the species at one of these parties, so I prepared the snacks and cleared out of Dodge. Whoops, I've got someone waiting for me. So long, Dan. Enjoy the bachelor party."

"Enjoy your movie," said Dan as he stepped over the threshold into the living room.

"Welcome, Dan," said the host, Josh Reubens. "You know my

brother, Abel."

"Yes, of course. How are you both?"

"We're fine," replied Abel. "Why don't you join my father? He's in the parlor on the sofa."

"That's an excellent idea," said Dan. "I think I'll do that." He strolled past a handsome group of four young men he didn't know and presumed they were Mark's friends from school. Arriving in the parlor, he spotted Meyer Reubens seated on the couch in a heated discussion with his business partner, Leo Schwartz. Meyer's hand gripped a swaying, half-full beer mug as he gestured throughout his speaking. Dan hesitated to butt in on their discussion, so he looked around for someone else to schmooze with and found Stewart Reubens.

"Hi, Stew, just met your sister on her way out the door."

"Oh, hi, Dan. "Yeah, Julie's has her usual movie date with that *sheygats* [Yiddish for a male non-Jew], Charlie Frye."

"They've been seeing each other for some time now, haven't they?" asked Dan.

"Yeah," said Stewart. "I'm afraid I'm going to have to get used to him. They've become an item now, and I even like the guy, but none of us want her to marry out of the faith."

*There are worse things*, Dan thought, but didn't say. "Maybe he'll convert," he offered as he scooped up a handful of cashews and popped a few in his mouth.

"I suppose one of them will have to," said Stewart. "But it better not be Julie."

The tone of the conversation was making Dan a little uncomfortable, so he switched gears. "I don't see Mark here yet. Say, Stew, isn't the guest of honor supposed to be at his own bachelor party?"

"Mark's expected any minute now. It's supposed to be a complete surprise for him, so he was given a later start time. Well, my beer cup has gone dry, and I see where you haven't had anything at all to drink yet. Come on out to the kitchen with me and we'll fix that. There's a couple of half-kegs of Michelob Ultra out there just waiting for us."

Stewart held a tall plastic cup under the tap, filled it until the foam billowed, and handed it to Dan. While Dan sipped the foam off the top, Stewart filled a second cup for himself. Just as he let go of the tap lever, they heard, "SURPRISE!" coming from the living room. Mark had arrived. Dan and Stewart drifted through the multitude of guests toward the guest of honor. As Mark made his way inside, he shook hands, hugged some friends, and received pats on the back from others. When he got close enough, Dan congratulated Mark with a firm handshake.

"Ah, Dr. Mark Schwartz. Doesn't that have a nice ring to it?" asked Dan.

"It sure does," he answered.

"Leo must be real proud of you."

"Yeah, my dad keeps saying, 'My son the doctor.' I keep telling him it's a Ph.D. in physics."

"Any career plans lined up for after the honeymoon?" asked Dan.

"I've got a number of irons in the fire—from teaching to industry to research. With all the preparations for the oral defense of my thesis, I haven't had time to pursue my career options. By the way, some of those options have geographic considerations, so I want Ivy to be a part of those decisions."

"We're going to miss her if you take her away from us, but we certainly do want what's best for the two of you."

"Thank you, but I won't know anything for at least a month or so. We'll let you know as soon as we make any decision."

One of his school chums tapped Mark on the shoulder and he turned away, so Dan looked around for a chair and found a straight-back one in the dining room next to Mel Silver, Katie's second husband.

"I've enjoyed Katie's *Boxcar Bertie* story," said Dan. "She's quite clever."

"You know it," said Mel. "She's always amazing me. Say, what's going on here?"

When Abel and a friend started to clear the dining room table of its deli sandwiches and snack spreads, Mel piped up and asked, "Hey, where are you going with all the food?"

"We're commandeering the dining room table for another purpose. Here, would you like something?" asked Abel as he held a platter of corned beef and pastrami sandwiches in front of the two men.

They had each taken one of their choice when four young men carried in a huge white gift box tied smartly with a red ribbon and a big red bow. They set it down in the middle of the table and stood back. Abel opened a laptop computer on the edge of the table and inserted a disk in the player slot. He then went to the wall light switch and blinked the lights several times, to get everyone's attention, before returning to the laptop. Abel started the disk and the room filled with exotic Middle East music as everyone gathered around the table.

Mark, the groom, was given the honor of pulling the ribbon free, and soon the box began to rock and sway in time to the music. Then, accompanied by a high-pitched flute, the lid moved free of the box, rising and falling in stages, until two attractive bare feminine arms lifted the lid toward the ceiling. Then, with a clash of cymbals and the rattle of tambourines, the lid slipped to the floor, and a woman's head with long black hair, a crystal tiara, and sparkles appeared. The music returned to the flute and clarinet as a near-topless form emerged slowly, enticingly, and snakelike from the box. It was a shapely, amply endowed, thirty-something woman, wearing only a G-string and pasties, who stepped from her cardboard trappings onto the tabletop. The large oval rhinestone embedded in her navel undulated independently from her seductive hip motion. The box was quickly removed to give the stripper more room to dance.

Meanwhile, the onlookers jeered, whistled, laughed, and ogled while the belly dancer demonstrated her skills. Her exciting bumps and undulating grinds synced to accommodate the ever-advancing music of Maurice Ravel's *Bolero*. Several of the more inebriated guests tried to touch her, but the experienced teaser danced perilously near and then retreated just soon enough to frustrate them again and again. She danced for at least twenty minutes before stepping down to the carpeted floor via an empty chair.

The dancer hung onto the chair and beckoned Mark with the curl of her finger to sit in this chair. When the shirt-sleeved Mark complied, she ran her fingers through his longish brown hair and then all over his chest. She blew in his ear and stayed to nibble a bit. The woman dragged her long hair across his face and swung her pastied nipples an inch from his eyes. She sat in his lap and vigorously wriggled for several seconds.

Meanwhile, Mark's face grew redder by the minute, and he was hard-pressed to hide his embarrassment. The woman finished by actually dragging her pasties directly across his lips. She stood up, took a bow, and darted out of the room. Everyone applauded, and she returned to the doorway to extend a long bare leg into the dining room. The very last thing she did was to throw her G-string into the room as she disappeared into the bathroom across the hall to put on her street clothes.

Dan and Mel, having sat so close to the table, had ringside seats to all of the erotic entertainment. The deli foods and snacks were returned to the table, along with cookies, cakes, and pies. A number of the guests made token, practical, and suggestive gift presentations to Mark.

The party slowly grew more boisterous as the drinking continued. Dan decided that it was time for him to leave. He looked at his watch and was surprised to learn that it was 11:30 already. He made his way through the milling guests to Josh and thanked him for the invitation before heading out the door into the night.

Walking to the car, Dan thought he detected furtive movement across the semi-dark street. Unsure, he wanted to stop, turn, and look more closely, except something inside him said, *No—keep going, it's only your imagination working overtime.* But imagination is a powerful influence when you're out walking at night. Fortunately, a few steps later, he did stop, turn, and see a young couple embracing—saying goodnight on what he presumed was her doorstep. Dan swallowed hard, and resumed the path to the Toyota.

*That damned Muddy Atkins is making me paranoid. Next thing you know I'll be needing a shrink.* He slipped into the front seat and looked up in the rearview mirror. A bag of nerves looked back at him. He started the engine and drove home.

As Dan pulled into a space in front of the bookstore, a strange man stood under a nearby lamppost lighting a cigarette. Dan gave him the once-over before getting out of the car. The man was about Muddy's size and build, but unfortunately, he faced the other way. Dan opened the driver's-side door and stepped out onto the sidewalk, slamming the car door behind him.

The other man reacted to hearing the door squeak open and then its slamming shut. He turned around full face, and Dan saw him clearly. It was the dreaded Muddy Atkins. Although Dan rushed toward him in hopes of forcing a confrontation, Muddy quickly disappeared into the night as he had done so many times before. *So close, yet just out of reach—teasing me like the skilled dancer had teased the young guys at the party with her sexy wares. But what is he trying to accomplish with all this stalking—teasing me and running off afterward? What's his connection to the manuscript? What's he trying to hide?*

Dan's hand shook as he put his key in the front door of the closed bookstore. It was after midnight when he set the alarm and climbed the stairs to the Sherman apartment. He found Rivka awake and reading a book when he reached their bedroom.

"What's wrong, Dan? You look like you've seen a ghost."

"A ghost would've been better."

"What on earth do you mean?"

"I just saw that scumbag Muddy Atkins."

## Chapter 24
## Feelings
### Monday, May 18th, 2009

Ivy opened her eyes and took her first peek at the new day—a day of promise announced by a bright, almost white, sunbeam parting the master bedroom drapes, stretching across the bedroom, and gracing her immediate world with light. She rolled over onto her left side and acknowledged the sleeping form of a finally reprieved Mark Schwartz, lying in bed beside her. She released a major sigh at the thought *he's my husband-to-be.* Though still facing away from her, his manly physique pleased her.

*Perhaps I was a little tough on the poor dear—slow to forgive him, banning him from my bed for five nights, but he needed to learn that lesson—be honest with me. I shouldn't fault him from sowing his oats. Most virile young men do. But I did miss him so. Any longer than five days and I would have been punishing myself as well.*

Ivy rolled onto her back once more and stared at the ceiling. *Less than a week to go before the wedding,* she thought. *I'm so happy I'm going to burst. I'm in love. It's so wonderful to be alive. Absolutely nothing can spoil the way I feel. Rivka would say I'm tempting the spirits if I say things like this loud enough for them to hear. She called it a 'kine-ahora.' I don't care. Even the evil spirits wouldn't dare defy me today.*

Feeling like an unleashed sprite, Ivy rose to her knees and leaned over Mark to plant a kiss on his cheek. She kissed him again.

He stirred. She nuzzled. He mumbled something and returned to dreamland. Deciding not to disturb him any further, she collapsed onto her back again, this time continuing to roll around until her bare feet touched the hardwood floor. Sitting there on the edge of the bed, she stretched her arms and legs into mobility and padded her way to the master bathroom. Minutes later, ready to brush her teeth, she stood before the medicine cabinet mirror.

She stared agape at the mirror in disbelief for over a minute and then released an ugly scream before she slumped back onto the toilet seat cover—a scream that brought Mark rushing into the bathroom, barreling headlong through the door to be with her.

"What's wrong, sweetheart?"

Ivy's eyes seemed frozen in space. She tried to speak, but couldn't. Then, in an almost involuntary reaction, her right arm lifted up with a shaking finger pointing toward the cabinet mirror.

Mark shifted his attention from the trembling Ivy to the mirror—and its message written in soap: *Tell him to quit reading and forget everything OR ELSE!* Mark didn't know what to make of the message's meaning, but he knew, for sure, it wasn't there the night before when he shaved.

He immediately sized up the importance of the situation. Someone had broken into the house and violated their privacy. He focused his attention back to Ivy, where he was most needed. He lifted her to a standing position and embraced her, alternately stroking and patting her back, attempting to comfort her. A kiss on the neck and then on the cheek seemed to help.

"There, there, sweetheart. I'm here. It's all right now. There's no one here now but us."

Ivy slowly stopped shivering and pulled her head back far enough to look him straight in the face. "How can you be so sure?"

"Trust me, dearest, anyone who'd leave a message like that doesn't stick around afterward to be caught. No, the message writer is long gone by now. You'd better believe it. But what does this message mean? And who is the 'him' in the message?"

"I believe the 'him' in the message is Dan Sherman," she replied. "Dan's been reading a biographical manuscript that's supposed to reveal a bloody family secret that someone in the Atkins family wants suppressed."

"That sounds pretty complicated," said Mark. "Does Dan know who this Atkins family member is?"

"He thinks it's the brother of the four surviving family siblings, a Muddy Atkins."

"Muddy?" repeated Mark. "That's a rather unusual name, and not very flattering."

"I agree, but that's what the Shermans call him."

"What's he been doing to Dan, anyway?" asked Mark. "And why has this Muddy character suddenly directed his displeasure toward you?"

"He's been stalking Dan for almost two weeks now," Ivy said. "Dan believes it's all about intimidation. Muddy wants to expand the threat to someone the Shermans care about. I suppose, in this case, that's me. Oh, by the way, this Muddy character also broke into the store one night looking for the same manuscript. He actually disabled the bookstore alarm system."

"I see," Mark said. "Why don't we both get dressed and go down and have some breakfast. Afterward, I'll go around the house and see if I can determine how the sonofabitch managed to get in."

Ivy nodded her agreement and gently shoved him from the bathroom while she finished putting on her makeup and pulling herself together.

Mark finished dressing first and made his way to the kitchen where he put on a kettle of water for Ivy's tea and plugged in the preloaded coffee pot for himself. Then he loaded the four-slice toaster with whole wheat bread, but purposely didn't pull down the starting lever. Plates and silverware came next. Finally, he brought jam, cream cheese, cheese slices, and butter to the table.

Before retrieving the morning paper from the front porch, Mark checked both the front and rear doors and all the first-floor windows to convince himself that they all had been locked from the inside. He wondered how the intruder had gotten into the house.

What Mark missed was a broken basement half-window on the left side of the house. Muddy had simply reached through the broken pane and released the window latch. He had climbed through the half-window and come up the cellar stairs into the house. Another flight of stairs and he stood staring down at the couple sleeping peacefully in their bed. The opportunity to do more damage crossed his mind, but leaving them a message remained his primary mission.

Mark met Ivy coming down the stairs as he returned to the kitchen. While he watched her push down the toaster lever, he poured coffee and tea into two mugs and carried them to the table. As soon as they were both settled, Mark asked, "Did you remember to lock the front door when we came in last night?"

"I thought I did, I meant to, but I really can't be sure. I can't believe I'd be that careless." Tears were returning to her already reddened eyes. "You mean it was all my fault?"

"We don't know that," offered Mark. "But he could have freely entered that way and locked it on the way out. I did a quick survey this morning. All the doors and first-floor windows were securely locked. I can't imagine him or her getting in any other way."

"I'm so sorry. He could have murdered us in our bed." She sniffled.

"We'll have to be especially careful about locking up in the future," cautioned Mark. He took a swallow of coffee and a bite of toast covered with cream cheese and a slice of American cheese.

"I will," she mumbled, as she wiped her teary cheeks with a tissue.

"That message really made no sense to me," declared Mark. "What kind of secret is worth all this effort to suppress?"

"There isn't any message anymore—I washed the mirror clean. I had to use one of your razor blades to get the thickest soap off. That's why it took me so long to come downstairs."

"Well, that means we can't take this intruder's threat to the police."

"I'm sorry," Ivy said in a small voice. "I didn't think about the mirror being evidence." She smeared cream cheese and jam on her toast before taking her first nibble and sipped away at her tea with a long face.

"It's all right, honey," he reassured her. "I suppose I should have taken a picture of it with my new iPhone 3Gs. I'm just as much at fault, so let's not cry over spilt milk as the cliché goes."

"You're so forgiving—another reason why I love you."

Fifteen minutes passed while the conversation halted and they finished breakfast. Mark walked to the counter and poured a second mug of coffee. On the way back to the table, he was the first one to break the silence.

"Are you going to tell the Shermans about *our* intruder and *his* message?"

"You bet I am," replied Ivy. "I'm concerned about the 'OR ELSE!' part of that message. I don't know who it's really intended for—Dan or me. I'm so scared."

"I can stay with you all day if you want," offered Mark.

"That won't be necessary. I have to go to work anyway."

* * * *

As soon as Ivy entered the bookstore, Rivka knew something was troubling her. "What's wrong, dear?"

"Well, it seems you folks don't have an exclusive on break-ins," said Ivy. "While we slept last night someone got into the house and wrote a threatening message on the master bathroom mirror, the one on the front of the medicine cabinet."

"We?" asked a surprised Rivka and then she wanted to bite her tongue for asking. *This is another generation, a freer one,* she quickly reminded herself.

"Yes, Mark slept over last night." Her cheeks flushed a slight shade of red as she confessed.

"What actually did the message say?...No, wait...Let me call Dan." Rivka turned her head toward the staircase and shouted, "Daniel! Daniel!"

In less than two minutes, Dan appeared, out of breath. He'd sprinted up the stairs from the Dungeon. The two women were standing beside the register counter. "What on earth did I do wrong now?" Looking at Ivy, he said, "She only calls me Daniel when I'm in trouble."

"I wouldn't say you're completely innocent in this case," said Rivka, "but I do think you'll want to hear what Ivy has to tell us."

In a trembling voice, Ivy said, "Someone got into my house last night and wrote a threatening message on the master bathroom mirror."

"Well, that brings a whole bunch of questions to mind," said Dan.

"What was the message on the mirror?" asked Rivka for the second time.

"I will never forget it as long as I live. It was: 'Tell him to quit reading and forget everything OR ELSE!' What scares me the most is the 'OR ELSE' part in capital letters. Who is the threat intended for—you, Dan, or me?"

"Don't you worry about that, dear. I'm sure this particular threat is meant for me," lied Dan. *Damn that little shit. Muddy threatening someone I care about. He's not going to get away with this.*

"Dan!" scolded Rivka, "I told you this blasted manuscript business was going to end up being dangerous—trouble we could have avoided. And now look what you've done. It involves poor Ivy, who shouldn't have to worry about anything like this. After all, she's getting married next week."

"Hey, I know. There's no way I could have predicted the sneaky little bastard would take things this far. All I wanted was an explanation of why those books disappeared. I'm sorry."

"You should have stopped reading and returned the original manuscript when I told you to, Mr. Wise-guy."

"Well, that's spilt milk now. There's only one thing to do."

"And what's that?" asked Rivka.

"I'm going to take the battle to the enemy camp right now and confront the little sonofabitch where he can't run away from me."

"Oh, Dan, now you're being drastic. Besides, that could be very dangerous. We don't know what he's capable of. I worry about

198

you when you start talking like that."

"Don't worry, dear, I know how to take care of myself." Dan reached for his jacket on the hook behind the door and stepped outside before Rivka could stop him.

**** 

Dan was already sitting in the driver's seat of the Toyota when he realized he had no idea where he should drive—he had no address for Muddy Atkins. *I don't want to face Rivka again. I'm not sure I have the courage to listen to her trying to dissuade me. I know, I'll call Cora. I have the whole critique group on my speed-dial.* He pulled out his flip-top cell phone and called Cora Bacon. *She would know where to find her own brother.*

"Hello, Cora. Dan Sherman here....Fine, thank you....The reason I'm calling is to get your brother Muddy's address. I'm trying to locate him....Why? He's stepped up his stalking campaign. I believe it's high time I confront him man to man....No, no violence.... Ah, room 233, Annapolis Waterfront Hotel on Compromise Street near the yacht club. Thank you so much, Cora. I'll see you on Thursday."

Dan started the engine and drove to West Street, around Church Circle, down Duke of Gloucester Street, and then onto Green Street straight to Compromise Street. He pulled up to the hotel's front entrance and turned the car over to the valet parking attendant. Inside the main lobby he located the elevators and the stairs. Seeking only the second floor, he chose the stairs. On the second level he followed an arrow directing him to the 230s and 240s. He stopped at room 233 and hesitated before knocking on the door. *Am I doing the right thing? Will this accomplish anything worthwhile? What the hell, I'm here already.* He ignored all of his reservations and knocked sharply, placing his finger over the peephole in the door, so Muddy wouldn't recognize him right off.

"Who's there?" came the reply.

"It's Daniel," he answered.

"Daniel who?" asked the voice.

"Daniel Sherman from the bookstore."

"Suppose I don't want to talk to Daniel Sherman from the bookstore."

"I don't mean you any harm. I just want to get a few answers."

"I still don't want to speak with you," Muddy said.

"Please, tell me why you're stalking me."

"To get you to stop nosing around in my personal business. Stop meddling in my affairs. Now go away!"

"All I want is a few minutes of your time to clear up some misunderstandings," pleaded Dan. "Tell me what's in the book that you don't want me to see, and I promise I'll forget everything. I'll have achieved my goal."

"Get out of here before I call hotel security or maybe even the police."

"I highly doubt that you'll call the police, Muddy. Don't you think they'll be interested in all the stalking and the breaking-and-entering you've been doing?"

"Out! Out! Out! I won't talk to you. Now get your ass out of this hotel!"

Dan turned away and headed back to the stairs, feeling that he tried his best, even though he failed to accomplish what he set out to do. He had arrived in anger and departed in frustration.

# Chapter 25
# A Meeting Casts Its Spell
Thursday, May 21st, 2009

nce more Thursday evening rolled around, and the Mystery Writers' Critique Group assembled around the great table. Yes, there were more stories to be read. Sometimes those stories revealed more than the author intended, facts and meanings that exposed myths and promoted truths well beyond the narrative itself. When such a reading casts its spell, a routine meeting can turn fateful. No one can prepare for this sort of thing. It just happens when important myths and truths come together.

Rivka had just put out all the snacks and drinks. The group had been chatting noisily for at least ten minutes when she called the meeting to order. "Joel has asked to read first, so go for it, Joel."

The consummate lawyer picked up his Mickey Mann brief and began to read aloud.

———

### Chapter 10. The Barmaid

"The prosecution rests, Your Honor," declared ADA Dulaney as he returned to the State's table opposite the defense table.

"The defense may call its first witness," offered Judge Hershfeld.

"The defense calls Ms. Effie Miller to the stand." Mickey stood and faced the rear of the courtroom.

The door to the hall opened. A gaunt, thirtyish woman with black ringlets framing hard facial features meandered to the front of the courtroom and hesitated slightly before taking the stand. In her silky red dress and gold necklace, she seemed more poised for a party than a courtroom. The woman was in no hurry to get anywhere. She was on display, with no way of telling whether the court would admonish, endure, or simply enjoy her tactic.

Mickey slowly followed the witness to the stand. "Ms. Miller, would you state your full name and occupation?"

"Lillian Euphemia Miller, but everyone calls me Effie, which is short for my middle name. There are too many Lils in my line of work, so I chose Effie. My line of work—I'm a barmaid."

A brief titter echoed through the courtroom.

"Ms. Miller, would you please tell the court where you work and what you do there," said Mickey.

"I'm usually employed at Happy Hilda's bar over at 19th and Elm streets. Eh, what does a barmaid do? Basically, I takes orders from them customers sittin' at tables and I brings them the drinks what they ordered."

"Were you working the night in question?" asked Mickey.

"Yes, sir."

"Were you aware of anything unusual happening in the bar that night" questioned Mickey.

"Sure, Billy Danser got knifed in the chest. Is that unusual enough?"

"Ms. Miller, please just answer the questions," he cautioned. "Can you tell the court what went on just before the knifing?"

"They was arguing up a storm. They used a few expressions I never even heard before." She looked out at the courtroom and grinned.

"Were you in the room when that argument erupted? And if so, exactly where in the room were you?"

"Yes, sir, I was," said Effie. "I was on my break, sittin' in a booth by the back door. You know, the way through to the kitchen."

"Is there another door to the street directly from the kitchen?" asked Mickey.

"Yeah, only it's not really a street," she replied. "It's more like a back alley to the street."

"I see, and how far were you from the two men who were arguing?"

"Oh, maybe twenty feet, give or take a few. They were standing at the bar."

"Was either man facing you?"

"They was face to face the whole time, but then Billy turned away, so I got to see both their faces."

"So you could identify both men?"

"Sure. It was Billy Danser and Grover Fox. They're regulars at Happy Hilda's."

"Were you paying attention to what they were arguing about?"

"Yeah, sort of. It was somethin' about Grover dissing Billy's sister. They was both swearing like old sailors."

"What else did you see and hear?"

"I saw a man get up from a table just the other side of them and, as he passed the two, he suddenly shoved a knife into Billy's chest and kept on comin' toward me. It was like all in one motion. He never stopped. He ran right past me into the kitchen. Then, when Billy fell, Grover, he ran after the guy into the kitchen and out the back door."

"Did you recognize this man?"

"I seen him before in Hilda's maybe a half dozen times, but I ain't got a name for him. Billy might have knowed him by name, though."

"Could you positively identify him if you saw him again?"

"No problem."

"Is that a yes or a no?"

"Yes."

"Your witness."

ADA Dulaney slowly got to his feet behind the prosecution's table. "The other person" defense theory ran through his mind. *Backed up by a reliable witness, too. It could ruin my case altogether. I need to recover from this in a hurry. Maybe I can shake this witness.* He moved out from behind the table and approached the witness. After clearing his throat he asked, "Were you really close enough to hear the exact words of their argument?"

"Yes, sir. I heard almost every foul word they uttered. Grover, he called Billy's sister a fat, sloppy, cheap whore a couple a times even. Billy, he called Grover a bastard and he use a few words I won't mention in this here courtroom. They was going at it all right, but these two guys are usually friends. They even go to ball games together. They both likes the Orioles."

"Friends, eh? Did you, by any chance, happen to hear what would turn one friend against the other? In other words, do you know what started this whole argument?"

"No, sir. I kinda tuned in late—after they started all their yellin' and stuff. I was just sittin' there in the booth with my glass of tonic water, mindin' my own business, before they got my full attention."

"I see. This mystery man you say stabbed Billy Danser, did he just come in or had he been sitting at his table for a while?"

"I served him a pitcher of Miller Lite about a half-hour before, maybe a little longer. I suppose he woulda come in just before that. I usually notice patrons what don't have something to drink in front of them, so he wouldn't have been sittin' there too long before that. I don't rightly know for sure."

"Was there anything unusual or disturbing about his looks or behavior that would indicate he might do what he did?"

"Objection," yelled Mickey. "Calls for a conclusion."

"Sustained," ordered the judge.

"I don't understand what you're asking," said Effie.

"I'll rephrase," said Dulaney. "Was he angry or agitated? Did he look like he was ready to stand up and stab someone or did  he seem passive or serene?"

"Objection," repeated Mickey

"I'll allow it," said the judge.

"I didn't notice," said Effie. "I said 'Hi!' and gave him the usual package smile and he nodded and smiled back. That's all I know."

"This unnamed stranger you said went running into the kitchen—how do you know he ran out the back door as well?"

Effie shrugged. "I don't know for sure. I just assumed he did. I guess I couldn't rightly see him do it."

"Yes, and perhaps you just *assumed* this other person altogether," suggested Dulaney, trying to capitalize on her word.

"Objection! The prosecution is badgering the witness," cried Mickey.

"Sustained," said the judge. "Ask a question, Counselor."

"What did this person of yours even look like?" asked Dulaney.

"He was about the same height as Billy when they was standing next to each other."

"An how tall was that?"

"I couldn't tell exactly because I was sittin' down. Maybe five-ten. No more."

"I see. Was there anything else distinctive about this man?"

"I remember him from before—he had a full beard and mustache. Sorta dark reddish beard with some gray around the edges. Hair the same, too. He was pretty hefty, but I wouldn't call him fat."

"You could see all this as he passed you in a dimly lit barroom?" asked Delaney.

"Yes, sir, I was lookin' right at him, and he fit exactly what I remember."

"Did anyone try to help the deceased? Maybe try to stop the bleeding?"

"Yeah. Leo rushed over and so did I, But it was too late. Leo tried to stuff a bar rag in him, but he had already bled out."

"Ms. Miller, you're not a doctor. How would you have known that?"

Effie flushed at the unexpected question. "I just assumed it. He looked kinda dead." The jurors suppressed a smile.

"Did someone at least call an ambulance and the police?"

"Sure, Anita Birches did. She was closest to the phone behind the bar from where she was sittin.'"

"Is there anything else you can tell us?"

"I can't think of anything right off."

"Thank you, Ms. Miller. No more questions," said Dulaney.

"The witness may step down," said Judge Hershfeld.

——

"Hey, this is getting exciting. We now have a mystery man," said Esther Reubens.

"I love all the questions and what she answers," said Katie. "This Effie is one tough babe."

"Thanks," said Joel. "It's my first shot at a full-length mystery novel. It sure beats writing briefs during my day work."

"Katie, didn't you say you had another chapter of *Boxcar Bertie*?" asked Rivka.

"Yes I do," replied Katie. She picked up her stapled chapter and began to read.

——

## Chapter 8. A Visitor or Two

Bertie had already made it onto her knees as Stan rolled in next to her. The train of boxcars had been moving faster than he expected by the time he threw himself at the open door. In fact, he almost missed his target altogether.

Bertie sensed it first. They were not alone—someone else was hidden in the deep shadows in the forward end of the boxcar. The cloud-covered night sky made it even more difficult to see through those depths. But she knew someone was there—she could smell the unwashed body from the distance.

"Who's there?" cried Bertie. "Come out where we can see you."

"None of your damn business," answered a hoarse voice with neither face nor form.

"We mean you no harm," added Stan. "We just want to know who we're dealing with."

"Just stay in yer end of the car, and we'll get along jes fine," said the same voice out of the dark.

"What if we don't want to do like you say and keep back here?" argued Stan.

"I've got a gun that will make sure you keep your distance," said the voice.

"How do we know you're not lying."

"Don't antagonize him, Stan," murmured Bertie, moving closer to the back end of the car. "I can live with his conditions. We'll keep our space and let him have his."

"I don't like being intimidated," said an angry Stan as he too moved to the rear. "But for your sake, Bertie, I'll go along with a truce. "You hear that up there?" he shouted.

"Yeah! A wise decision," replied the unknown voice.

Bertie and Stan settled into their corner at the end of the car. They took turns at who sat up and who lay their head in the sitting lap. Each of them snatched an hour or two of sleep this way. The train made stops in New London, Connecticut, and Providence, Rhode Island, but it wasn't until the approach to Boston that daylight began to fill the car, affording some visibility. Bertie was taking her turn to be on watch. In the sitting position, she couldn't move because Stan's head was in her lap. She noticed something weird at the opposite end of the car. Not only was the sitting form becoming clearer, there seemed to be another form lying flat on the car's wood flooring without benefit of straw.

*Seems like they're both asleep,* Bertie thought. *I don't see a gun anywhere. Maybe he was bluffing. Why didn't the other person speak?* Her eyes strained through the still-dim light trying to see more detail. *The guy on the floor hasn't moved. It doesn't even look like he's breathing. Jeez, everything appears wet under him. I wonder if it's blood and the guy is actually dead.*

Bertie wanted to wake Stan, but she had to do it quietly and carefully. If he woke with a loud start, she'd wake the guy across the way as well. She looked down at Stan and stroked his cheek with her forefinger. His hand flew up immediately to brush away the annoyance. He tried to sleep through the brushing but she persisted. Each time she stroked, he was a little more awake until one eye after the other popped open and stared into her face. She then put a finger to her lips and whispered a *shushing* sound. Then she said in soft tones, "There are two people across the way from us. It looks like at least one is sleeping and the other one is dead."

Stan lifted his head for a quick look, then sat up straight. "How do you know the other guy's dead?" he asked.

"Check out the pool under him," whispered Bertie. Looks like blood. "I think the one we spoke to murdered the other guy, so we have to be careful. We can't claim *not* to have seen the dead man, so if he wakes up and sees us gawking at what he's done, he'll have to deal with us. I think we have to move first and get the upper hand."

They both got to their feet and slowly, silently approached the smelly stranger. As they got closer, the smell got worse. Stan stood at the ready to pounce, but the guy awoke and stared back at him. Suddenly, he produced a gun.

Stan jumped at him anyway and deflected his hand so the shot went wild, ricocheting through the car several times before embedding itself somewhere in the wood siding. The two men wrestled for the gun and two more wild shots circuited the car. Finally, the gun came loose. As they both scrambled for it, the gun scooted out the boxcar door. In a wild attempt to recover his weapon, the smelly stranger accidentally followed it out the door and disappeared.

Bertie and Stan looked at each other in mixed shock and relief. As the train approached the Boston suburbs it began to slow. Neither one had repacked their belongings. They were stuck in a boxcar with a bloody murder victim.

——

"Hey, you're not going to leave us there, are you?" asked Frieda. "A week is a long time to wait for more."

"How are you going to get them out of that mess?" asked Rivka.

"There're more chapters to come," said Katie. "I'm glad I got you guys hooked. Isn't that what it's all about?"

"It's still not fair," said Esther with a mock pout.

"Good girl, Katie," said Dan. "You got 'em going. Suspense is what it's all about."

"Good job, Katie," said Rivka. "I know Tom has more that he wants to read, so let 'er rip, Tom."

Tom rearranged some of the pages in front of him and began.

———

### Chapter 4. The Accident

On starting day Tom was paired with Frank Mulhaney, a square-shaped man, who would be more attuned to playing right guard for the Baltimore Colts except for his over-the-belt, beer-belly protrusion. His eyebrows were thick and immovable and set over watery gray eyes. His speech was rough, but his mien was all business. And he insisted on taking the wheel. The first day they drove around Alexandria and Arlington for almost sixty Northern Virginia deliveries. There were a half-dozen more in the District of Columbia. The next day they kept to Baltimore with nearly a hundred individual deliveries.

The third day took them to Annapolis. The fifth delivery of the morning brought them to a quiet neighborhood and Slate Street in particular. They stopped at 2320 and delivered a long, thin cardboard box to apartment 3A. The woman answering the door signed Tom's receipt box, and he shuffled down two flights to the street to climb into the cab's passenger's seat.

As Frank pulled away from the curb at 2320 Slate Street...

———

"Why is that specific address so darned important that you repeat it twice?" asked Frieda.

"Have a little patience and you'll see," said Tom.

"Wait a minute. Did you say 2320 Slate Street in Annapolis?" asked Cora.

"That's right," replied Tom, a little annoyed at being interrupted so close to the climax of his story.

"That's one hell of a coincidence," declared Cora. "My brother, Muddy Atkins, and his former wife, Anne, had a second-floor apartment at 2329 Slate Street in Annapolis. Isn't that too bizarre to believe? And this delivery was across the street?"

Tom waited for the "wows," "yeahs," and "no-kiddings" to die down before continuing.

———

As Frank pulled the truck away from the curb at 2320 Slate Street, Tom noticed the line of parked vehicles on the left side of the one-way street.

"Where to next?" asked Tom.

Seeing the traffic light at the next corner turn green, Frank accelerated and took only a split second to glance down at his delivery order book. "Next is 67 West Street, Suite 204," he replied, quickly returning his attention to what was ahead in the road. But it was already too late.

Tom cried, "Look out!"

The truck had just rolled abreast of an unmarked white panel truck when driver and passenger were both stunned by what suddenly flew in front of their truck's grill. Big as life, the two men saw a young Caucasian woman dressed in pink, with outstretched arms, fly up in front of their windshield and slide back down off the truck's hood, then underneath the truck. Frank panicked. His foot tapped the accelerator for an instant, then slammed on the brake. The heavy truck came to a jerking halt, but not before they felt the tires *thump-a-thump* over something extraordinary in the road. He slipped into Neutral, then Park, and next applied the emergency brake as a matter of routine. The forty-four-year-old Frank sat there shaking for several seconds, then burst out of the door, sliding his shoes down onto the macadam street. Tom also hustled down from his side of the cab and rushed around to the other side of the truck.

Sure enough, a woman's body lay beneath the cab. There was no way Frank could move the truck without further mutilating the body, so the two men grabbed the woman under her arms and dragged her to the opposite sidewalk. Once free of the street, Frank felt for her carotid artery. Sensing no signs of life, he stood up straight and scanned his environs for anyone else who might have observed the accident scene. No one. Not a soul in sight. Frank felt a second wave of panic wash over him. He bolted for the cab, climbed into the driver's seat, and slammed the door.

"You can't just leave her here on the sidewalk!" called Tom, still standing over the woman's body. He stared at the woman intensely until he'd memorized her every mangled feature. "You can't just leave her here!"

"The hell I can't? You just watch me," shouted Frank. "Get in quick before someone sees us."

"Shouldn't we call it in?" Tom asked weakly.

"Not unless you want to lose your Commercial Driver's permit," said Frank. "I need mine to make a living. The woman's dead! Permanently dead! Ain't nothing we can do about it sticking around here. Get in before I leave you here, too."

Tom reluctantly shuffled over to the passenger side and climbed up into the cab. Frank released the emergency brake and drove off.

Strangely, there was never any mention of a hit-and-run accident in any of the local papers. They checked carefully every day for several weeks afterward. The two men thought maybe the police had suppressed all mention of the incident as a strategy leading to their arrest. The arrests never came, but the guilt lived on, especially with Tom.

———

There were tears in Tom's eyes as he put down his pages and continued to speak.

"This is my whole confession. We left the scene of an accident, an accident neither of us could have avoided. We're guilty—aren't we?"

Silence. No one knew what to say.

"Well, aren't we?"

## Chapter 26
## Fruits of the Critique

Tom repeated his pained question. "Well, aren't we? Wasn't it a separate crime for the two of us to leave? Frank shouldn't have taken his eyes off the road while moving in the first place. But because I chose that particular moment to ask him 'Where to next?' I'm fully culpable as well. I've lived with this thing for the past twenty years, so now you see why I wrote this confession. I have no one to ask for forgiveness except the good Lord, and I sincerely hope that is enough. I have suffered a good deal poring over my crime, but I am not so remorseful that I wish to be punished any further than I have already suffered." He fumbled for a handkerchief and blew his nose.

"I've met with Frank Mulhaney, the driver of the truck, several times in recent weeks, and he's stubborn as hell about it, still demanding that I not confess publicly. He even got physical, threatened me with his fists. How Frank deals with his own conscience is his business. I can understand and respect his decision to maintain the status quo. I realize, of course, that my confession necessarily implicates Frank, but for my sake and the sake of my troubled soul, for some time I've needed to tell someone and get it down on paper."

"If it's for your sake alone, why commit it to paper?" asked Dan.

"I've done it only for the purpose of clarity and completeness in my own mind. It's not a real confession unless someone else hears it and sees it," replied Tom. "However, that said, I hope what I've read to you will remain in this room. I'm depending on your discretion, all of you, because Frank has threatened me if I reveal his part in all this, or if I somehow implicate him in any way. I believe he will make good on his threats. I'm not so afraid for myself, but for my wife, Laura."

Silence prevailed in the room. His confession had moved everyone. Tom pulled out his handkerchief, dabbed at his eyes, and blew his nose again as he waited for someone else to speak.

"Are you absolutely sure the woman was dead?" asked Dan. "Could she have gotten up and walked away, for instance?"

"Absolutely sure," said Tom. "There weren't any signs of life. Frank even checked her carotid artery and then shook his head and said 'Nothing there.' And from what I saw was left of the woman, there was no way she could have gotten up and walked away."

"Then who would have any reason to remove the dead victim of a hit-and-run accident from the scene?" asked Dan. "I'm beginning to think that maybe this wasn't a run-of-the-mill, hit-and-run accident. Maybe there's more to this that we're not seeing."

"Are you thinking some kind of foul play?" asked Joel.

"It's entirely possible. We just don't have any idea who or why yet," replied Dan.

"Dan, the missing victim is only part of the problem. Tom and Frank were both wrong to leave the scene," declared Rivka. "But worse than that, there's no excuse for Frank to take his eyes off the road even for a split second, as you called it." She paused, cocked her head, and frowned as she searched for the right words.

"Tom, you knew it was wrong right off," added Rivka, "but in the end you were strongly persuaded by Frank to leave. As I see it, the alternative would have been for him to leave you behind so you could call the police. I don't see Frank letting you do that. Do you? I sincerely believe you have already served your time as a punishment for leaving the scene. Whether the police or even the legal system would see it that way is another thing. However, there is neither a body, nor a record of an accident. So who's to say a crime was even committed?"

"Me and my conscience, I suppose," replied Tom.

"What was the date again?" asked Cora, her brow wrinkled with concern.

"May 8th, 1989," confirmed Tom. "What about it?"

"Oh-oh! I see where time and place seem to be coinciding here," said Cora. "Across the street and the approximate date—it's too much to disregard. Anne, my brother's wife, disappeared just about that time. Muddy always claimed she ran off and left him and didn't want to be found. The police thought otherwise, but they never could pin anything on him, because she apparently took her coat, hat, purse, and a drawer full of costume jewelry with her. Add to that, they had no body. Their investigation fizzled."

"You still think there's something fishy there?" said Joel.

"Now I think maybe the police were right," Cora added. "Maybe he did 'do her in'. Two months into their marriage, they were at each other's throats, arguing up a storm for the smallest thing. I wonder that the marriage lasted as long as it did. If Anne's still alive and well somewhere and rid of him—good for her. I hope she's happy at last."

"From all that, I take it you were never that fond of your brother," said Dan. "He's certainly made our lives troublesome as well."

"I see what you mean, Dan," said Cora. "Otherwise, I can't conceive of why Muddy would be interacting with *you* at all. I wouldn't think he'd even be acquainted with you, except from what *you've* told me, Rivka. My little brother has been stalking you guys, and you believe he's a suspect in your bookstore break-in. I can believe almost anything about him, He's been in trouble for one thing or another ever since he was able to walk and talk. Maybe having two older sisters to constantly tease him had something to do with his wayward development. But I don't understand why he would wreak his terrible vengeance on you two."

"Well, Cora, ever since I borrowed your father's manuscript, and even after I returned it mostly unread, he's been turning up like a bad penny wherever I go," explained Dan. "As for the break-in, I think he was trying to steal the manuscript copy from us, but for the life of me, I have no idea *why*. It would appear that the break-in was a desperate move on his part, but it failed anyway—he never found my copy. We didn't report it to the police because there was no harm, no foul."

"Dan, I don't understand two things," said Joel. "What's your interest in this manuscript? And why would Cora's brother covet it so desperately?"

"My interest?" repeated Dan. "Well, when our very own bookstore copy, two library copies, and Arthur's personal copies all turn up missing—you have to admit we have a mystery, something I, personally, can't resist. I believe Cora's brother is trying to hide something—perhaps some family black sheep or bad seed, a wrongful deed, some secret location, or more likely something hidden in their family's house. If Muddy wanted to learn some specific things from the book, reading a single copy would have been sufficient to gain those facts. Removing multiple copies from public circulation points more toward attempting to hide something."

"Maybe," Cora burst in, "the sale of our house has exacerbated my brother's situation and pushed him to take action to protect his secret."

Dan nodded his bushy head vigorously. "That could certainly be true, Cora. Knowing that I had borrowed the manuscript and copied it could have made me his target."

"Maybe the secret of the book, the hit-and-run, Anne's disappearance, her missing body, and Muddy Atkins are all somehow connected," suggested Rivka.

"Good grief! Do you think this guy actually threw his wife in front of our truck?" asked an anxious Tom. "And then hid the body somewhere after we left the scene?"

"A missing body and no trace of a hit-and-run accident could explain why the papers never carried any story," offered Dan. "The fact that you and Frank deserted the scene would have given him no one to blame but himself. In fact, even worse for Muddy, he might have been targeted as the only suspect in foul play. The scene also raises the question whether the victim was even alive when she hit the windshield."

"Oh, she was alive alright," declared Tom. "That face was so full of animated fright and surprise she couldn't have been dead already."

"Could you possibly identify that face from a photograph?" asked Dan.

"I'm pretty sure I could," replied Tom. "That face and that instant are so frozen into my brain—they've been there solid for the last twenty years. I visit the poor young woman nightly in my nightmares. Oh, if you could only get ahold of this Anne's photo."

"There should be plenty of them in our family photo albums," offered Cora.

"It doesn't sound as though the police were even involved until Muddy reported Anne missing," continued Dan. "If we could prove all this, neither Frank nor you would have anything to fear from the police."

"Dan, you're making a lot of assumptions you haven't really proved yet," said Rivka. "Muddy Atkins can sue you for filing a false report if you take this to the police now."

"She's right, Dan," said Joel. "You don't have any proof, at least, not yet."

"My sister Rae thinks Muddy's an out-and-out psychopath," said Cora. "My sister Gloria says he's downright evil, but being twenty years younger, she continues to coddle him anyway. Even my father believed Muddy had a rotten streak. We all thought his twenty years with the Merchant Marines would have made a responsible man out of him. It appears as though that didn't happen, so whatever inconvenience or punishment takes place now is of his own doing."

"As I see it," offered Joel, "unless you find the woman's body, you can't confront the man, nor do you have enough evidence of interest to bring to the police. As far as the police are concerned, it's either a case they've investigated exhaustively or simply a cold case hardly worth opening now."

"So where's the body?" asked Tom. "And is it who you think

216

it is? This Anne somebody?"

"Anne Atkins was her name," said Cora. "If she's alive, I'll bet she has a new name to go along with her new life. I really liked Anne and I wish her well."

"That's rather optimistic," said Dan. "From what I've heard here tonight, I have to conclude that, if there is a body, it's got to be Muddy's wife and, most probably, it's hidden somewhere in the Atkins house. That would be the secret room mentioned in Arthur's book. The one where munitions were stored during the Revolutionary War. The one where the family hid slaves during the Civil War. The one where hard liquor was hidden during Prohibition. And now the one that has held Anne Atkins for the last twenty years."

Rivka's cinnamon-colored eyes flashed with anxiety. "You don't even know if that room still exists," she said. "Nor do you have any idea where it is. You're talking about a supposed body that's probably lain around for more than twenty years. I'm not sure there would be enough body to identify after all that time. Although, I suppose there's always DNA to rely on."

"I've been sitting here all evening listening to you folks talk about a body being hidden in our house, the house my husband and I just bought and moved into," said Helen Margoles, her voice tremulous. "That's not a very comforting thing for me to know. In fact, if our beautiful new house is haunted, I don't know whether I want to sleep there tonight."

"No one said anything about any ghosts or any place being haunted," said Cora. "My two sisters and I have been living in that house all our lives without any eerie or disturbing effects. Rest assured, you can sleep there."

"Rest assured, my foot," mumbled Helen.

Rivka felt a pang of sympathy for their newcomer. "Helen, I truly understand how you must be feeling. Now that you've added your thoughts, I seem to recall your husband's preparation for the move you made. Didn't you tell me he took the area measurements of every room in the house?"

"Why, yes, Lee did," replied Helen. "And because he did,

everything had its place, and the entire move went beautifully. He's such a perfectionist."

"Were those measurements in the form of a diagram, say, a floor plan, by any chance?" asked Dan.

"They were all laid out like a blueprint," answered Helen. "He printed it out from his computer and directed traffic during the move-in. The movers carried everything in and set them down just where he told them to."

"Do you think he'd print it out and mail or email a copy to me?" asked Dan. "And would you object if we came over and looked for any hidden space some time in the next few days? I know it's an imposition, but I do want to get to the bottom of this."

"Come over, Dan. Any time, as long as you call first and give us some warning. I'm just as anxious to get this thing resolved as you are. Oh, shoot, I don't think I'll sleep a wink tonight with thoughts of a dead body on the premises."

"Then don't think of it as a haunted house," suggested Katie. "Consider that a ghost adds a measure of character and a dollop of charm to a house. And who doesn't love a ghost story?"

"Don't joke, Katie, I've got the creepy crawlies already," said Helen.

Rivka looked at her watch. "Hey, critiquers, we're running almost an hour late tonight. Thank you all. Meeting adjourned."

# Chapter 27
## What Really Happened
Monday, May 8th, 1989

At 7:15 that fateful morning some twenty years earlier, Muddy and Anne, his wife of eight years, were arguing in the Atkins kitchen in their second-floor Annapolis apartment. The argument was largely of Muddy's making, finding fault with her cooking and housework. "You can't do anything right!" Powerful allergies had laid claim to his sinuses that morning and, by painful association, his poor temper as well. He, of course, turned *his* discomfort toward destroying *her* self-esteem.

When Anne had endured quite enough of his belligerent tirade, she complained, "I'm your wife, not your damn slave. Treat me with some respect. Just because your sisters were so cruel to you growing up, doesn't mean you have to take it out on me."

Threats and name-calling followed. Those became slaps and slaps turned into blows. When Anne found herself beaten and on the floor, her eyes became glazed with surprise and pure anger. Then fear set in. She clawed her way across the floor to the nearest corner and and sat cowering there.

Muddy looked down on her with a sneer and said, "You dumb bitch! I'm not through with you yet."

"You sonofabitch," she cried. "One of these days I'm leaving you for good and I ain't coming back."

"Go ahead, leave. Ain't no one here gonna miss you."

219

Seeing her suffer seemed to give him satisfaction and somehow she sensed this.

Anne slowly turned toward the empty corner behind her and, using her bare hands on the two adjoining walls, she wriggled her slight body up enough to stand on her feet. She edged along one wall until she reached her lightweight spring coat hanging on a clothes hook next to the door. The determined twenty-eight-year-old woman slid her arms into it and pulled it tightly about her.

Without facing him again, she took her purse from the doorknob and slipped out of the kitchen, slamming the door to the hall in her wake. She flew down the stairs and out onto the concrete stoop. Muddy gave chase into the hall. Downstairs, holding the outside door wide open, Anne turned to face him and gave him the classic "finger."

"Wait!" he yelled after her. "Get back up here now, you dumb bitch! You don't even know what you're doing. You'll be sorry."

"You rotten bastard," she cried out. "This time I'm leaving you *for good* and I ain't *never* coming back." She slammed the door shut and spun around toward the street. Anne Atkins had declared her independence and disappeared from his view.

Angered even more, he scrambled down the stairs, out onto the sidewalk, and sprinted after Anne until he caught up with her. Muddy grabbed both shoulders and spun her around to face him. By now his adrenaline was pumping furiously. He slapped and backhanded her several times before she restrained him with a powerful kick to his privates. She tried to run. Though Muddy doubled in pain, he recovered soon enough to pursue his rebelling wife. His face was contorted with hatred as he caught up with Anne once more and grabbed her from behind. Using every bit of flowing adrenaline, he picked tiny Anne up off her feet and threw her into the middle of Slate Street. Her arms and legs were flung wide as she sailed through the air, screaming.

Muddy couldn't possibly have known that a truck would mysteriously appear out of nowhere and take Anne's life from her—a coincidence he wanted no part of. *Oh-oh. That friggin' truck is stop-*

*ping. I'd better hide in my panel truck.* He retreated around to the panel truck's rear doors, quietly unlocked them, and climbed into the darkness. Closing the doors behind him, he maneuvered into a position where he could hear and see, but not be seen.

Muddy watched as the men from the truck dragged Anne from beneath the vehicle to the sidewalk. *One of them is acually checking for her pulse. He's shaking his head—apparently, she's dead. She couldn't have survived such a blow anyway. Now they're arguing.*

Instead of feeling the dread of losing his wife or the guilt of having cost her her life, Muddy sought to shift the blame away from himself as he had done thousands of times before in his past. At first he thought, *Those two truck drivers will be the perfect patsies and take the blame for hitting Anne—a poor defenseless woman, who suddenly ran out in front of them—a simple case of manslaughter.*

When he saw the big truck drive off it became a whole different story. As Muddy hopped down from the back of his panel truck, he checked to see if there were any witnesses. Slate Street was surprisingly deserted at 10:20 on a Monday morning. Nor did he see anybody spying out of windows as he slowly scanned the canyon of residential buildings.

Muddy looked down at Anne's pale face and bent body, a look completely devoid of remorse. Surprisingly, there was little blood. His anger was gone. A calculating demeanor took its place. *Who's to say I didn't run over my own wife? The neighbors must have heard our arguing. I wouldn't stand a chance with the police. I've done some pretty terrible things in my time, but nothing like this.*

The fear of getting caught overrode any guilt, and at that moment abject terror possessed him. Muddy grabbed his wife's body under her arms and dragged her into the back of his panel truck. After retrieving her purse and shoe from the street he began to think, *How and where to dispose of these things?* Suddenly, it came to him.

Muddy Atkins drove to the home where he grew up, now simply his father's house. His sister Rae still lived there, but today she would be at school teaching. Of course, he could count on his father, Arthur C. Atkins, being away, off researching another of his family history books.

Muddy remembered his private playroom, a secret cache that he believed no one else knew about. He'd accidentally discovered this space as an eleven-year-old boy. He never told anyone about finding the room. It had remained his secret to this day. It was the perfect place to deposit Anne's body. As long as the Atkins family home remained in family hands, he needn't worry about it being discovered.

Muddy drove up the driveway to the back door of the house and carried Anne into his first-floor hidden room. It took him a little under an hour to wrap the corpse in dry-cleaners' plastic bags and duct tape. He laid her out flat at the rear of the room. The thick spider webbing annoyed him every inch of the way. In spite of the air vent to the second floor, the room still smelled musty and damp. He decided to cover that vent with duct tape as a necessary precaution against the leaking odors of decomposition ever reaching the rest of the household.

A confident Muddy drove back to his own apartment, feeling he'd done all he could to hide his wife's body. He'd tell the police that she walked out on him after an argument and didn't want to be found. He'd add that he wasn't interested in finding her. The neighbors, glad to hear about an end to their loud arguments, would probably support that theory.

Now Muddy had to make sure that what was left of her things supported his "runaway wife" explanation. He thought it out carefully. *What would a runaway wife take with her?* He upended her costume jewelry drawer into her purse and added two pairs of glasses. Then he took out the middle-size valise from its set of three. In it he placed her bulging purse, two of her outfits, a pair of shoes, and a hat. He even tossed in a bra and two pairs of nylon panties. *All good*, he congratulated himself. *Tomorrow I'll put the filled valise in the hidden room with the body.*

## Chapter 28
## Nasty Exchange
Friday, May 22nd, 2009

Bonding among siblings can often be questionable, and the reasons may well be rooted in their early childhood behavior. That bonding can vary all the way from genuine warmth and need to mere duty, and even to sheer violence. The bonding between mother and child is more absolute. The bonding occurring in the Atkins family is a model of this entire range of feelings. Adding alcohol serves only as a magnifier in this particular incident.

The doorbell rang at Gloria's apartment at 1:00 p.m. She was surprised to find Cora standing in the hall with a small carton in her hands.

"Hi, Sis," said Cora. "The movers delivered some of your things to my place by mistake, despite all we went through to prevent slipups."

"Come on in," said Gloria. "I was just about to pour myself a mug of coffee. Should I pour one for you?"

"Sure, why not?" answered Cora as she settled into one of the captain's chairs at the kitchen table. "I'm not interrupting anything, am I?"

"No, no. The baby's asleep, and I was planning to soak in the tub for awhile, but I suppose that can wait. I guess our move took a hell of a lot out of me. Anyway, to what do I owe this glorious visit from you?"

"Really, Gloria, don't you want to hear my news?"

"Sure, what news is that?"

"Our critique group had quite a meeting last night," declared Cora after a few minutes of silence.

"Oh, what was that all about?" asked Gloria. "And how does it affect us?"

"It seems that our brother has been stalking Dan Sherman, the bookseller. Dan even believes that Muddy broke into their store one night to steal back Daddy's manuscript. He's concluded that Muddy wants to hide something that's in it." Cora paused a few seconds to let this sink in. "Then another one of our group, Tom Dwyer, told his story of a hit-and-run incident that took place in front of Muddy's Slate Street apartment on the day that Anne disappeared. Because the hit-and-run body disappeared, the group thinks that maybe Muddy chased or pushed or threw Anne out in front of Tom's truck, and when the truck drove off, Muddy had to dispose of the body or he'd be blamed. Dan also says that, according to Daddy's book, there's a hidden room somewhere on the first floor of our old house. The group has concluded—well, more like speculated—that Muddy stashed Anne's body there in that hidden room."

Gloria gasped. "Oh my God! You really think Muddy is capable of all that? How do you even know the hit-and-run victim was Anne?"

"I just got through showing photos of Anne from the family album to Tom, one of the hit-and-run drivers, and he picked her out of the groupings immediately," said Cora.

"You really believe this of Muddy?" asked Gloria.

"I wouldn't have believed it, Gloria, except I know he has a charging bull's temper, and those two fought like cats and dogs every day of their marriage. Maybe it went a *skosh* too far, and he accidentally killed her. Maybe he chased her into the street, but hiding the body tells me he was responsible for her death in any case."

"I suppose so, Cora, but I just can't see him committing outright murder."

"Gloria, being the kid sister, you've always been the one to stick up for him, but you've also done your share of teasing and egg-ing him on. What gives?"

"I felt sorry for him. Daddy always came down pretty hard on him. He just never understood Muddy. I've even invited him over for supper tonight."

"Why would you do a thing like that?"

"He's living in a tiny hotel room and eating out while he's waiting to go to sea again. I thought he'd appreciate a home-cooked meal."

"Will you be safe?" asked Cora. "Do you want me to come over and sit in?"

"No, no, he's our brother," said Gloria. "I'll be fine."

\* \* \* \*

The doorbell at Gloria's apartment rang again at 5:30 that evening, and this time it was her brother at the door. They quickly exchanged greetings, and she invited him to wait in the living room. Instead, he went directly to her liquor cabinet in the kitchen, removed a bottle of Beefeater's Gin, and set it on the counter. Gloria handed him a glass half filled with ice and a cold bottle of tonic from the refrigerator. Muddy poured from both bottles and stirred with his finger. He took the mixed drink and headed for the blue velvet recliner in the living room, where he made himself comfortable.

"Dinner will be ready in ten minutes," she called from the kitchen.

"What are we having?"

"Pork chops, glazed carrots, and mashed potatoes. And apple pie, if you behave yourself."

"You're spoiling me," he said. "Any beer? That would make a perfect go-along to dinner."

"There should be a bottle or two of Heineken in the fridge." Gloria rushed about the kitchen, attending to Bunny in her highchair, then turning over the chops in the broiler and microwaving the carrots and potatoes. Finally, everything came together, and she called Muddy to the table.

Kissing Bunny on the top of her head, Muddy took a chair opposite Gloria with Bunny on his left. "Hey, Bunny Wunny, how the hell are they treating you?" He added a chuck under the baby's double chin and got a glaring look in return from Gloria.

Dinner went well, accompanied by the two bottles of Heineken and some light conversation, mostly about Daddy and how little he paid attention to all of his children. While Gloria did the dishes and put Bunny to bed, Muddy retired to the living room once more, where he fixed one gin and tonic after another. He'd consumed four, heavy on the gin, by the time Gloria rejoined him there.

"Hey, Bro," she said. "Maybe you ought to go easy on all that sauce. You'll need to be sober to drive back to your hotel."

"None of your damn business, Goneril Baby," he mumbled in increasingly slurred terms.

"What did you just call me?" she demanded.

"Goneril Baby," he returned. "Ain't that the name our mamma gave you?"

"Yeah, but you know how much I hate it. She had that crazy obsession with *King Lear* when she named us. You got off real easy with Budreau. But why the devil are you calling me that now? Why are you turning on *me* now?"

"When we were kids, you all teased me mercilessly. You were the worst. I hated you then and I hate you now, Goneril Bitch."

"Muddy, you have a bad memory. I'm so much younger than you, I was nicer to you than Rae and Cora were."

"You're a liar, bitch."

"You come over here and eat my food and guzzle my liquor and then insult me?"

"Yeah, Goneril Bitch!"

"You sure can dish it out, Muddy, but can you take it?"

"What do you mean?"

"Those men in white coats are coming to get you, Muddy. They think you're crazy. They already know you killed Anne and hid her somewhere in our old house."

"How could they know that when we all know she ran off somewhere twenty years ago? She's alive. Even the police believed me, Goneril Bitch."

"You opened the can of worms yourself when you stole those books and began stalking the bookseller guy. Cora told me they've figured the whole thing out, and now the men in the white coats will be coming for you. She belongs to that critique group with the Shermans, and they know all about you and how you killed Anne and hid her."

"Stop it!"

"But you can't stop them. The men in the white coats are coming. Can't you hear them? Listen, I hear them."

"Stop, Goneril," he screamed, as he stood and staggered toward her. Getting up, he knocked over his full glass of gin and tonic. He paid no attention to it—just kept coming at her like some fictional monster with neither heart nor brain.

Gloria tried to back away, but he kept coming until he reached out and gripped her neck with both hands in a chokehold. She screamed long and loud, and now the baby could be heard crying in the background. He shook Gloria's whole body in his chokehold, then threw her backward. She careened off the coffee table, fell to the carpet and lay there silent and immobile. The baby's crying sounded more frantic, as though she knew of the violence in the front room.

Muddy looked down at Gloria and suddenly felt free of his sister. *She won't demean me any longer. I don't want to be here anymore—I need to leave now.* Muddy stumbled across the oriental carpet to the door and fled the building. He climbed into his rental car, shut the door, and sat for a few minutes until the whole reality came to him. *So now they know I killed Anne, but if there's no body, I don't think they can prove a damn thing. I've got to go move the body somewhere. But where? Maybe deep water. Maybe dig a hole someplace. I've got to get there before they do.*

He started the car and drove away, maneuvering in a zig-zag corrective, overcompensating pattern, scraping and side-swiping a car here and there. He found a handy parking space half a block from the house and nosed into the space on a peculiar angle that left the trunk extending perilously out into the street by several feet.

Sliding out of the driver's seat, Muddy stumbled around the

front of the rental car toward the curb and onto the sidewalk. He leaned against the wrought-iron fencing on his left, making his way from the parking space toward the former Atkins home. Reaching the property line, he climbed over the fence and staggered up the lawn toward his old home. There were lights on, mostly on the second floor rear. *They're in bed and not likely to hear me,* he reasoned. He approached the left side of the house, removed a loose section of wood latticework, and slithered into the crawlspace beneath the house, replacing the lattice behind him. In the minimal light Muddy crawled on his hands and knees until he reached a spot just below where the hidden room lay. It took him a few minutes to find the external release lever for the trapdoor. A single yank dropped one edge of the door to the ground. He centered himself under the opening and then stood up straight, which put the upper half of his body in the secret room. He lifted himself into the room and then pulled the door up behind him with the pull rope. He turned on the low-wattage room lighting and saw the plastic wrapped around Anne's body. He examined the twenty-year-old multilayered wrapping. It was no longer clear, but cloudy and very brittle to handle.

* * * *

Hitting her head on the coffee table as she fell to the living room floor had left Gloria unconscious for twenty minutes. When her brain finally stirred, she remained stunned, immobile for several more minutes. Though her child's pleading cries echoed in her ears, she couldn't seem to focus on reality no matter how hard she tried. The rear of her head hurt worse than the overall stinging headache. Her hand went back there and returned with bloody fingers. But a mother's instinct soon connected with her child's distress and commanded her to full consciousness. Gloria struggled unsuccessfully to sit up, so she dragged her body to the sofa, where she pulled herself up, first into a sitting position and then up onto the cushioned sofa itself. She hoped the wooziness would soon pass. The room swirled around her in bits and flashes—sometimes in long, unstoppable sequences. Her cell phone lay on the end table within easy reach, but without seeing clearly, she had to feel around for it. Once in hand, she slipped the phone into a jeans pocket. Then, exhausted, her head fell back, the room moved again, and she came close to falling unconscious once more.

Bunny had been quiet for several minutes, but hearing her mother's moans and sounds of motion may have instinctively frightened her. Patience is not an infant's virtue—Bunny resumed her screaming. Gloria shook her head, trying desperately to clear its cobwebs. *The baby, the baby, my head, my baby, the bleeding.* She sat up and grabbed the decorative runner from the coffee table. She wrapped it crudely around her bleeding head and tucked in the ends. Leaning forward, Gloria tried to get enough leverage to stand, but couldn't until she pushed down on the coffee table. Then, in a bent-over stance, she went hand-over-hand, groping furniture, walls and whatever lay along the way until she reached Bunny's room. At last she clutched the crib rail.

Barely able to stand, she scooped up Bunny and sank into the big rocking chair nearby. She clutched the child to her breast and rocked her until the agitated crying turned to deep sobs, then to the rhythmic breaths of contented sleep. Gloria pulled the cell phone from her pocket, and poked in M-Y-B-U-N-N-Y and CONTACTS. Near the top of the list, she selected Cora's name and called her.

Cora answered on the third ring tone.

Voice quavering, her sister said, "It's Gloria. I'm hurt. I told Muddy we know about Anne. Cora, he tried to kill me. I'm hurt bad."

"Where are you?"

"At home. Bunny needs me. Help us!"

"I'm on my way as soon as I call 9-1-1." Cora hung up.

Gloria dropped the cell phone on the floor and fell into a stupor with the child's head across her shoulder.

The Emergency Medical Technicians arrived at Gloria's apartment eight minutes later and prepped her for transport to Anne Arundel Medical Center. One EMT collected a blanket from the crib and took charge of Bunny and the baby's bottle. Gloria and Bunny were delivered straight to the Emergency Room.

## Chapter 29
## Pursuit

As soon as Cora had finished the phone call to the EMTs, she called Rae, and both of them decided to go straight to the hospital. Cora arrived first. She had just finished imparting the admissions data when Rae showed up in the ER waiting room. They were unable to gain any information about their sister other than she was in surgery.

Traumatic experience changes most people, some only temporarily, some permanently. Rae, the normally cold and calculating sister, started to show real signs of emotion. Worry lines formed on her brow, an occasional tear escaped, and she clung to Cora like glue. That is, until a hospital social worker brought out Bunny and her bottle. The woman placed baby and bottle in Rae's lap, after learning of their family relationship. Bunny softened Auntie Rae up even further when she clung to Rae's neck. Sometimes sisters smell and feel alike even though they don't look alike, and that was good enough for Bunny—she slept through most of the ordeal.

Forty minutes later, Cora, the normally emotional sister, turned cool and logical when it suddenly occurred to her that she should be contacting the police about the awful beating Muddy gave her sister. *He's my flesh and blood, but the beating was an out-and-out criminal act.* She called the police hot line, and after a preliminary exchange of questions and answers, was referred to Detective Sergeant

Michelle Monahan. The female detective agreed to meet them at the hospital. Twenty-five minutes later, Monahan sat in a straight-back tube chair across from the two sisters in the ER waiting room.

"Mrs. Bacon, Ms. Atkins, are you sure your sister will be willing to file assault charges against your brother?"

"Positively," replied Rae. "Look what the bastard did to her."

"Well, most likely," replied Cora a moment later. "Although she's always taking his part, so she may not want to press charges."

"Which is it, ladies?" asked Monahan. "Am I wasting my time here?"

"No, of course not, Detective," answered Cora. "She'll press charges even if I have to twist her arm a little."

The detective cast her a disapproving look. "No, it can't be by coercion."

"Just an expression," explained Cora. "I'm sure Gloria will press charges against him."

"Can you both be sure that it was Budreau Atkins who assaulted your sister."

"Yes," said Cora. "She called and told me just as soon as she regained consciousness. He attacked her and choked her. And now she's in there fighting for her life."

"Yes," said Rae. "I believe Muddy is an out-and-out psychopath, utterly evil through and through."

"Muddy?" questioned Monahan.

"Yes, ma'am," replied Rae. "Buddy was the obvious nickname for Budreau, but our father changed it to Muddy after all the trouble he caused the family."

"Has this Muddy ever assaulted anyone else before this?"

"Yes," said Cora. "I remember he beat up a neighborhood boy when he was fifteen. Our father bribed and muscled Muddy's way out of that one."

"Does he have a police record?" asked Monahan.

"I don't know—I don't think so," said Rae.

"Any idea where I might find your brother?"

"While he's in town, he's been staying at the Annapolis Waterfront Hotel, room 233," replied Cora.

"Can you describe your brother to me?" asked Monahan.

"Lanky...over six-feet...maybe 180 pounds...black hair," offered Cora.

"Don't forget his full black beard," said Rae. "And he's a Merchant Marine seaman."

"Thank you! Is that everything, ladies?" asked Monahan.

"Cora, aren't you going to mention anything about Anne?" asked Rae.

"Who's this Anne?" asked Monahan. "Someone else he assaulted?"

"It's actually a police cold case from twenty years ago," said Rae. "It's been rumored that he's currently trying to remove the body of his late wife, Anne, from a supposedly hidden room in our former home."

"Rumor? Body? Hidden room?" repeated a much confused Michelle Monahan. "What's all that about?"

"Muddy's wife disappeared some twenty years ago," said Cora. "Back then, the police first thought Muddy had done the poor woman in. But Muddy claimed his unhappy wife ran away from him of her own free will. The lack of a body, and the fact that her purse, clothes, and jewelry were gone as well, gave a measure of credibility to Muddy's abandonment story. After a number of dead ends, eventually the police gave up."

"We're pretty sure it's not just a rumor," said Rae. "Recently, after listening to some new information, a number of people now believe that Muddy murdered Anne and hid her body somewhere in our former home and it's been there ever since. Our house has been in the Atkins family for over 200 years. It was recently sold to the Margoles family, so we think he might be at the house right now trying to move Anne's body out of a hidden room somewhere in the house."

"Do you know where this hidden room is?" asked Monahan.

"No," answered Rae. "We only know of the room's existence from my father's book of the family's history. The room was used to hide weapons during the Revolutionary War, to hide slaves during the Civil War, and to hide liquor during Prohibition. So we know for a fact that it does exist. My father was a faithful historian."

"Why didn't you two tell me all this right off?" asked Monahan.

"That's the part we can't prove, but we are almost certain it's true," said Cora. "You'll have to hurry if you want to catch him in the act."

Michelle Monahan flipped her notebook closed and made a call to her captain. When she was through talking, she picked up her jacket, left her card with her cell number, and bid them both goodbye.

The two sisters and Bunny continued their vigil for Gloria. Cora sat for another half-hour before thinking about calling Dan and Rivka. She looked at the time on her cell phone. *Only 9:30. They should still be up. Muddy might try to take revenge on Dan. And I should let Dan know what happened to Gloria.* She poked in the number.

"Bookstore, we're closed just now, but we'll be happy to serve you in the morning," repeated the answering machine.

But Cora kept hitting the redial button, and the phone rang and the message repeated on and on. *Damn, I can't reach the Shermans,* she thought.

"Hello, bookstore," Dan picked up the phone after nearly two dozen rings.

"Dan, this is Cora Atkins. Muddy just beat Gloria up. She's in the hospital. She told him that we all know he killed Anne and hid her body in our old home. I've also called the police and spoke to a Detective Sergeant Michelle Monahan. She came here to the hospital and I told her everything. But now I regret that I didn't tell her your name and about your part in all of this. I'm afraid Muddy might take his revenge out on you."

"Where are you?"

"I'm still at the hospital, waiting for word on Gloria."

"Cora, if Muddy is aware of what we all know about him,

won't he try to move the body?"

"Sounds about right to me," replied Cora. "That's what I told the detective."

"Muddy must be at the house right now," said Dan. "Did you tell the detective about the secret room?"

"Yeah, I told her all I could —about what Muddy did to Gloria, about Anne's disappearance, and about the hidden room." Cora thought she'd said enough, but had a sudden new thought. "Won't Helen and Lee be in danger if they cross paths with Muddy?"

"Let's hope that doesn't happen," said Dan. "Meanwhile, I've been going over the floor plan that Helen Margoles sent me, and I have a pretty fair idea where the room might be. Do you have any way of getting in touch with this detective?"

"Yes, Detective Sergeant Monahan left her card with a cell number on it," replied Cora.

"Would you call her and explain about my part in all this? Oh, and tell her I'll meet her there in fifteen minutes with the floor plan. I can help with the hidden room part."

"Sure, I'll call her right now," Cora said.

Dan called Helen and informed her that he and the police were coming to find the hidden room. Unfortunately, and predictably, the call upset her. The family's privacy had been invaded.

* * * *

Dan pulled into the parking space behind an unmarked police car with its blue light flashing on top. Both cars sat under a bright street light. He introduced himself to Detective Sergeant Michelle Monahan, and the two of them went to the front door. Leland Margoles answered the doorbell and let them in. They found Helen sitting on the couch in the living room in a state of distress.

"Lee," said Dan, "I've been using your floor plan to locate the secret room on the first floor of your home." He pointed to an area bounded by the living room, two bedroom closets, and a hall. Weren't you the least bit curious about this unaccounted-for space?"

"I noticed it," replied Lee, "and meant to ask one of the sisters about it. Then in the midst of moving, I forgot all about it."

"According to Arthur Atkins, there has to be an access from the first floor as well as one from the crawl space beneath the house," offered Dan.

Monahan had been listening and said, "If there's more than one access, I had better get some additional manpower here." She stepped into the hall and made the call. In ten minutes an all-black cruiser, with its flasher bar alternating blue and white, parked on the street behind Dan's Toyota. Two uniformed officers got out and set up street barriers. Then, with flashlights, they began a methodical search of the grounds near the perimeter of the house.

Meanwhile, Dan and Monahan thoroughly searched the hidden room's perimeter indicated on the floor plan. All they needed now was an entrance. They examined every alcove and closet along the way, hand-touching and pushing, plus inspecting with a flashlight, everything that might trigger an opening to the hidden room. An hour and a half later, they were still stymied, so they retired to the living room to talk things over. They didn't give up altogether, as there were times when each of them thought they heard movement beyond the bordering walls.

## Chapter 30
## Death Rules the Night

**H**ours earlier, within those same walls, the drinks he'd consumed and the adrenaline drain finally overtook Muddy, leaving him little choice but to lie down on the cot he'd installed during his boyhood hideout days. He slept longer than he meant to, and when he awoke, he knocked over the cot getting to the trapdoor. He needed to pee in the worst way, and he was clumsy going about it. Muddy dropped the trap and slithered down to the ground in the crawl space. He found a grassy spot to satisfy nature and, on the journey back to the trap door, he noticed a flashlight beam dancing its way across the lawn.

Crawling closer to, and looking through, the latticework on the living room side of the house, he made out one of the uniformed officers. Peering toward one side of the house, he saw blue and white flashing lights. Over his shoulder, another flashlight beam appeared, and he was sure there was a cop attached to that one, too.

*Gloria was right—they've come for me. Now I'm trapped. No, not yet. There's still a chance. I've got to move Anne's body or they'll find us together.* Muddy slithered through the opening once more and pulled up the trap door. He righted the cot and sat down to think. He could hear voices beyond the wall, many of them, but they were muffled and incoherent. *Maybe I can hide on the roof—on the widow's walk at the top of the house. They'll never think to look there. Yeah.*

Muddy dragged Anne's wrapped body close to the back of

his former bedroom closet. Over time, the wrapping had begun to badly disintegrate. His dragging of the body across the floor added more rips, tears, and shreds of plastic. But Muddy didn't notice.

The short piece of wall hinged at the top of the closet was held in place at the bottom by a single, spring-loaded plunger-type doorstop. His earlier patching and sealing of the molding merely hid the tripping mechanism that was still accessible from the hidden room side. Muddy tripped the plunger and stepped back to allow the wall to rise out of his way. Then he stepped over the molding, again dragging Anne's body behind him. He checked the hall first to see if the coast was clear, then picked up the body and carried it to the great staircase. Brittle plastic, rotted cloth, and even decomposed body parts escaped from the wrapping and fell on the floor as he carried her to the top of the house. He was so fixated on his task that he failed to notice the prominent trail he left behind.

* * * *

"What was that?" cried Helen from the living room.

"It came from the hall," said Leland.

Dan and Detective Monahan were nearest the door to the hall. They rushed out, too late to see Muddy, but just in time to find the macabre debris and trail left behind.

"He's in the house," cried Monahan. "And headed to the upper floors." She took off in hot pursuit.

"He's taking Anne's body with him," said Dan. "Where can he be taking her?"

"Up to the roof. Maybe even the widow's walk," said Leland.

Monahan was halfway up the stairs when she pulled out her phone and barked a command to the officers outside. "Get some light on the top of the house. Use the cruiser spots."

Leland started up the stairs, following her. Dan decided it was safer to step outside and watch the action from the street. Besides, the climb involved three tiring flights of stairs, and he didn't know what he could do to help once he got up there. More than likely, he'd be in the way. Terrified, Helen scurried after Dan.

Muddy reached the closeted access to the house roof and

set Anne's body down on a landing rest bench. The desperate man turned the key in the lock, opened the door, and carried the body into the closeted staircase. Hearing someone on the stairs, he locked the door behind him and dropped the skeleton key into his pocket. Gloria's words kept running through his head: *They're coming to get you. They're coming to get you.* The sounds on the other side of the door confirmed it.

Soon there was a pounding on the door, the last barrier between him and *them*. Muddy climbed the final steps, opened the overhead hatch to the widow's walk, and stepped outside, pulling Anne's broken body in its tattered wrappings up and out after him. He carried her to the center of the walk and looked down into the blinding spotlights.

* * * *

Outside, in front of the huge house, Dan looked up at the widow's walk. Nothing appeared to be happening, yet he somehow knew the chase would end there. Someone touched his hand, and he looked down to see Rivka standing at his side.

"Rivvie, what are you doing here?"

"Helen called me. She told me what was happening and she needed another woman to talk to—moral support, most likely. I just had to come and keep her company." She squeezed Dan's large hand, and he squeezed back. Helen gripped her opposite arm.

* * * *

Leland arrived at the top landing behind Detective Monahan. He retrieved the spare key from atop the door frame and unlocked the door to the closeted staircase. They burst in, and Monahan saw the open hatch. She raced up the stairs to the widow's walk and started through the hatch. With one foot on each side of the hatch opening, she heard Muddy's frantic screaming, "Get back! Let me be. Get back!"

Muddy saw Monahan emerge from the hatch. *They're coming for me. They're coming for me.* This was all he could think of. He raised what was left of his wife over his head and screamed into the blinding light, "Is this what you want?" With a violent thrust, he threw Anne's

238

body out into the empty space in front of him.

As Monahan closed in, she saw Muddy climbing up and balancing on the broad railing of the widow's walk.

"Wait!" called the detective. "Don't jump!"

"Too late!" cried Muddy. But even if he had wanted to change his mind at the last second, the choice to live or die no longer belonged to him. The rotted wood railing collapsed. Muddy lost his footing. He bounced over the eave into the lights and landed on the lawn three floors below.

* * * *

"Oh, no!" cried Rivka, squeezing her eyes shut.

"It's Detective Monahan up there, but she was too late," said Dan, pointing to the frustrated Michelle standing behind the crumbled railing. He tried to get a closer look at the two bodies, but one of the officers stopped him less than ten feet away. Still, Dan couldn't help himself. His eyes strained to fix on the gruesome remains of Anne's body—bones spilling out of the shredded plastic wrap. His stomach churned. He turned away.

Rivka shuddered. "Could we go home now?"

Dan shook his head. "Not before I have a look at that hidden room. I want to satisfy my Arthuritus, if you'll excuse the pun."

Rivka picked up on his attempt to lighten the impossibly tragic mood. Turning to Helen, she said, "Ooooh, see what I have to put up with?"

Helen cracked a small, short-lived smile.

"It'll only take a few minutes, Rivvie," said Dan. "After all, it was the big secret that Muddy Atkins was trying to keep."

Dan led Rivka and Helen back into the house and to Muddy's old bedroom, using the trail of decayed matter to guide them. Neither of the women wanted to go any farther, but Dan stepped into the closet and through the opening in the rear wall. He performed a quick inspection of the hidden space and that satisfied his curiosity. The three returned to the front room, where they found Leland and the detective in tense, quiet conversation.

Dan's phone rang. It was Cora calling from the hospital.

"Do you have any news yet?" he asked.

"Yes, Gloria is out of surgery and in the recovery room. She's not awake yet. The doctor says they drained the cranial area and once the rest of the swelling goes down she'll be out of immediate danger. But they won't know how much damage she incurred as a result of the concussion. We can only hope it'll be minimal."

"That's good news," Dan said.

"But wait!" Cora blurted out. "What's happening there? Did they find the hidden room? What about Anne's body?"

Dan hesitated and sucked in a deep breath. "Yes, they found the hidden room. But....Cora...I have very bad news. Muddy went up to the widow's walk of your old house. He was carrying Anne's body and threw it off the roof. Then...he intended to take his own life. He was about to jump when the railing beneath him collapsed and he fell to his death. I'm so sorry."

Cora clicked off. The phone went dead.

Rivka, standing next to Dan, placed a comforting arm around his shoulder. "That was tough, darling. You handled it well."

Dan gave her a grateful bear hug.

The Shermans realized they had no more reason to stay. They said their goodbyes to the Margoles, but not before Dan thanked Leland for his help. "Your precise drawings made all the difference," he said.

Holding hands, the Shermans left for home.

## Chapter 31
## Mark and Ivy's Wedding
Sunday, May 24th, 2009

More than two centuries ago marriage was not about the bonding of a couple seeking love and companionship. It was a way of cementing alliances and gaining relatives—more labor hands to work the fields. In many cases, the young man and woman had no say in their own lifelong arrangements. Today's marriage was definitely about love, understanding, trust, and companionship—the ultimate bonding and the result of months of difficult planning.

Dan awoke forty minutes before the alarm commenced this special day. He bounded out of bed and rushed into their only bathroom, a definite headstart to avoid Rivka's usual dominance of the tiny space. Showering and double shaving—first with the electric shaver and then a dry scraping with the bladed razor—ensured smooth cheeks that would last him all day. He slipped into striped boxer shorts, an undershirt, and a ribbed-front white dress shirt. He added a clip-on bow tie to the collar. So far, so good. Then he heard movement behind him.

"Good morning, dear." said Rivka. She smooched a kiss on the back of his neck and darted into the bathroom, closing the door behind her.

Next, the substitute father of the bride reached for the rented gray tuxedo hanging on the open closet door and pulled off the protective plastic. Parting the jacket front, he slipped the trousers off the hanger and carried them to the bed where he sat down to put them on. He sat there daydreaming for several minutes, contemplating his part in the day's events. Then Dan lifted his left foot and deposited it into the left trouser leg, but it would only go down so far—something blocked its passage. He tried the right foot—same problem.

Dan's bellowing cry of frustration was loud enough to reach Rivka in the shower. He heard the water stop and saw her appear at the door with a bath towel wrapped about her torso.

"Dan, any louder and you'll wake the whole damn neighborhood. What's wrong?"

"My pants! I can't get my feet into either leg opening. They're blocked."

She took one look at him sitting on the bed in a formal top with red and blue boxer shorts and started to giggle. "But you're a big boy now. You should be able to manage putting on your pants by yourself."

"The legs are sewed shut," he carped.

Rivka padded across the carpet, took the trousers from him, and ran her arm down each of the legs. "I see."

"They fit fine on Thursday when I tried them on in the tuxedo shop," said Dan.

"They were way too short. I asked the clerk to let them out another inch and a half. She must have sewn them herself rather than let the tailor do it."

"What am I going to do? The wedding is this afternoon," he moaned.

"Never fear, 'Mottle Kamzoil the Tailor' is here." Rivka extracted her sewing basket from the bottom drawer of her dresser and sat on her vanity table stool while she used bobby pins to mark the length and a pair scissors to clip the incompetent stitching. Turning the trousers inside out, she separated the legs and sewed the leg ends around using a proper precise stitch. About halfway through the task, her bath towel slid down around the stool. She looked up and caught his expression, a broad grin. "What?" she asked.

"Just a thought—I've heard of the cockeyed seamstress but not the naked seamstress."

* * * *

Ivy could sense the importance of this day just as soon as her eyes popped open. The empty pillow next to her reminded her that three days ago she had nixed Mark's sleepovers until after the big event. She had missed his being there, but the past night was the last night. She glanced at the alarm clock and cocked her head slightly. *Oh, my gosh—7:30 already. The alarm didn't go off. Today of all days—I've got so much to do. And Rivka will be here at 8:30.* "I'm getting married!" she said aloud, throwing her hands in the air.

Because the bedroom's dimness didn't quite match her high expectations for the day, she bounded out of bed and padded barefoot to the easterly window to check the weather. There were several dark clouds, and the day before had been teasing, with on-and-off drizzling. The wedding venue was outdoors, but there were huge tents for that eventuality. A sliver of sunlight shone off in the distance—*a ray of hope. Nothing is going to spoil my wedding day, absolutely nothing!*

Beside the bed, the bride donned her slippers and headed for the master bathroom. A shiny clean cabinet mirror caught her attention. It brought back the unpleasant memory of nearly a week ago. *Maybe we'll get a new medicine cabinet and mirror sometime soon.*

Last night on the phone, Rivka had told her a few details about Muddy: his depraved treatment of his wife, the secret room, and his own grisly end. Ivy felt a jubilant surge of relief. Rivka's report couldn't have come at a better time—they were free of him forever.

She showered, powdered, perfumed, put on her best underwear—all with great care, and then she donned a lightweight robe. *If I hurry, I might just sneak in a little breakfast before Rivka arrives.*

Down in the kitchen she sipped her tea and munched on a blueberry muffin for several minutes until she heard a knock at the front door, followed by the ringing of the doorbell. Ivy let Rivka in and poured coffee for her. They sat together at the kitchen table, reviewing the schedule for that morning. At 9:00 Penny Fortune, a stylist and owner of the Good Fortune Hairdressers, would arrive to fashion a hairdo worthy of a royal bride. Between 10:30 and 11:00 the bridal bouquet would arrive from Special Day Florists, and Rivka would answer the door. At 11:00 Rivka would apply polish to freshly trimmed nails. At 11:30 Rivka would help Ivy into her wedding gown and then don her own matron of honor dress. At 12:30 the honorary father of the bride would arrive with a clean Toyota to convey the three of them to the William Paca House. At 1:45 p.m. she and Mark would sign the *ketubah*, a Jewish marriage contract, to be witnessed by Rabbi Moshe Goldfish, Dan Sherman, and Leo Schwartz, father of the groom. At 2:00 the wedding would commence, presided over by the rabbi.

At 12:30 Dan, in his altered gray tuxedo, arrived to drive the bride and Rivka to the main event.

* * * *

Mark had moved the alarm clock that usually sat on his night table to the dresser across the bedroom to ensure that he'd get out of bed to answer its call. He didn't want to be late to his own wedding. He bolted out of bed to quash the irritating sound and turned on the radio to the local weather station while he dressed. Partially cloudy, with scattered showers wasn't exactly what he wanted to hear, *but the show must go on. In fact, we'll say our vows under a tent if we have to.*

While preparing for cumulative exams and his doctoral dissertation, Mark had had little time to participate in the wedding plans. He appreciated the fact that Ivy had demonstrated her ability to handle the planning so well. Of course, having the Shermans to assist through all of it didn't hurt, but he was proud of the woman he was about to marry. Mark supposed that Dan and Rivka would become *mishpokhe* [Yiddish for the extended family] after the ceremony. He could only guess how much they had done for Ivy.

Mark showered and shaved. He donned his underwear, solid-gray socks, and dress shoes. Taking one look at the plastic bag containing his tuxedo, he shook his head. *That can wait until after break-*

244

*fast. No use risking spots or a spill.* He slipped into his terry robe and headed for the kitchen and the waffle breakfast Alice had prepared especially for him. It had been a while since Mark had sat at the same breakfast table with his father and Alice.

"Well, Mark, it's been nice having you home again, even if it was only for the last few days," said Leo. "Now you and Ivy are about to make a home of your own."

"Seriously, Dad, you and Alice have been living together for some time now. I know that the two of you love one another, so why don't you guys make it official?"

Alice and Leo looked at each other with blank expressions; first one, then the other, burst out laughing.

"It *is* funny," replied Alice. "Your father and I were just discussing the possibility last night. I think you two have been a good influence on us."

"Let's just say we've entered negotiations on the matter," replied Leo. "I've already been through two marriages that didn't end well—one in death and the other in divorce. Oh, well, they say that the third time is a charm. Anyway, we'll let you know."

Mark drained his glass of orange juice. "Wow, sometimes miracles do happen."

"If you need any help while you're job hunting, remember we're here for you," said Leo as he reached for another waffel and began spreading marmalade on top.

Alice got up to pour more coffee for the three of them and said, "You're changing the subject again."

"Thanks, Dad," replied Mark, spearing a forkful of waffle. "I've got the first few months covered out of savings, so I'm not forced to accept the first offer I get. I want to be able to choose the ideal career path for me."

"Does an ideal job even exist?" posed Leo.

Mark set down his coffee cup. "You know what I mean— challenging work, worthy compensation, decent working conditions, reasonable location, and room for advancement. I've got my doctorate in an expanding field, and I sure don't want all that to go to waste."

Leo smiled at his son's naive expectations.

Shortly after 11:30, Josh, his best man, walked in the back door, looking sharp in his gray tuxedo. "Hey, everyone looks great, especially you, Alice—the rest of us look like penguins. We've got one hour to get this show on the road."

"I'm supposed to wear this tux because I'm the father of the groom," complained Leo, "but all I get to do is sit in the front row like the rest of the audience."

"Aw, quit your griping, Leo," answered Josh. "You're a part of the wedding party and you're going to be photographed with them."

"Aren't you gentlemen forgetting something?" asked Alice. She had one hand behind her back.

"What?" asked Mark.

"The rings, the wedding rings, guys. Can't have a wedding without 'em." She passed a small black velvet box containing twin wedding bands to the best man, and he slipped it into his right-hand jacket pocket.

"And don't forget where you put them." She laughed.

At 12:30 Josh conveyed them all to the Paca House front steps.

\* \* \* \*

The sun had inched its way from behind the black clouds much earlier, and the ground at Paca House had dried sufficiently to support an outdoor ceremony. The bride's group arrived first, and Ivy was ushered into one of the first-floor rooms for an individual photo session, while the others waited for the groom's group, which arrived a short while later. The entire bridal party endured a forty-five minute photo shoot, using Governor Paca's colonial parlor as a backdrop, particularly the ornately carved fireplace and mantle. The bridesmaids and groomsmen took another ten minutes to photograph.

Mark and Ivy had pooh-poohed the custom of the bride not being seen by her groom until she walks down the aisle. They thought it was unfair to make guests stand around for an hour after the ceremony, waiting for the wedding party to be photographed.

So, with photographing done, the groom's party was exiled across the hall to the colonial dining room for prayer, meditation, and even expected interruptions for modest humor. Meanwhile, Ivy moved to a large throne-like chair in the colonial parlor. In that way the bride and groom were greeted separately by the arriving guests. There was also a table in the dining room for wedding gifts.

At 1:45 the groom and best man were sent outside to stand next to the *chuppah*, a canopied trellis under which the wedding ceremony would take place. Standing near the little bridge on the lawn between two blooming gardens, the portable trellis was covered with a huge *tallit*, or prayer shawl, and trimmed with white roses. Guests were arriving every minute now, filling the white wooden folding chairs. A red carpet had been laid down the center aisle from the rear entrance to the *chuppah*. Rabbi Moshe came down the center aisle and set up a lectern and small table in front of the *chuppah*.

At precisely 2:00 a recording of "And This Is My Beloved" from *Kismet* played through the sound system while Leo slowly led Alice down the aisle to seats in the front row next to Esther and Meyer. Janice and Wayne Sachs followed them. The music switched to "Sunrise, Sunset" from *Fiddler on the Roof* while three groomsmen— Stewart, Abel, and a schoolmate of Mark's were paired with three bridesmaids, Julie, Brenda, and Barri. Together, they paced their stroll down the aisle, separated by gender, and formed a line on each side of the *chuppah*. Matron of honor Rivka came down the aisle alone to stand opposite Josh. A musical fanfare preceded Mendelssohn's *Bridal Processional* and everyone stood. Ivy took Dan's arm and together they traveled down the red carpet to culminate in a fatherly kiss at the far end. Dan took an aisle seat in the front row while Ivy stepped under the *chuppah,* joining Mark facing the rabbi. The music faded to silence.

Rabbi Moshe stood at the microphone. He greeted the entire bridal party and all of the guests with a welcoming prayer—praising and thanking the Lord for bringing them to this season and this glorious event. At the rabbi's direction the bride and groom each signed the *ketubah*, the marriage contract, which lay on the little table. Then, facing each other, Mark made loving eye contact with Ivy as he un-veiled her. She moved closer to him and circled about Mark three times, creating an imaginary wall of protection around the couple.

The rabbi poured and blessed a cup of wine and handed it to Ivy and then to Mark for each of them to drink. "The two of you drinking from the same cup symbolizes a willingness to share your lives together," he explained. "By accepting rings from one another, Ivy and Mark, you will have pledged yourselves to a lifelong union regardless of incurred health and wealth."

"I will," said Ivy, reciting the pledge while Mark fitted a gold band on her ring finger.

"I will," said Mark, repeating the pledge as Ivy slipped a like ring on his finger.

"This ends the *Kiddushin*, the betrothal portion of the cer-emony," declared Rabbi Moshe. He then read their *ketubah,* first in Hebrew and then in English. "Now we enter the *Nissiun*, the nuptuls portion of the ceremony." It was time for reciting seven blessings over a second cup of wine. The seven began with blessing God's creations and ended with blessing the marriage couple. Rabbi Moshe handed the cup first to Ivy to drink, and she passed it to Mark. When he finished drinking, Rabbi Moshe wrapped the plastic cup in a napkin and set it on the floor. Mark raised his right foot over the cup and stomped down, smashing it.

"The smashed cup symbolizes the destruction of the temples and the repeated sufferings of the Jewish people over many millen-nia," explained the rabbi.

But the crinkling crushing of plastic was also a signal for the guests to start singing "*Siman Tov u'Maz'l Tov*"—"Good Sign and Good Fortune" over and over again as the newlyweds retraced their steps on the the red carpet back to the rear door of Paca House. Tradi-tionally, this was a short quiet time—a time to become modestly ac-quainted, a seclusion to contemplate the marriage they've pledged.

When all the guests were seated at tables under the tents, the newlyweds appeared once more at the rear steps of the colonial build-ing. Francine Miller, acting as emcee, stepped up to the microphone.

"It is my great pleasure to introduce for the very first time—Mr. and Mrs. Mark Schwartz," said the emcee. The guests responded with spontaneous applause as the newlyweds paraded to their seats at the wedding party table.

As soon as the newlyweds were seated, Rabbi Moshe said a *HaMotzi*—a blessing over kosher bread called *challah*. "Blessed is the Lord, our God, who brings forth bread from the earth," he repeated in English.

"The rabbi couldn't trust the venue to be kosher, so he brought his own challah," whispered Dan to Rivka.

A recording of "Tennessee Waltz" brought the newlyweds to the portable parquet dance floor that had been laid down at one end of the first tent. They waltzed to the end of the song and then to chosen music. Members of the bridal party cut in to dance with either the bride or the groom. The song "*Havah Nagilah*" rang out over the sound system. "Come, let us be glad and rejoice. Awake, friends, with a joyful heart." A few of the more enthusiastic guests formed a ring and began dancing the hora. Afterward, music of more moderate tempo encouraged other dancers, until the festive meal was served.

Dan was returning from the restroom when Cora Bacon approached him.

"I have something for you, Dan," said Cora. She handed him a brightly decorated gift bag with handles.

"Uh-uh," he said. "I'm not in charge of gifts. All wedding gifts belong on the dining room table inside Paca House."

"This is for you, Dan, something you said you were missing."

"What is it?"

"Look inside and you'll see," encouraged Cora. "Yes, here and now."

Dan spread the bag open and slid a book out. "Hey! It's a copy of your father's book!"

"Not just any copy, mind you," she said. "Look inside the front cover."

Dan did just that and discovered what she meant. "Our bookstore pricing label. It's our missing bookstore copy! Thank you,

Cora. How did you happen to recover it?"

"It was among the things left in Muddy's hotel room," she replied. "Our copies and the libraries' copies were also retrieved by the hotel management. They were kind enough to let us know."

With a broad smile, Dan said, "You realize this is the very book that started this whole mystery adventure." Cora nodded and stepped away. He called after her. "By the way, how is your sister Gloria doing? Has she recovered from Muddy's beating yet?"

"Oh, yes, she's doing fine. She gave us quite a scare. The hospital discharged her two days ago and Rae took care of Bunny in the meanwhile. Thank you for asking." Cora walked off.

While dessert was served, the dancing resumed except when interrupted for spontaneous speeches. At one point Josh took the microphone and gave the best man speech, roasting the groom and toasting the newlyweds.

Leo took the mike from Josh and gave a fatherly speech, including an appropriate mention of Heddy, his first wife and Mark's mother, who had died while they still lived in England. Mark was only three at the time.

The music and dancing continued until the couple appeared at the rear door of Paca House to wave goodbye to everyone. As the newlyweds left the house, a number of the guests rushed to the front lawn to see them off in their brand-new Chevrolet Malibu, a gift from Leo. It was to be a cross-country driving honeymoon.

Dan and Rivka stood on the middle landing of the front stairs to watch them pull away from the curb. Wayne and Janice stood one step below them. They turned around to face the Shermans.

"I want to thank you for making this trip so precious for us. Meeting us for dinner almost every evening and helping us to get to know everyone has been outstanding," said Wayne, holding out his hand. Dan shook it warmly.

"And don't forget how much we appreciated being included in the wedding processional," said Janice. "You are both so dear to us. We'll never forget you." She reached out with both arms, encircled Rivka, and pulled her in for a hug.

"Oh look, there's a JUST MARRIED sign on the trunk and four tin cans attached to the rear bumper," said Rivka.

"I know. I just saw Abel and Barri carrying the sign and cans out to the Schwartzes' car a few minutes ago," said Dan, as the newlyweds disappeared from their view.

"It's going to be hard not seeing Ivy every day," said Rivka, wiping the tears from her eyes.

"I agree. We've sort of adopted her, haven't we?" said Dan. "Well, we're halfway there. Why don't we just go to the car and head on home?"

"Oh, there's Helen Margoles," said Rivka. "I'd like to say hello." Rivka reached out and tapped Helen on the shoulder when they reached the sidewalk in front of the old Governor's House. "Hi, Helen. Have you got the Margoles home all fixed up yet?"

"Almost," she replied. "The builder knocked out the living room wall abutting the hidden room and made it part of the living room. The trap door is also gone. We're waiting for him to finish plastering and painting. I simply couldn't abide living in a house with ghostly trappings. The memory of them once being there is bad enough. The thought of Atkins falling to his death from the widow's walk still haunts me at night. Leland thinks I'm being silly."

"I don't think you're being silly," said Dan. "We all have to live with our pet phobias. Mine is that I'm afraid I won't find a reasonable solution to a problem. I guess that's the ghost of the engineer left in me."

# Epilogue

The following article appeared in the police-beat section of the *Annapolis Journal-Gazette* on June 19th, 2009.

# Police Close 20-Year-Old Cold Case

According to Annapolis Police spokesperson Lt. Ron Baker, a 1989 missing-persons cold case turned into a current homicide investigation when the body of Anne Atkins was discovered at 605 E. Prince Street. According to witnesses, her remains had been thrown by her husband, Budreau "Muddy" Atkins, from the widow's walk of the home at that address. Her decomposed remains were wrapped in plastic. A second body appeared on the front lawn when the railing on which the husband was standing collapsed, sending him to his death.

The husband had reported his 28-year-old wife missing on May 8th, 1989, saying she had left him after repeated arguments. The original police investigation concluded that Budreau Atkins had been telling the truth. However, the current investigation revealed that he had thrown her to her death in front of a moving truck on Slate Street back in 1989. The couple resided on Slate Street.

Watching the truck leave the scene of the crime, the husband panicked and hid his wife's body in a secret room in the Atkins family home at the Prince Street address. The recent sale of the Prince Street house prompted the husband to move the body.

The truck driver and passenger, cited for a misdemeanor—leaving the scene of the accident—were not prosecuted, due to the three-year Maryland statute of limitations. Nor were they the direct cause of the felony bodily injury.

**The End**

**Rosemary and Larry Mild**, cheerful partners in crime, coauthor mystery and thriller novels and short stories. Many of their wickedly entertaining stories appear in anthologies: *Kissing Frogs and other Quirky Fairy Tales*; *Dark Paradise: Mysteries in the Land of Aloha*; *Mystery in Paradise: 13 Tales of Suspense*; and *Chesapeake Crimes: Homicidal Holidays*. In 2013 the Milds waved goodbye to Severna Park, Maryland, and moved to Honolulu, Hawaiʻi, where they cherish time with their daughter, son-in-law, and grandchildren.

**Email the Milds at: roselarry@magicile.com**

**Visit them at: www.magicile.com**

## The Paco and Molly Mystery Series (#1)

*Locks and Cream Cheese*—In scandal-ridden Black Rain Corners, a Chesapeake Bay mansion harbors locked rooms and deadly secrets. A wily detective and a gourmet cook tackle the case.

## The Paco and Molly Mystery Series (#2)

*Hot Grudge Sunday*—Bank robbers and conspirators derail the sleuths' blissful honeymoon at the Grand Canyon. Can they nail the suspects after they themselves become targets?

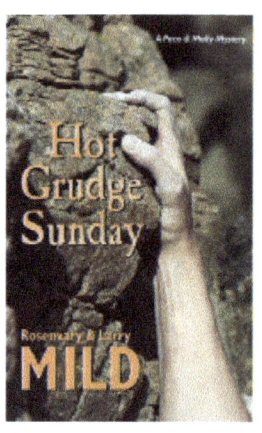

## The Paco and Molly Mystery Series (#3)

*Boston Scream Pie*—A teenage girl's nightmare triggers a sinister tale of twins, two feuding families, and a blonde bombshell who hates being called "Mom."

**Available on Amazon.com and all e-readers.**

## The Dan and Rivka Sherman Mystery Series (#1)

***Death Goes Postal***—Rare 15th-century typesetting artifacts journey through time, leaving a horrifying imprint in their wake. Dan and Rivka risk life and limb to locate the treasures and unmask the murderer. Not quite what they expected when they bought The Olde Victorian Bookstore. **(Also available as an Amazon Audible Audiobook.)**

## The Dan and Rivka Sherman Mystery Series (#2)

***Death Takes A Mistress***—A young Englishwoman is murdered by her lover. Years later, her daughter, seeking revenge, journeys from London to Annapolis, MD to find the killer and her father. But to which family does he belong? Dan and Rivka set out to expose the true villain.

## The Dan and Rivka Sherman Mystery Series (#3)

***Death Steals A Holy Book***—Dan and Rivka inherit a rare Yiddish translation of a 14th-century holy book, but it is stolen and their book restorer is murdered. Can they recover the book and nail the culprit?

**Available on Amazon.com and all e-readers.**

## The Dan and Rivka Sherman Mystery Series (#4)

*Death Rules the Night*—Dan wants to know why all copies of an important book are missing, not only from the bookstore, but also from all the local libraries and the author's bookshelves. Who is trying to hide the book's secrets and what are they? Can stalking, threats, and even murder sway Dan from solving this mystery? Rivka fears for their lives.

*Cry Ohana, Adventure and Suspense in Hawaii*—A car accident, blackmail, and murder tear apart a Hawai'ian *ohana* (family). Kekoa, the teenage son, witnesses the murder and is forced into life on the run. Danger erupts at a Filipino wedding, a Maui resort, and the Big Island's volcanic steam vents. Can the family re-unite and bring down the killer?

*Honolulu Heat*—Leilani and Alex Wong anguish over son Noah, an idealistic teenager who teeters on both sides of the law. He meets Nina Portfia, his dream girl, but they unwittingly share horrific secrets. Noah finds himself immersed in a bloody feud between a Chinatown protection racketeer and a crimeland don who, ironically, is Nina's father.

**Available on Amazon.com and all e-readers.**

*Murder, Fantasy, and Weird Tales*
—Delve into tales of the brave, the foolhardy,
and the wicked on their journeys to the
unknown in Hawai'i, Japan, Cambodia, Italy,
and elsewhere. Art lovers, hit women, a
vampire, a lively hologram, and others reveal
their secret compulsions.

*The Misadventures of Slim O.
Wittz, Soft-Boiled Detective*—"If
you're looking for a truly bumbling gumshoe,
you want me, Slim. I'm frequently behind
the eight ball and seldom paid. In eight
complete mystery stories I always bump
into criminals. And you're right: my case
record is remarkably shaky."

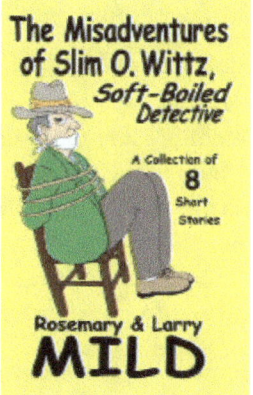

*Copper and Goldie • 13 Tails of
Adventure and Suspense in Hawaii*
—Sam, a disabled cop, now a PI, and his
canine sidekick, Goldie, ply the streets of
Honolulu in a Checker Cab, looking for
fares and solving all sorts of crimes they
encounter. 13 exciting short story adventures.

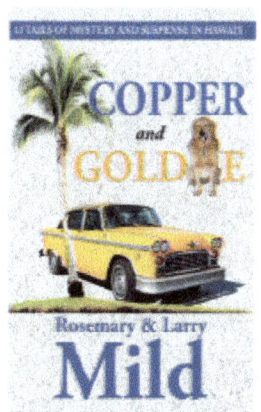

**Available on Amazon.com and all e-readers.**

*Miriam's World—and Mine*
—Miriam Luby Wolfe, a junior at Syracuse
U., spent her fall semester in London
exploring her talents: singing, dancing,
acting, and writing. But she never made it
home. A terrorist bomb destroyed her plane
over Lockerbie, Scotland. Learn about
Miriam, the Pan Am families, the bombers,
and the political fallout.

*Love! Laugh! Panic! Life with My*
*Mother*—Don't we all have mixed
emotions about our mothers? Rosemary
Mild's mom was super-achieving, but tough
to live with. Luby Pollack was a journalist,
popular book author, and psychiatrist's wife.
Always the heroine, and sometimes the
villain, from the viewpoint of her loving but
ornery daughter.

In My Next Life I'll Get It Right—
is a collection of personal essays ranging from
the hilarious to the serious—keen, sometimes
wicked, observations on everyday life. And…
wishful thinking mixed with tough reality,
See how Rosemary views her two marriages,
the good and the not so good. Join her as
she takes on sailing, skating, Jazzercise,
football, and more—and feel for a mother's
heart-wrenching loss.

**Available on Amazon.com and all e-readers.**

*Unto the Third Generation*—Two young people, each unaware of the other, volunteer to become cryonauts—physically frozen in a life-suspension experiment. Leonard, a steel worker, and Francine, a waitress, postpone their destinies for untold generations. But their lives are in jeopardy —depending upon two world-shaking events.

*Charley and the Magic Jug and Other Short Stories*—Climb the mountain to the secret cave with Charley. Watch three brothers face a sweet but certain death. Learn how a tiny pill can changes lives. Get away through time with thieves. See what the winds reveal in "Tsunami." Follow Casey as he chases the ladies in "On the Prowl." And witness so much more in a score of short stories.

### Also by Larry

*No Place To Be But Here*—It is not only Larry's own story, but that of his family. Join him as he tells how his two wives, three children, and five grandchildren have shaped his life as much as he has molded theirs. Tragedy is certainly no stranger as he deals with death, cancer, murder, and global terrorism, not only on the written page, but in his own life.

**Available on Amazon.com and all e-readers.**

www.ingramcontent.com/pod-product-compliance
Lightning Source LLC
Chambersburg PA
CBHW070435120726
47910CB00003B/789